D0442696

CITY OF WIND

CENTURY
QUARTET
BOOK III

Pierdomenico Baccalario
Translated by Leah D. Janeczko

Random House   New York

This is a work of fiction. Names, characters, places, and incidents either are the product of the author's imagination or are used fictitiously. Any resemblance to actual persons, living or dead, events, or locales is entirely coincidental.

Translation copyright © 2011 by Leah D. Janeczko
Jacket art copyright © 2011 by John Rocco

All rights reserved. Published in the United States by Random House Children's Books, a division of Random House, Inc., New York. Originally published as *La città del vento* by Edizioni Piemme S.p.A., Casale Monferrato, Italy, in 2007. Copyright © 2007 by Edizioni Piemme S.p.A. All other international rights © Atlantyca S.p.A., foreignrights@atlantyca.it

Random House and the colophon are registered trademarks of Random House, Inc.

Visit us on the Web! www.randomhouse.com/kids

Educators and librarians, for a variety of teaching tools, visit us at www.randomhouse.com/teachers

CenturyQuartet.com

Library of Congress Cataloging-in-Publication Data
Baccalario, Pierdomenico.
[Città del vento. English.]
City of wind / by Pierdomenico Baccalario ; translated by Leah D. Janeczko. — 1st American ed.
p. cm. — (Century quartet; bk. 3)
Summary: In their continuing quest to save the world from evil forces, Mistral, Elettra, Harvey, and Sheng meet again in Paris, where they must search for the mysterious veil of Isis reportedly hidden in the heart of the city.
ISBN 978-0-375-85897-0 (trade) — ISBN 978-0-375-95897-7 (lib. bdg.) — ISBN 978-0-375-89228-8 (ebook)
[1. Good and evil—Fiction. 2. Adventures and adventurers—Fiction. 3. Paris (France)—Fiction. 4. France—Fiction. 5. Mystery and detective stories.] I. Janeczko, Leah. II. Title.
PZ7.B131358Ci 2011 [Fic]—dc22 2010029137

Printed in the United States of America
10 9 8 7 6 5 4 3 2 1

First American Edition

This book is for my grandmother,
who sees the stars from very close up.

CONTENTS

THE SECRET — 1

1. The Bees — 5
2. The Omens — 15
3. The Spy — 24
4. The Return — 30

FIRST STASIMON — 34

5. The Luggage — 36
6. The Train — 40
7. The Poison — 57
8. The Plot — 62
9. The Door — 67
10. The Tower — 71
11. The Café — 78
12. The Perfume — 82

SECOND STASIMON — 98

13. The Clock — 100
14. The Music — 109
15. The Breakfast — 113
16. The Flowers — 124

17. The Alchemist   130

18. The Guardian   139

19. The Zodiac   150

20. The Message   154

21. Zoe   165

22. The Balloon   172

23. The King   177

24. The Square   182

25. The Coin   186

26. The Observatory   193

27. The Bookshop   201

28. The Crash   205

THIRD STASIMON   222

29. The Meeting   224

30. The Music Box   235

31. The Fall   241

32. The Reawakening   252

33. The Traitor   258

34. The Veil   264

35. The Ship   273

36. The Goodbyes   282

37. The Observer   286

*They will discover the secrets of my writings and will interpret them.
Whilst some they may keep hidden, those that are of benefit to mortals
they will inscribe on stelae and obelisks.*
fr. 23,66

*"Mother," said Horus, "grant me the understanding
of this sacred text so that I be not unenlightened."
And Isis replied, "Hearken, my son."*
fr. 23,70

Hermes Trismegistus, *The Maiden of the Cosmos*

CITY OF WIND

CENTURY
QUARTET
BOOK III

THE SECRET

ON THAT NIGHT FIVE YEARS AGO, THERE ISN'T A SINGLE STAR IN the sky. Shanghai is covered with clouds, thick drizzle falling from them, a damp veil concealing the city's lights and reflections.

A black car moves slowly through the city traffic. At each stoplight, tiny beads of rain form on its tinted windows. Sitting in the backseat beside the gray-haired man, the woman stares out the window. Not even the faintest noise makes its way into the car.

"I'm pleased you had a good trip," says the gray-haired man. His name is Mahler. Jacob Mahler.

"It wasn't a pleasure trip," the woman replies. "It's my job."

The man smiles. "And spending three months aboard a Siberian icebreaker isn't exactly the most enjoyable way to travel to Shanghai."

"Exactly," she says, cutting the conversation short.

The man stares out the window in the opposite direction. The two remain in silence for almost a quarter of an hour.

Finally, Jacob Mahler says, "We're there."

They've pulled up to the main door of a tall building. Mahler gets out first, quickly making his way around to the other side of the car to open the door for the woman. They walk through the thick drizzle, which hides the building's true size. It seems to be immense, like a giant obelisk of mirrors and black steel.

They go inside.

They reach an elevator whose door is decorated with intricate hieroglyphs. They go up to the sixty-third of the building's sixty-four floors.

Mahler ushers the woman into a study with a picture window overlooking Shanghai. A breathtaking view.

There's a man in the study. His back is turned toward them, his arms crossed behind him in an unnatural position. A night-blue Korean suit, a collarless shirt and well-polished shoes. When he hears them come in, he turns around. He's wearing glasses with black Bakelite frames.

He doesn't smile.

He doesn't hold out his hand.

He doesn't say hello.

He nods at the woman to sit down. Jacob Mahler leans back against the far wall. She sits down and stares at the floor, biding her time.

"It's very simple," she finally begins. "I know a secret. For a long time, I wasn't sure whether or not to tell anyone about it. But many years ago, I decided to keep quiet. And that was a mistake."

"Many years ago?" the man with the black-rimmed glasses asks. His voice is unusually hoarse. "You don't look so old."

"Looks can be deceiving," the woman replies. "How old do you think I am?"

If there's any teasing in her question, the man doesn't seem to notice it. His answer is totally void of emotion. "Forty."

"I'm more than twice that old."

"Surprising. Why should I believe you?" The man's gaze is ice-cold.

"Because you know it's true. Because my age is a part of the secret I know about. Those who need to protect it, like I do, have the gift of living long lives."

"To accomplish what?"

"To pass the secret down to those who come after them."

"Are you the only one who knows about it?"

"No. There are four of us."

"Who are the others?"

Plastic, the woman thinks. *This is like talking to a plastic mannequin. There's absolutely nothing human about this man.* She shifts nervously in her chair. "At this stage, their names aren't important."

"Maybe not to you. To me, they're essential."

"Then call us the Four Wise Men. Or better yet, the Four Magi."

For the first time, the man's eyes narrow with a trace of cold interest. "I know what the Magi are. Are you telling me it's that old? Two, three thousand years old?"

"The secret dates back to that era, yes."

"Does this secret have a name?"

"We call it Century, because it's handed down every hundred years, more or less. The secret's connected to something that's destined to return."

"Like comets."

"Exactly."

A long silence follows, disturbed only by the faint tapping of raindrops against the windowpanes.

"Why would you sell me such an important secret?"

"Because you're willing to pay for it. You're very wealthy. And now's the time to do it."

"What do you mean?"

"Soon, the four of us are going to pass down the secret to the four who'll come after us."

"And once you've passed it down?"

"We can finally die."

The man tents his fingers below his nose. He shakes his head almost imperceptibly, as if to shoo away a fly. Then he takes off his glasses and rests them on the desk in front of him. "I'm listening."

"Can I ask you something?" says the woman.

"It depends."

"Your name. Is it your real name?"

The man shakes his head. "Is Zoe yours?"

1

THE BEES

Five years have passed.

Tiny insects are dancing outside the window, hovering up and down in lazy spirals, forming circles in the air. They're handfuls of dots scattered in the sky.

They're bees. The bees of Montmartre, the historic artists' district of Paris.

On the sixth floor of a building on rue de l'Abreuvoir, surrounded by the sound of the buzzing bees, Mistral smiles. Her elbows are propped on the windowsill, her chin resting on the palms of her hands, her dreamy eyes lost in the endless whirl of activity. The beehive is just below the roof, in the shelter of the gutter. A few months ago, the bees' home was practically invisible, just a little hexagon of wax. But when she returned from her trip to New York, it was already as big as an egg carton, nestled between the copper gutter and the overhang.

"Almost two hundred thousand kilometers . . . ," Mistral whispers, watching a forager bee fly off and disappear down the street below. That's how far a hive of bees needs to fly, sucking up nectar from flower to flower, to make one kilogram of honey. A real race against time before the start of winter.

Do they have enough flowers? the girl wonders, lost in thought. Just in case, she always keeps little plants and fresh flowers on the windowsill.

It's afternoon. As she has on many other afternoons spent watching the bees, Mistral imagines with horror that someone in the building might notice them and, with a single swipe of a broom, destroy seven months of hard work done by ten thousand bees. That's according to the calculations, drawings and notes she's made in her sketchbook.

A plump yellow bee hovers over a bunch of violets. Mistral watches the insect alight on a blossom and hears it buzzing as the petals stir sweetly between its feet. Fascinated by this beautiful sight, she picks up a pencil and her sketchbook and draws it. She can see the grains of yellow pollen on its tiny legs. It's incredible how a simple bunch of flowers can contain an entire universe. . . .

Beyond her window, Paris spreads out in all its glory, with sparkling rooftops, the white cupola of Sacré-Coeur and, on the other side of the Seine River, the Eiffel Tower. Gleaming in the distance like stone bellflowers are the spires of Notre Dame.

"Mistral!" her mother calls from the living room. "It's late!"

Mistral's so accustomed to being alone at home that she's almost startled. "Oh! My lesson!" she says, putting down her sketchpad and rushing out her bedroom door. She hurries over to her mother, who is rummaging through her purse, looking for her keys.

Her mother glances at her wrist to check the time but realizes she isn't wearing a watch. "Darn it! Where did I put it?" she exclaims, rummaging through her purse again. "Mistral, we really need to go!"

The woman's perfume lingers in the air. One of the sweet kinds that even the bees would gladly follow. Cecile Blanchard is a perfume designer.

Mistral walks into the other room.

"Don't you need to take anything with you?" her mother asks, still looking for her watch.

"No."

"Aren't you kids using a book? Sheet music?"

"I'm having a private lesson today. I just need to sing."

The mother and daughter quickly shut the apartment door behind them. They run down the spiral staircase to the ground floor.

The main door to the street is open wide, letting in gusts of hot air, which are drying up the puddles left behind when the doorkeeper mopped the floor. The street is steep and rippling with heat.

The tables outside the corner café are deserted. The only sound is the distant hum of traffic from the Saint-Martin area and, for an instant, the sharp, shrill call of a bird.

"Did you hear that?" Mistral asks, holding back a shiver.

"What?"

"That bird."

Cecile didn't hear anything. She walks briskly down the sidewalk and over to the apple-green Citroën parked crookedly on the street.

Mistral peers around. The coast is clear. The bees are buzzing, unseen, above her. Birds dart across the sky.

For a moment, she thought the bird's call sounded like the plaintive warble of a violin.

"You realize this is all nonsense, don't you?" Linda Melodia grumbles from her bed at Rome's Fatebenefratelli Hospital, gesturing at the other patients in the room to emphasize her irritation. Linda is sporting a perfect hairdo, an immaculate linen nightgown and a pair of flowered wooden clogs. She looks more like she just checked out of a vacation resort than into a hospital.

Elettra tries to calm her down. "The doctors said—"

"Doctors! That's just my point!" Linda booms. "What do doctors know? Nothing! I met a doctor once, and believe me, that was more than enough for me!" She looks around, furious. "I'm going home. I'm getting my things from the locker and going home."

"Auntie, you can't! They still need to examine you."

"I'm perfectly fine."

"No, you aren't perfectly fine."

"I'm telling you I'm perfectly fine. I've never been allergic to anything in my life, and I don't see why I would be now."

"You fainted yesterday."

"Anyone would've fainted with all that dust around," Linda protests, "and that mildewed furniture and that mountain of clutter. . . . If only one of you would give me a hand!"

"What, clearing out the basement?"

"I've been meaning to do it for years, and the time's finally come."

"If only you could do it without passing out from exhaustion. . . ."

Linda grumbles, gets out of bed and turns to leave the room. She can't seem to decide whether to stop and chat with some of the other patients. Then she whirls around and walks back to her niece. "I have no intention of going through with the exams! I'm getting my things and going home."

"It'll only be a few days. Besides, you need to rest."

"Heaven knows what's in the refrigerator. . . ."

"Dad and I are getting by just fine."

"Wipe the inside of the pots with a little lemon juice before putting them in the dishwasher. And don't overload the dryer or else it'll—" Then, as if attracted by radar, she points up at a crack in the wall. "Would you look at that! Is this what they call public hygiene?"

"You'll survive. Lots of people do."

Linda focuses on the household chores again, as if it's a comforting mantra. "Use the half-hour cycle, nothing longer. Afterward, leave the door open and—"

"Let it air out, I know. How could I forget? You've reminded me a hundred times already."

"Are you trying to tell me I'm a nag?"

"No, Auntie. Just a teensy bit obsessive."

Linda seems to calm down. She steps over to the window and looks outside nervously. "By this time tomorrow, I'll be radioactive," she says with a sigh.

"They're just going to take a couple X-rays," Elettra remarks patiently.

The woman dangles her fingers over her impeccable coiffure and wriggles them around like worms. "Vrrrr . . . Vrrrr . . . Radioactive. All because I was feeling a little under the weather."

"You weren't just under the weather, Auntie. You were unconscious for over an hour!"

"If I really have to be radioactive, I'd at least like to get my radiation from a microwave. That way, I can hold an egg in my hand and it'll end up hard-boiled. . . ."

"That's the spirit!"

"I'm going home," Linda starts up again, springing away from the window. "I don't care one bit about those exams. I'm perfectly fine."

"Just take your mind off things, think about something other than chores and it'll be over in no time, you'll see."

"Take my mind off things, of course. . . ." She looks at Elettra and changes the subject. "What about you?"

"What about me?"

"Is your mind still on that good-looking American boy?"

"Auntie . . ."

"Long-distance relationships are the best kind. All it takes is a quick phone call now and then to tide you over. There's no need to have them in your hair every afternoon, loafing on the couch watching TV while you slave away in the kitchen baking a cake for them."

"Auntie! Harvey doesn't watch TV!"

"And you don't bake cakes, for that matter. You kids have

more important things to do. Like playing with those wooden tops, for example."

"Auntie, please . . ." Elettra peers around. "You swore you wouldn't talk about that with anyone."

"You certainly are lucky! If that had happened to me . . . ," Linda says, her voice trailing off.

Elettra smiles. She looks at her aunt from behind her long black curls. She's tempted to make one of her customary comebacks, but this time she agrees completely. She really is lucky to be with Harvey.

"Left! Right! Left!" yells Olympia, the boxing trainer.

At her every command, Harvey slams his fist with a thud into one of the air mitts the young woman's holding up in front of her. Harvey punches hard, moving rhythmically, giving it all he's got. He clenches his fists tighter and tighter, moving them one after the other in rapid succession.

"Left! Right! Right! Left!"

Two minutes go by.

Two and a half minutes.

And then, finally, three.

Olympia lowers the mitts and Harvey stops. He's exhausted, his head hanging, his body covered with sweat.

"Nice work!" his trainer compliments him, resting her hand on his shoulder. "I thought you were going to rip my arms out of their sockets."

Harvey slumps back against the ring's colored ropes. His lean, muscular body twitches. His silky blond hair is sticking to his forehead. He spits out his mouth guard and slowly waves a gloved hand in front of his eyes. "Everything looks blurry," he admits. "I'm seeing stars."

"That happens sometimes."

They slip out of the ring.

"Did you really mean it, about your arms?"

"Yeah, it was like you were possessed or something," replies the young woman with short hair and cocoa-colored skin.

He nods. "Good."

He lets Olympia pull off his boxing gloves and heads toward the old locker rooms.

"You should cool down a little before you jump in the shower," his trainer warns him.

But Harvey doesn't listen to her. As he gets undressed, his elbows and knees tremble and ache. He's gotten stronger since he started coming to the gym. He's also walking tall, proud. He steps into the shower, his mouth gaping as he tries to endure the cold. The icy water hitting his sweaty skin has the same effect as a slap, but Harvey takes it as a challenge. He needs to learn to endure exhaustion and pain. He lets out a gasp and clenches his teeth. When he gets out and dries off, his arms are so weak that he can barely pick up his gym bag.

"See you Wednesday," he tells Olympia.

His trainer nods, already working with two students who are skipping rope.

Harvey walks out of the gym and heads to the subway entrance in a daze. Perched on the subway stairs is a crow with a cloudy eye.

"Hey, Edgar," Harvey greets the bird before going down into

the station. The tame crow flies off and disappears into the hot sky over New York.

"No!" Sheng yells into the phone. "I'm not going back, Dad! I don't care. No, don't make me talk to—aaaah!" He rolls his eyes and lowers the phone. When he holds it back up to his ear, his mother is already pouring forth a stream of words broken by sobs.

"Mom," Sheng begins, trying to reason with her, "of course I want to see you again! But instead of always asking me to go back, why don't you come visit me for a while? What do you say? The people are really friendly here in Rome!"

In the other room, the three young sisters of his cultural exchange program host family are blasting their stereo again.

"No. Those aren't tanks. . . . It's just music, Mom. Still, this music's going to drive me—"

The phone on the other end of the line is handed back to his father, who's adamant.

"Just a few more weeks, Dad! Four—"

"Two!"

A long silence follows.

"Okay, Dad. Two weeks. Then I'll go back to Shanghai. Yeah, I know you need me there. Bye. You too. Bye."

When Sheng hangs up, he doesn't know whether to tear the room apart or burst out crying. He feels totally overpowered by his father and completely misunderstood by his mother.

He looks into the mirror and stares at his blue eyes and perfectly white teeth. Tonight, maybe for the first time in his life, Sheng doesn't feel like laughing.

I have a mission to accomplish, he thinks, looking at his reflection seriously. *I'm important. I'm Sheng. The world needs me. There aren't six billion other Shengs. There's just one.*

"And that's me," he adds out loud.

The fact remains that this one and only Sheng has to go back home soon. And he really doesn't want to.

2

THE OMENS

WALKING THROUGH THE STIFLING, WINDLESS AIR OF AVENUE DE l'Opéra, Mistral thinks about how long it's been since she last saw the others.

Almost three months have passed. A seemingly endless period, which they've all spent reflecting on their adventure, what they've learned so far and what they have yet to discover. A period spent looking over their shoulders, trying to figure out the meaning of the stone they found in New York and the message from the top with the bridge engraved on it: There's some connection between Siberia and Paris. They've also been reading and studying, trying to figure out the secret that the objects have the power to reveal.

Professor Van Der Berger, the briefcase, the map of the Chaldeans, the Ring of Fire, the Star of Stone, the tamed crows that flew to their rescue down in the abandoned subway station in New York . . .

Mistral smiles, tiny beads of perspiration glistening on her forehead.

It's getting hotter and hotter, she thinks, peering up at the majestic opera house and then along the building's closed windows, which are dotted with boxy white air conditioners.

The asphalt under her feet is soft, almost spongy, like it's about to melt. Fortunately, she finds a moment of respite when she steps into the cool air of the music school's atrium.

Mistral walks through the courtyard, which is full of bicycles. Her clothes are sticking to her skin. She turns the corner and reaches the stairwell, where a man wearing a baseball cap comes running down the stairs. He bumps into her, knocking her against the wall.

"How rude!" Mistral snaps. *Why are people always in such a rush and so impolite?*

The building has no elevator. As she's climbing the long, long flight of stone stairs, Mistral hears pigeons cooing outside the skylights, waiting for it to cool down enough for them to fly off in search of crumbs.

Below the doorbell to Madame Cocot's music school, Seven Notes and Seven Steps, is a plaque with staves and musical notes on it.

Pythagoras invented the seven-note scale, Mistral thinks distractedly.

Madame Cocot's powdered face appears from behind the door. "Mademoiselle Blanchard," the woman says with her customary abruptness. "I was beginning to think you weren't coming."

"I'm sorry I'm late—"

"Never mind about that," Madame Cocot says, waving her inside. "We have a lot to do today, and I want to talk to you about something," she adds, disappearing behind a white pillar. "Something very important, Mademoiselle Blanchard."

Mistral glides across the white porcelain floor, slips off her yellow flats and chooses one of the hundred colorful pairs of house slippers the teacher keeps lined up in the foyer. Then she follows Madame Cocot into the piano hall. Gathered in the corners of the room are the ruffled ends of the linen curtains covering the skylight. Other curtains, with bold stripes, are stirring in front of the French doors leading out onto the terrace.

Outside the picture windows, the slate rooftops of Paris glimmer in the sunshine like black mirrors, and place de l'Opéra looks like a swimming pool made of white marble.

"You're aware of the high standards I set for my pupils," Madame Cocot says as she sits down at the black wooden piano, stacked with workbooks, notebooks and all sorts of sheet music. Once she's made herself comfortable, the old woman looks like a porcelain doll from some Russian collection. "You're also aware that in a few days' time I'll be going to Biarritz to be a judge at a competition."

"Are you trying to tell me I'm terrible?" asks Mistral. "That you don't want to teach me anymore once you come back?"

Madame Cocot looks up at the girl from her low stool. With her expression, she'd like to let Mistral know that the problem is exactly the opposite: The girl's voice is so beautiful that it sends a shiver up her spine, and her talent is so rare that it takes her breath away. But as Madame Cocot isn't very good at communicating through facial expressions, she simply hands Mistral a pamphlet.

"I've already discussed this with your mother, but she didn't give me permission," she adds.

Mistral doesn't understand. The pamphlet the woman handed her is from the Paris conservatory of music and dance.

"I'm sorry, but . . . she didn't give you permission for what?"

"Mistral, you aren't terrible. You're extraordinarily gifted! That's why . . . Well, you're right. I don't want to teach you anymore . . . because I'd like them to do it."

"The Conservatoire de Paris?"

"The advanced training faculty at the Conservatoire de Paris, to be precise."

"But why didn't my mother give you her permission?"

"She said that it's your talent, so it should be up to you to decide. We can request an audition, if you like. Otherwise, pretend I never said it." Madame Cocot sighs. "Although that would be a shame. . . . Well? What do you think?"

"I don't know what to say. Do . . . Do I need to decide right now?"

"No, no! You have all the time you want. Until September twenty-eighth, that is. That's the deadline for auditions. Meanwhile," she says, tapping out a brisk arpeggio on the piano keys, "we need to do a little practice."

There are two women in Piazza in Piscinula. One is rather old, wears tattered clothes and lives in a makeshift hovel beside the Tiber River. From time to time, a gold earring glimmers through her stringy hair. The Gypsy woman is reading the palm of an attractive young woman, who's stealing glances left and right, as if she's worried someone might see her.

"I see mountains . . . ," the Gypsy woman says, reading her palm. "You're going to go on a journey. A very important journey . . ."

When she notices Elettra arrive, the Gypsy woman looks over just long enough to nod, her eyes reassuring the girl that nothing unusual happened while she was away from the hotel. The woman has been watching over the Domus Quintilia for six months now, receiving Aunt Linda's discarded clothes or some of her mouth-watering treats in exchange.

Elettra nods back, takes her keys out of her jeans pocket and unlocks the front door. In the courtyard of the Domus Quintilia, the creeping ivy is at the height of its splendor and the tender, drooping branches of the fig trees are casting quivering shadows over the old well. The wooden terrace looks like the keel of a ship that's been pulled up onshore to dry, and the four statues guarding the courtyard have been bleached by sunlight. No cars are parked there, not even her father's old minibus.

Elettra climbs up the few steps leading to the entrance, crosses the reception area and reaches the foot of the stairs. She glances over at the door to the basement, which is hidden behind tall houseplants.

"Auntie!" she calls out. "I'm home!" She runs up the stairs and reaches the bedroom on the first floor. Her Aunt Irene is sitting in her wheelchair out on the terrace, where she's working in the shade of the canopy. Beside her are a pitcher of mint syrup and a bowl of sliced Sicilian lemons. Her gray hair is up in a bun held in place with a turtle-shaped barrette.

On another small table are lots of colorful little bowls filled with sliced strawberries, bananas, peaches and kiwifruits, chopped pistachios and walnuts, plus at least five different flavors of syrup, all ready to be mixed together to make Aunt Irene's legendary summer fruit salad.

"Well? How's Aunt Linda doing?" the elderly woman asks, resting a hand on her niece's wrist.

Before she answers, Elettra reaches over the wheelchair and grabs a giant strawberry. Her long black hair tickles her aunt's nose, making the woman laugh. "Mmm . . . Fine . . . Mmm," she finally replies, chewing the strawberry.

"Have they done the exams?"

"No. This afternoon. But she's already fed up."

Irene smiles. "And she wants to come home."

"She figures everything's falling to pieces around here," Elettra says, nodding. "Mmm . . ." Another strawberry. "Where's Dad? Did he go see that friend of his?"

For some time now, in his attempt to finish his first bestselling spy novel, Fernando Melodia has been back in touch with an old friend who works for the police, hoping to find inspiration.

"He might have. Sheng called. He says he has to go back home."

Elettra groans. "His dad must've called again."

"Something like that, yes . . ." Irene folds her hands on her lap. "He'll be here soon."

"Okay. Anything else?"

"No other messages. Wait, I take that back. Mistral called. She said the weather in Paris is wonderful, and she wants to know when you'll go visit her."

"Tomorrow."

"Seriously?"

Elettra laughs. "No, but it would be nice."

"Why don't you go, then?"

"With Aunt Linda in the hospital and Dad all wrapped up in his book?"

"Your aunt will be home soon, better than ever. As for your

20

father, you know the only thing he does in this hotel is mix up the reservations." Aunt Irene goes back to slicing fruit. "So all you need to do is tell him the trip would be an opportunity for him."

"An opportunity?"

"He wants to write a book, doesn't he? Well, then, he needs to see Paris, the world's most literary city!"

Elettra nods enthusiastically. "Good idea."

There's a knock at the door.

"That must be Sheng," says Irene.

"Do you think after six more months here he'll finally learn to use the doorbell?" Elettra jokes, heading downstairs to let him in.

In New York, at 11 Grove Court, the grandfather clock at the end of the hall chimes the moment Harvey unlocks his front door.

"Dwaine . . . ," the boy whispers to the clock, which always makes him think of his brother, who died last spring.

The hallway is ice-cold from the air-conditioning. There's no trace of Mrs. Miller in the kitchen. Harvey's father, on the other hand, is in his study, arguing with someone on the phone.

"We're talking about an increase worthy of a seaquake!" shouts Professor Miller, a skeptical climatology expert. "And about a plain that'll have turned into a desert in only ten years! Does that sound normal to you?"

Catastrophes. His favorite topic, thinks Harvey. He goes up to his room and drops his gym bag on the floor. If he lies down on his bed right now, he'll never make it downstairs for dinner, and he doesn't want his parents to start asking questions. He needs to hold out for a couple more hours.

Too tired to do anything else, he pulls his boxing clothes out of his bag, plugs the bathroom sink, turns on the faucet and quickly washes them. Then he walks back into the bedroom and, groaning from the pain, reaches up to pull down the ladder leading to the attic. He climbs up with the agility of a seventy-year-old and hangs the wet clothes beside his other gym outfits, which he washes and leaves out to dry without his parents knowing about it.

The attic is his secret hideaway. It's where he's hidden the Star of Stone, a rock just slightly bigger than a football, and three of the four seeds he found inside of it. On the walls, he's hung geographical and stellar maps, relief maps of meteor craters, charts with data on the planet's health and anything else he thought might come in handy.

"I'm coming . . . I'm coming . . . ," he murmurs to his carrier pigeon as he goes over to its cage. He changes its water, which has turned yellow, gives it more birdseed and strokes its soft neck with the back of his hand. He laughs, thinking how useless the pigeon is now. Ermete trained it to fly from Harvey's house to the apartment he had rented in Queens, but after Ermete was evicted and moved into a new place, they weren't able to train it to fly anywhere else. The new tenants still can't figure out why every once in a while the pigeon comes to tap on their window with its beak.

The two friends now use more traditional ways of keeping in touch, like meeting in Central Park at prearranged times to share their latest discoveries, but they're always left with the same question: What is it they're supposed to do in Paris or Siberia? Over the past three months, they haven't come up with an answer, but maybe it's not so important after all.

Harvey looks at a black-and-white photograph of Elettra, one of the dozen or so snapshots he's hung up on the attic walls. It's his personal spiderweb of memories. He rests a finger on her cheek and whispers, "Good night, Elettra."

At least once a week, Sheng has the same dream. He's in a jungle with the other kids, a silent jungle. They make their way out of it and dive into the sea. They swim and swim until they reach a tiny island covered with seaweed. Waiting for them on the beach is a woman. Her face is covered by a cloak, and she's wearing a close-fitting gown with all the animals of the world printed on it. In one hand, the woman's holding a pail. In the other is something Sheng can't see. He tries to get out of the water, but he can't. It's like he's being dragged down. Then the woman turns around and Sheng can finally see what she's holding in her right hand.

That's when he wakes up.

3
THE SPY

THE GRAY-HAIRED MAN LOWERS THE BINOCULARS HE'S BEEN USING to spy on the apartment on the opposite side of avenue de l'Opéra. He takes a step back, surprised, and hides behind the flowery curtain, trying to avoid touching the horrible plasticized fabric.

The girl has just opened the French doors to the terrace and stepped outside. As far as she can tell, the man's just a shadow behind one of the hundred windows across the street. But to him, she's something unexpected. Calm and still.

She's singing, and her mesmerizing voice is ringing out, growing sharp, then rich, crisp, then round with captivating simplicity.

The man closes his eyes for a few seconds, savoring the sound. Then he looks at his watch and gets back to work. He's seen everything he needs to see. Jacob Mahler takes one last look at Mistral, shuts the window behind him and puts the binoculars back into his violin case.

He hurries across the room, grabs the doorknob and then freezes. Outside, he hears footsteps that stop on his landing. Jacob Mahler leans against the wall.

Someone rings the bell.

"Claire? Are you back?" a woman hollers. Just to be sure, she knocks on the door.

"No. She isn't back," Jacob Mahler hisses under his breath, still leaning against the wall. He stands there, perfectly still, until the woman goes away. When he finally steps out onto the narrow landing, he smells the unpleasant scent of citron.

"Thanks for letting me use your apartment, Claire . . . ," he murmurs, closing the door behind him. He puts on his baseball cap and leaves.

"I don't want to, you know? I just don't want to!" Sheng yells, pacing up and down Elettra's room.

Sitting cross-legged on the bed, she tries to cheer him up. "Come on, Sheng. He's your dad. He must have a good reason for telling you to go back."

"That's the whole problem! Want to know what the reason is?"

"I'm all ears."

"He can't stand being home alone with my mom, and she can't stand being home alone with him, either," Sheng says, picking a tennis ball up off the floor and turning it around in his fingers. "Basically, I'm like a lightning rod for my parents. They use me for protection when they're going through stormy times."

"Don't you think you're exaggerating a little?"

"You know what the worst part is?" He throws the ball against the wall and catches it when it bounces back. "I just stand there being a lightning rod. I go along with it. At least, I used to. Because now . . ."

"Now?"

"Now . . ." The ball bounces against the floor. Sheng follows it and ends up in Elettra's bathroom, in front of the big mirror surrounded by lights. "Look at me!" he moans. "I don't even have the guts to tell them point-blank what I really think about going back to Shanghai."

"Then let's go to Paris."

"Huh?"

"Paris. We've been talking about going for three months now. After all, the top told us that—"

Sheng shakes his head. "No, no, that's a terrible idea. If my dad found out . . ."

Elettra gets up from the bed. "Too bad. That means I'll have to tell Mistral you don't want to come." She walks over to the door.

Sheng runs after her. "Wait!"

"Yeah?"

"When do you want to leave?"

"Harvey?" Professor Miller is sitting at the desk in his study, looking unusually disheveled. Books out of place. Papers scattered on the floor. A tie flung over the back of a chair.

"Hey, Dad," Harvey says.

"Your mom's at one of her charity meetings. Let's go out for dinner, just the two of us."

"I'll cook, if you want."

The man shakes his head. "This is my chance to try out that Ethiopian restaurant. She still refuses to eat with her hands."

"It's now or never," Harvey agrees.

Professor Miller gets up from his chair and tosses a handful of papers over his shoulder.

"Something the matter?" Harvey asks.

"The climate's gone haywire," the professor says, summing up the situation. He looks down at his wrinkled shirt. "Can I go out dressed like this?"

"Yeah, sure."

They walk out of the room.

"So what do you mean it's gone haywire?" Harvey asks as they go downstairs. "Is it the greenhouse effect?"

They walk out into the garden.

"No, the greenhouse effect is perfectly natural," his father says, sighing. "Cows and goats do more damage with their dung than most of our trucks put together. But something's not right. Too many melting glaciers, tropical storms in places where it didn't even rain a few years ago, droughts where they grow rice, migrating birds that can't find their flyways anymore, whales that end up beached without any explanation. And behind all of this is one, single problem."

"Which is . . . ?"

"There are four billion more people on Earth now than there were fifty years ago."

"Well, good thing they're people and not cows or goats," Harvey says, grinning. "Otherwise, it'd be goodbye greenhouse effect, hello broiler effect!"

His father chuckles.

They've just reached the Ethiopian restaurant. While they're waiting, Professor Miller drums his fingers on the table nervously. "Oh, by the way," he says, "some of my friends got back to me about those questions you asked. They all sounded intrigued. Still sure you want to go into journalism?"

Harvey tries not to let the question bother him. Every chance

27

his father gets, he tries to talk him into becoming a scientist. "Yeah, why?"

The professor riffles through his pockets and finds a crumpled slip of paper. Another unusual sight, given that he usually keeps everything meticulously organized in numbered file folders. "I showed a botanist friend of mine the seed you gave me. He asked where I found it and said he'd like to buy it."

"Not a chance. What'd he tell you?"

"It turns out it's an extremely rare species of *Ginkgo biloba*, one of the world's most ancient trees. In fact, he claims it's a seed from a prehistoric tree, a real museum piece."

"Any news about the stone?"

The professor pulls out a second slip of paper. "I sent the fragments you gave me to a friend in France. She believes it's meteoritic material and quite anomalous."

"Anomalous meaning . . . ?"

"Meaning she'd like to see a larger sample."

Harvey frowns.

"She'd be willing to invite you over to the *collection des minéraux* laboratory at the University of Paris so you can personally watch all the analyses she conducts on it."

Meanwhile, their food arrives: two platters lined with thin bread and piled high with super-spicy chunks of lamb.

"Now we're talking!" says Harvey.

Laughing, the father and son learn how to pick up the food using only their hands and the bread. In a few moments, their lips are burning.

"Well, then," Professor Miller finally says, "what should I tell her? Are you going?"

"To Paris?"

"They'll pay for your trip."

"You wouldn't be coming?"

"I'd love to, but I've got a lot on my mind right now. The data coming in from the Pacific is completely off the charts. I wish I could go there and verify everything in person. . . ."

Harvey smiles. "So why don't you?"

"Don't tempt me."

"Well, you're temping me with Paris."

"I'd be very pleased if you accepted my friend's invitation," Professor Miller confesses.

For the first time in years, Harvey sees his father's eyes brimming with pride.

"This friend of yours . . . is she good-looking?"

His father smiles. "Oh, you know . . . archaeologists."

Harvey thinks it over for a minute. "Okay," he answers. "Tell her I'll go."

4
THE RETURN

◯

AFTER THE LESSON, MISTRAL LEAVES THE BUILDING, HER HEAD full of dreams and the keys to the music school in her pocket. Madame Cocot gave them to her in case she wants to do some extra practice while the music teacher is out of town. "Give it some serious thought," the woman told her, tweaking her cheek.

Walking under a sky speckled with clouds, the girl decides not to go home by Métro. She feels like being outside. She walks slowly, enjoying the mingling aromas of flowers, freshly baked bread and French cuisine, which are just a few of the many ingredients in the perfume of the Parisian streets.

When she reaches the ivy-covered entrance to her building in Montmartre, the doorman steps out of his ground-floor apartment and calls her over. He gives her some envelopes and a package wrapped in manila paper. To the girl's great surprise, the package is addressed to her.

MISTRAL BLANCHARD
RUE DE L'ABREUVOIR 22

As she's climbing the stairs, she slides her finger under the edge of the paper and peeks inside. It's a book.

ARGOT: THE SECRET SONGS OF ANIMALS

Mistral rips off the paper. On the cover is a golden music box, its lid ajar. Bursting out of it like a bouquet of flowers are dozens of different animals riding rainbows. On the first page is an inscription. The book is in French, but the note is written in English.

New York, June 12

My dear Mistral,

I found this old book of Alfred's while I was tidying up the apartment. Our mutual friend Vladimir, the antiques dealer, told me you love to sing, so I thought I would send it to you as a little memento of New York.

Agatha

"Agatha!" Mistral says aloud, her voice echoing through the stone stairwell. Grateful for this unexpected gift from Professor Van Der Berger's old friend, whom they met in New York, Mistral flips through the book, which has beautiful color illustrations. It describes the calls of various animals and, more importantly, explains how to imitate them.

How wonderful! Mistral thinks as she starts climbing the stairs again, engrossed in the book.

SONG FOR BEES, SONG OF THE WHALES . . .

Having reached her apartment door, she looks at the cover again. *Argot.* The mysterious language that animals use to warn each other of danger, track down their den, find a place to hide . . .

She slowly turns the key in the lock. And then she stops.

"Mom?" she calls out, standing stock-still. She opens the door, making as much noise as possible, and calls out to her mother again.

She's done this ever since she walked in one day and found her mother kissing a man. An embarrassing and shocking surprise. Her mother apologized, but there was no reason for her to. She isn't married. Mistral has never had a real father, and her mother raised her alone, trying to juggle her daughter and her perfume career. So there's nothing wrong with her trying to live her own life once in a while. But then why is it, Mistral wonders, that every time she suspects her mother is seeing someone, she gets a knot in her stomach and feels a sense of dread? Whenever that happens, she reminds herself that she's always been the most important person in her mother's life.

Her mom is often away on business, and Mistral has to spend a lot of time on her own, but she appreciates how much her mom has sacrificed for her. They're lucky that Cecile's job as a perfumer is going so well, that she's had such a successful career. Mistral has grown up lacking nothing, living in the penthouse of a beautiful, ivy-covered building overlooking Paris.

Mistral loves their apartment, with its light wood parquet floors that creak beneath her bare feet, exposed ceiling beams painted white, rounded doors, dining room chairs all deliberately different from one another, straw baskets used as stools, unframed paintings on the walls and white couches arranged in a circle in the living room. . . .

Once she's certain no one's home, Mistral walks in and goes to her bedroom. She rests the book about argot on her lilac-colored brass bed and steps over to the window to check on the bees.

The apartment smells like lavender. On the bathroom mirror, she finds a note from her mother:

> I won't be back for dinner.
> Love you,
> Mom

Mistral sighs. She looks at the little bear painted on the countertop, at the butterfly-shaped bathtub decals that look like they're flying out from the drain. They decorated the room to-gether when she was five years old. Mistral still remembers her mom's paint-splattered hands like it was yesterday.

She takes the note off the mirror and goes back to her room.

The phone starts ringing.

It's Harvey.

A few minutes later, Elettra calls, too.

It's no coincidence. They're coming.

33

FIRST STASIMON

"Hello, Vladimir."

"Hello? Zoe? Is that you?"

"How are you?"

"No, how are *you*, blast it! I've been looking for you for months! Where on earth have you been?"

"Away on business."

"But why now, of all times? You realize it's begun, don't you?"

"Yes."

"And that it began in Rome?"

"I know."

"Then why didn't you come back? Where were you?"

"Just out traveling the world, as usual."

"But where, exactly? Couldn't you have at least called? Wherever you were, didn't they have phones?"

"There's no reason to be so angry."

"But where were you?"

"Siberia."

"You went back to Tunguska?"

"Wherever I was, I'm back now. I'm in Paris."

"The kids are on their way there."

"Good."

"Do you remember Alfred's instructions?"

"Of course."

"Alfred's dead."

"I know."

"How'd you find out?"

"He was the first one I called. And he didn't answer."

5

THE LUGGAGE

The Charles de Gaulle Airport in Paris is filled with light. The international terminal has picture windows that overlook the runways and the long gates. When newly arrived passengers pick up their suitcases, they can see the people waiting for them on the other side.

Harvey follows the other passengers from his flight and reaches the baggage claim area. He yawns and stretches, tired after all the hours spent sitting on the plane, watching movies on the screen mounted on the seat back in front of him. He watched them in French with English subtitles, hoping to learn something.

The conveyor belt on the luggage carousel beside him starts to turn.

Someone stands out from the crowd of businessmen, vacationing families and overweight retirees in sweatsuits. Someone wearing a Hawaiian shirt and cargo pants. It's Ermete De Panfilis, who's limping along and rubbing his sleepy eyes. To celebrate his return to the Old World, the owner of the Regno del Dado went to a duty-free shop and bought a pair of flashy tortoiseshell sunglasses, which sparkle on his almost completely bald head. The shades match his faux crocodile backpack, which he bought at a sale at Macy's and claims is a must-have accessory. Inside the backpack, cushioned in layers of rolled-up newspaper, are the Star of Stone and Ermete's wooden top. In Harvey's pocket is another top.

Harvey and Ermete don't say a word to each other. They're playing it safe and traveling separately.

As the empty conveyor belt squeals along, a voice over the loudspeaker announces something in French, which only a sprightly man with an orange plastic visor on his head and a bulky guidebook in his hand manages to understand, to the delight of his three young daughters. If Harvey remembers correctly, they were sitting next to Ermete on the plane and didn't keep quiet for a single second during the whole trip. The girls bounce over to the next carousel, where their flight number appears a moment later. The mouthlike opening in the wall spews out the first suitcases with a thud.

Harvey looks through the glass doors, trying to figure out which of the people waiting on the other side is his father's friend. Is she the tall, ditsy-looking woman whose clothes make her look like a flowered lampshade? Or the young woman chewing pink gum? What if it's the old woman who's pinned an airport worker against the wall with her luggage cart?

The girls' happy shrieks turn Harvey's concentration back to the conveyor belt. All three of them are grappling with a suitcase bigger than they are, which threatens to drag them away. Harvey sees his wheeled suitcase approaching. This is the first time he's barely had to wait for his luggage. *Vive la France!* he thinks.

Making sure Ermete notices, he grabs his bag, turns his back to the carousel and the three screaming girls and heads off toward the exit, suitcase in tow. The glass doors open with a sigh.

"Mr. Miller?" a man's voice addresses him a moment later. It belongs to a young, tall, thin man wearing a white shirt and a black tie.

"Yeah, that's me." Behind him, the glass doors open and close again.

"Would you follow me? Mademoiselle Cybel is waiting for you."

"Mademoiselle Cybel?" Harvey smiles. "I think you're making a mistake. I don't know anyone named—"

The metallic glimmer of a knife peeks out from the man's pocket, and in the blink of an eye it's pressed up between Harvey's shoulder blades. "No. No mistake, Mr. Miller. Don't say a word. Just come with me, please."

Still standing beside the luggage carousel, Ermete can't believe his eyes. Who on earth is that guy? And why is he escorting Harvey away, walking only two inches behind him?

Harvey makes a fist with his right hand and spreads out his fingers three times fast, three times slow, three times fast.

Morse code. SOS.

There's no time to lose. Ermete limps out of the international arrivals terminal without waiting for his suitcases.

"Here we go again," he grumbles, not taking his eyes off the two. "I haven't even left the airport yet and somebody's already being kidnapped." Having made his way past the air-conditioned area and through exit 20, the engineer is hit by a blast of hot air. His Hawaiian shirt clings to his potbelly like a second skin.

The stranger has already walked Harvey across a two-lane street. They're heading toward an old Citroën with tinted windows and an appliqué on its hood that makes the front of the car look like a crocodile snout.

Ermete mutters something under his breath. If they get into that car, it's all over.

He looks around. A hundred paces away, people are waiting in line at a taxi stand. The engineer whirls around and heads toward the cabs. He glances back and sees Harvey being pushed into the crocodile car.

Ermete half-runs, half-limps up to the taxi stand. He cuts through the line, causing a chorus of protests.

"Excuse me!" he shouts in Italian. "Excuse me! This is an emergency!"

"Les Italiens!" someone fumes, as if that explains everything.

Ermete darts between a woman and her taxi, nudging her away with his backpack. "Excuse me!" he shouts again. He gets into the car and slams the door shut before the woman even has the chance to react. *"Segua quella macchina!"* he hollers to the taxi driver, who has a long, greasy mustache.

The man folds up his newspaper and rests it on the seat beside him. *"Pardon?"*

Just then, the Citroën crocodile passes by them. Ermete waves his arms, points at it and repeats, in English, "Follow that car!"

"Mais oui!" barks Greasy Mustache Man, throwing the car into gear. Ermete plops back in his seat and puts his faux crocodile backpack down next to him. Only then does he think about his suitcases, which are sadly going round and round on the conveyor belt inside the airport.

6
THE TRAIN

"HAO! JUST FOURTEEN HOURS AND FORTY-NINE MINUTES TO GO," says Sheng, always the optimist, the moment the TGV leaves Rome's Termini train station. He stays focused on his watch for a moment and then turns his attention to his travel companions, Elettra and Fernando Melodia.

"We'll be there before you know it," Elettra's father remarks, setting up his things on the little table in their compartment.

"This is the first time I've taken the train since I came to Italy," Sheng adds.

"Well, it's a good thing it's not an Italian train," Elettra points out. "Although there's no guarantee it won't break down anywhere between here and the border, at the Fréjus Tunnel . . ."

They're taking the train to Paris because Elettra's father refused to go there by plane. He wanted to travel with wheels under his feet. Besides, he claims that train rides get the creative juices flowing, which is exactly what he needs right now. He's come prepared with an incredible supply of notebooks, pens and pencils, along with a stack of books to use for inspiration.

"So, how's your novel going?" Sheng asks him, earning a nasty glare from Elettra.

"Fine, fine, I suppose," Fernando says, rather evasively. "Let's say that . . . well, you could say I've pretty much finished the second part."

"*Hao!* That's great!"

"What I really need to do now is build up to the finale. And write the first part, of course."

Sheng and Elettra exchange baffled glances. The Chinese boy decides to dig deeper. "Um . . . how could you write the second part without even writing the first part?"

Fernando gnaws on his pencil. "There aren't really any rules about how to go about it. People just write whatever comes to mind, don't they?"

"You see, Sheng," Elettra cuts in, swaying slightly with the movement of the train, "my dad's a genius. And like all geniuses, he needs to work in his own, special way."

They laugh.

Later on, when they've almost reached Florence, someone raps on their compartment door. A second later, a ticket collector wearing a white shirt and a black tie asks them for their tickets. "First time going to Paris?" he asks, smiling, as he hands them back.

"*Hao,* yeah!" Sheng replies.

"On vacation?"

"No," Elettra says flatly. She can feel energy building up inside of her, which naturally happens whenever danger's near.

The ticket collector leaves, closing the door behind him.

Five paces down the corridor, he dials an internal extension number and whispers, "I found them in car 12. Notify Paris."

When things get incredibly complicated, Ermete can rest assured they'll get even more complicated. The phone call he receives the moment he switches on his cell phone is a perfect example of this.

"Listen, Mom, I know you worry, but believe me, I landed safe and sound," the engineer moans, trying to calm her down. He pins the phone between his shoulder and cheek as he counts out euro coins into the French taxi driver's hand. The thirty-plus-kilometer cab ride from the airport to the square they're in now is making a dent in his savings. "No, I'm not mad at you! No. I just don't have time to talk right now, that's all. . . ."

"C'est bon," the taxi driver says, holding up his free hand. He pours the river of coins onto the passenger seat with a loud jingle.

Ermete grabs his backpack, slips out of the backseat of the cab and stands there on the sidewalk. He has no idea what street he's on, but the crocodile Citroën Harvey was in pulled up right in front of a restaurant on the corner.

"Mom, listen," Ermete says, exasperated, "if I told you what I was doing . . ." He presses his back up against the wall and moves over a few steps, trying to figure out what's going on. The name of the restaurant, CYBEL, CUISINE DE TER, is written around the picture of a woman wearing a little tower-shaped hat. Ermete takes a few more steps along the wall, camouflaging himself behind some pots of succulent plants drenched in sunlight.

"Mom!" he repeats into the phone. "I'm . . . Oh, how can I explain this to you?" Suddenly, he stiffens. He's just spotted Harvey's

42

kidnapper inside the restaurant. "Sorry, I need to go." Ignoring his mother's whining protests, he switches off his cell phone.

Trying to act casual, he strolls over to the menu written in flowery handwriting on a blackboard beside the door. He pretends to scan the names of the various dishes, while actually trying to figure out what's happening inside. Through the corner of his eye, he notices a certain commotion going on in the restaurant.

He looks at his watch and realizes it's still set to New York time. Does he need to move the hour hand forward or backward? And by how many hours? He thinks it over. There aren't any customers, so lunchtime must've ended a while ago, and it's still nowhere close to dinnertime. It might be four o'clock, or five at the latest.

He immediately makes a call. "Mom? What time is it? Yeah, what time is it? Yes, right now! Not a month from now . . ."

There's a long pause.

"Of course I don't know. Why else would I ask you? Are you going to tell me, or do I need to send you a written request? No, Dad's watch stopped working at least twenty years ago. Don't start up again with the stuff about it needing a new battery. It's broken, got it? Broken!"

A brief pause.

"Four forty-four. Okay, thanks." He says goodbye and hangs up, noticing that it's a palindromic number. He finds coincidences like this totally irresistible.

He spots two other young men with black ties walking through the restaurant.

"Okay," Ermete mumbles, stepping away from the menu board to walk around the block. "What do I do?"

He tries to think. They've got Harvey. Harvey has one of the tops and a cell phone on him. . . .

He dials the boy's phone. It's off. Then he realizes that by calling Harvey's cell phone, he probably just gave the kidnappers his number, too.

"Think, Ermete, think!" he tells himself, walking around the building. "You should know how to handle this by now. After all, this is the third kidnapping we've been through."

The first time, it happened to Mistral. The second time, it was his own turn. The very thought of it makes his bones ache.

Where the heck am I? he wonders. He's in a neighborhood of low, clean buildings, its streets paved with medieval cobblestones. He remembers crossing the Seine. The restaurant isn't far from a little square and a bigger street. The sun blazes down mercilessly, casting no shadows. Nearby is a bone-dry fountain, its drain clogged with pigeon feathers. A sign at the corner of the two streets reads RUE GALANDE.

Then Ermete notices a little Algerian café on the other side of the square. It looks like a good spot from which to keep an eye on the restaurant. Outside of it is a wobbly plastic table with a greasy yellow plastic tablecloth, a peeling sign showing an assortment of ice creams in funny shapes and a mosquito zapper, which is switched on. Ermete sits down on one of the two chairs next to the table.

A few minutes later, a North African man with a necklace of aluminum skulls looks out from the doorway and says something to him in French.

Ermete gestures to explain that he doesn't understand.

The man speaks again, this time in English. "No table service."

Ermete is panicked. He needs to stay within sight of the restaurant. He's tempted to argue, but the sight of the man's studded bracelet and big muscles makes him change his mind.

When he steps inside, he's hit by a wave of Saharan heat. They're out of ice cream. All they make is lamb shawarmas.

"I'll have a shawarma . . . and an ice-cold beer." As he's ordering, the engineer keeps glancing over at the restaurant.

"We don't have any."

"Okay. A warm beer, then."

"We don't serve beer," the North African says. "Only yogurt drinks."

"Fine," Ermete says quickly. "Then I'll take a yogurt drink." He turns to hurry outside.

"Pay in advance, please."

This is insane, Harvey thinks. *This is totally insane.*

The door of the elevator he was shoved into has just opened up onto a dimly lit, muggy room that looks like a tropical garden. Cascades of leaves hang from the ceiling. A carpet of grass covers the whole floor. Roots are underfoot everywhere. Growing from the walls are strange pitcher-shaped plants and orchids in different colors. Lined up on a slate countertop resting on two crude lava rocks are a dozen giant plants with plump, shiny leaves.

And there's a woman wearing a silk gown.

The owner of this naturalistic nightmare is an enormous woman with a misshapen neck, a string of gray pearls partially hidden among its folds. She has big, watery eyes that look like they're melting down onto her cheeks. Her lips are pudgy and fiery red. Her bare, saggy arms quiver like jelly with her every move. She's layer upon layer of flab.

The woman is in the process of dropping a large termite into one of the plants. The second the carnivorous plant detects the insect, the little green lid at the top of its pitcherlike body snaps shut.

"Bon appétit!" the woman cries cheerfully. Then, noticing Harvey, she greets him in terribly snobbish English. "Goodness gracious! He's arrived at last, our dear Mr. Miller Junior . . . Mr. Miller Junior."

Harvey just rode all the way from the airport trying to communicate with the man in the black tie, who's standing behind him now. And for what? To come see this old whale of a woman? *Whoever these people are, they're making a big mistake.* "Nice place you got here," he says with a sneer.

The woman gestures to the man wearing the black tie, who instantly disappears, as if swallowed up by the grassy mantle covering the floor and the creeping ivy covering the walls.

"Do you mean it? You like it?" the woman trills, despite her throaty voice. "Well, you haven't seen anything yet. You haven't seen anything yet."

Harvey is alarmed to notice things moving through the leaves and grass. Are there animals in here?

The woman steps behind the slate counter, her gown rustling. "Keeping up this little tropical ecosystem in the center of Paris takes a lot of work," she continues, "but you're right. You're right. It is a nice place. A very nice—"

"You know who I am," Harvey cuts her off, not caring if he's being rude, "but I've never had the pleasure of meeting you. And I don't know why you brought me here."

She spreads out her arms. "So you could see, with your own two eyes, Mademoiselle Cybel's *maison secrète*! Mademoiselle Cybel's *maison secrète*!" she exclaims twice, letting out an icy laugh that makes her double chin quiver. "If you only knew how many people have begged me to show them my secret realm. . . . If only you knew. They'd do anything to see my collection of *Nepenthes albomarginata*. . . ." With this, she points at the pitcher-shaped, termite-eating plants. "Or my sweet, adorable droseras . . . my sweet, adorable droseras," she coos, sprinkling a handful of ants over the giant plants lined up on the counter. Their sticky leaves contract and trap the insects, which wriggle their legs in vain.

Harvey turns away but freezes the second he notices a black spider as big as a fist scurrying through the foliage. Panicking, he looks at his feet, which are sinking down into the damp grass, and thanks his lucky stars he's wearing gym shoes.

"Listen, Mademoiselle . . . Cybel," Harvey says, taking a deep breath, "I'm really happy I got to see your green room, or whatever the heck you call it, but now, if you'll excuse me—"

"It's unlikely I will," the woman says with a frown. "It's very unlikely I will." She leans down behind the counter, making the kind of sound a hippo makes when sinking down into a mud hole. When she reappears, she's holding a little white mouse by its tail. "Where's Marcel? Where's Marcel?" she asks, looking around. "Oh, there he is!" she exclaims, her big, watery eyes glimmering. "Stand still, please, Mr. Miller Junior. Marcel's by your foot. Right by your foot . . ."

47

Whatever Marcel is, Harvey instantly turns into a pillar of salt. Mademoiselle Cybel flings the mouse across the room. Something that Harvey thought was a root turns out to be a big snake. It shows its fangs, catches the mouse and slithers away into the grass.

"My baby anaconda," Mademoiselle Cybel explains, beaming. Then she adds, "You look pale, Mr. Miller Junior. Very pale. Is it from your long journey? Or do animals disgust you?"

Harvey doesn't answer. He just clenches his fists and tries to figure a way out of there.

The woman walks toward him, her silk gown rustling. "Goodness gracious! Of course, that would be natural for a city boy. What would you know about the world, except for what you read in the papers or see on TV? Amusing. Very amusing. Especially because . . ." Mademoiselle Cybel walks right past Harvey and over to a little door partially hidden behind the creeping ivy, "I'm the one who decides what appears in the papers and on TV!" She rests her hand on the doorknob and looks over her shoulder. "Are you coming with me, Mr. Miller Junior, or would you rather stay here and keep Marcel company? Unfortunately, he's not much of a conversationalist when he's eating."

Harvey decides to follow her.

"I've heard very interesting things about you. Very interesting things," Mademoiselle Cybel says, once they're in the next room. It looks perfectly normal to Harvey. White walls, a desk, glass flooring.

"Like what?"

"For instance, that you're very brave. Very brave."

Mademoiselle Cybel goes over and sits down behind the desk.

48

Shafts of white light are streaming in through a large window that overlooks the square. On the walls are thousands of little screens showing people the size of passport photos and a swarm of little blinking green and red lights.

Harvey takes a step forward and then stops in his tracks.

"Come along," Mademoiselle Cybel trills. "Come along. They won't bite. It's just an aquarium."

Harvey shakes his head with disbelief. Beneath the transparent flooring are dozens of piranhas, which are thrashing against the glass, snapping at Harvey's feet.

"You're out of your mind!"

"Perhaps," the woman admits. "But what does it matter?"

"My friends are going to come looking for me," Harvey tells her, forcing himself to ignore the crazed dance of the fish beneath his feet.

"Are you so sure of that? Paris is Paris! If someone wants to disappear, they can disappear very easily here. What's the word they're always using these days? Ah, yes . . . privacy. We French are very fond of our privacy. Besides, who is it you expect to come looking for you? Your parents, from New York? Your friends, from Rome?"

"H-how did you—" Harvey stammers.

The woman's buttery face quivers, and her eyes bob around like cherries in a gelatin mold. "Yes, yes! Go on! Do go on! Goodness gracious! 'How did you know that?' That's what you want to ask me, isn't it? Isn't it? Well, it's very simple: I'm well informed! Very well informed! Have you ever wondered how newspapers are written? Or television newscasts? Who is it that gives them all those facts, all those things to write?"

"Sources," says Harvey.

"Sources? Bah!" the woman snaps, holding back a laugh. She runs her hand over the fleshy folds of her neck and strokes her string of pearls. "You're still very young, boy. Very, very young."

"So what? I'm going to be a journalist one day."

"Magnificent! Magnificent!" Mademoiselle Cybel trills, clapping her hands together like a walrus. "Then perhaps we'll work together! After all, you'll need my help!" she says, pointing at the thousands of tiny screens on the walls, the green and red lights, and the crawling text beneath it all.

"I d-don't understand . . . ," Harvey stammers.

"How could you? These are my own, personal private eyes!" A keyboard has appeared beneath the woman's fingertips. "I need to find an American boy by the name of Miller who's taking an international flight from New York to Paris? *Click-clack.* I notify my flight attendants by text message. *Clack.* And the moment you step foot on any flight . . . *Click.* I know about it. I need to track down a thirteen- or fourteen-year-old girl with curly black hair who's coming here from Rome, probably in the company of a Chinese boy? *Click-clack.* How will they be traveling? By car? I text my friends at the Mont Blanc, Fréjus and Great St. Bernard passes. Just to be sure, another message goes to the Franco-Italian border at Ventimiglia. *Click-clack.* What if she takes the train? Heavens! We immediately notify the staff working on the TGV. Would you mind taking a look around while you're checking the passengers' tickets? Oh, how nice! Here's the answer! Boarded in Rome. Car twelve. One girl, one Chinese boy and one adult male. Voilà!"

Mademoiselle Cybel continues relentlessly as the little green

50

and red lights blink on and off. "Want to know what's going on in the world? Then ask waiters, ushers, doormen, taxi drivers. Fashion shop clerks. Flight attendants. Janitors. Ticket collectors. Sailors on cruise ships. Baristas. Piano bar musicians. All it takes is a little cash and they can fatten their meager paychecks in exchange for a possible scoop. And who's behind it all? Who's behind it?" The woman leans over the desk, making her double chin sag like the droopy sail on an old galleon. "Mademoiselle Cybel and her spiderweb of snitches! Her spiderweb of snitches!"

Harvey can't believe his ears. A network of everyday spies that no one would ever suspect. A massive network that no one could ever escape. "But that's . . . that's horrible!"

"Not everyone would say that. Not everyone," Mademoiselle Cybel replies, melting back into her chair. "Those who come to me, that is, a good deal of all those who want to keep up-to-date on all the latest gossip and find out what's going on in the city, appreciate the efficiency of my private eyes."

"Which explains why I'm here . . ."

"Exactly! Exactly!" the woman gurgles.

"So who asked you to find me?"

"Ah, client confidentiality, Mr. Miller Junior! Client confidentiality! Although I think you can probably figure that out for yourself. . . ."

"Let me guess: some mysterious man who lives in Shanghai."

"Exactly! Exactly!"

"What do you guys want from me, anyway?"

Mademoiselle Cybel opens a drawer with her pudgy hand and takes out a sheet of paper. "Five toy tops, a wooden box and anything else you might have. If you don't have them, you'll need to tell me who does. Elettra? Mistral? Your Chinese friend, perhaps? Come to think of it, I don't know his name. . . ."

"Genghis Khan," Harvey says with a sneer, grateful that the reservations at the Domus Quintilia hotel were mixed up and that they've been playing it safe over the past few months. These people obviously don't know who Sheng is, and they don't consider Ermete part of the kids' group.

"Amusing. Very amusing!" Mademoiselle Cybel says, snickering. "I'll let my client know. But now, Mr. Miller Junior, would you be so kind as to empty your pockets? My men have already searched your suitcase. They didn't find any of the things we're looking for, just your horrible white tube socks. White tube socks! And you Americans want to rule the world?"

The wooden top hidden in his jeans pocket suddenly feels as heavy as lead. "Even if I did have something, why should I give it to you?"

"Because you have only two alternatives, Mr. Miller Junior. Only two alternatives," Mademoiselle Cybel replies, slipping the sheet of paper back into the drawer. "The first is to cooperate with me and spend the next few days enjoying the beautiful Parisian summertime. The beautiful Parisian summertime."

"And the second?"

"The second is to refuse to cooperate," Mademoiselle Cybel says, tapping her foot on the floor, "and have a little party with my tropical dearies in the aquarium."

Tack-tack-tack. The piranhas thrash against the glass floor beneath Harvey's feet.

* * *

The shrill, irritating ring of the telephone shatters the silence on rue de l'Abreuvoir, making Mistral start. She's lying belly-down on her bed, where she's been completely absorbed in the book about the secret language of animals. She rolls over with acrobatic grace, stretches out her long, slender arm and picks up the phone. The line is staticky.

It's Ermete.

"Oh, wonderful!" the girl exclaims in her lovely Parisian accent. "You're here!" But the tone of the engineer's voice makes the smile on her lips vanish instantly.

The static on the line grates on her ear like chalk on a blackboard. While Ermete's telling her what happened, Mistral is suddenly assailed by the memory of Jacob Mahler, of being held captive in the house in Rome and escaping in Beatrice's yellow Mini.

"Where are you?" asks Mistral. She opens her old cherrywood wardrobe and takes out a skirt with red, white and black circles on it, pulling it up over her long legs with a bounce. "Oh, no! Rue Galande. Yes, I know where it is," she says. "That will take me a while. Please, stay where you are. No, of course not. I won't tell anyone. I'll be there as soon as I can."

Jacob Mahler is sitting at a table at the café from which he's been spying on the girl. When he sees her run out the front door of her building, he puts down his newspaper, takes off his earphones and jots down RUE GALANDE in his notebook. Then he checks his map of Paris, rests his digital recorder on the table and copies down the number of the cell phone that just called her. Beside it, he writes a name: ERMETE.

He motions to the waiter.

"A cassis," he orders calmly. There won't be any other phone calls for a while. Or any more strange static on the line, either.

"Oh, no!" Sheng cries as the train leaves the Turin station. "Here, read this."

Elettra's eyes scan the message that just appeared on her friend's cell phone.

"Bad news?" Fernando Melodia asks, shuffling through his blank sheets of paper. Then he tucks his pencil behind his ear and stares out at the ring of Alps rising up behind the ugly buildings on the outskirts of town. He narrows his eyes, deep in thought. "The mountains . . . I could add a chase scene down some twisty mountain roads. Maybe on motorcycles . . ."

The two kids look at him, their faces as stony as sphinxes.

"Never mind," Fernando says, guessing their thoughts. He crumples up yet another sheet of paper. "No motorcycle chase through the mountains."

The train zips along below a series of electrical cables that look like spiderwebs. Elettra jumps to her feet and turns to Sheng. "Feel like getting a snack?"

The Chinese boy follows her out of the compartment. They both try to act natural, but the moment they're out of earshot . . .

"They got Harvey!" exclaims Elettra.

"That means they were watching him."

"He shouldn't have left New York!"

"And we shouldn't have left Rome!"

"And Mistral shouldn't leave her house!"

"Man, were we stupid."

Elettra can't get over it. "We should've known! We were totally predictable. They knew we'd be meeting up right about now."

"Huh? Why?"

"It's June nineteenth."

"So what?"

They walk into the dining car, and the door closes behind them. There are lots of little tables and a small counter behind which a waitress is trying to keep a dignified balance. They can see the mountaintops through the windows.

"Think about it, Sheng," Elettra explains. "We met in Rome right before New Year's Eve. Then we met up again in New York at the end of March. . . ."

"March twentieth, the spring equinox."

"Exactly. And now it's only two days until the summer solstice."

"So what?"

Elettra feels like banging her fist on the counter. "So this stupid train needs to get us to Paris, and fast! Really fast! Why didn't we fly there?"

"Because your dad—"

"I know, I know. But just the thought that Harvey . . ." Elettra's voice trails off. Her fingers are sizzling with energy. "Do you think they're going to hurt him?"

"No, they don't want to hurt us."

"What do they want, then?"

"You know what they want. They want the things the professor left us, plus the things we found after that."

The energy in Elettra's fingers grows stronger. "They can read

55

us like a book. Just like the professor." She rests both hands on the counter. A flame bursts up from the espresso machine, making the waitress shriek.

The three of them stand there, gaping. Elettra slowly takes her hands off the counter.

"Two bitter orange sodas, please," Sheng says, smiling.

7

THE POISON

"Help me, I'm begging you!" Ermete moans to Mistral the moment she shows up in the square in the Latin Quarter. "I can't take it anymore."

He hands her a bundle of greasy paper. Sticking up out of it is a gigantic shawarma brimming with lamb, lettuce, onions, cucumbers, tomatoes, yogurt and spicy sauce.

"This is the third one they've made me eat so far," he explains, "and I don't have the guts to say no."

Mistral peeks inside the brasserie. The smell of cooked onions and meat wafting out of it is so powerful it could wake up a mummy. Now that the girl's holding the sandwich, Ermete points at the restaurant across the square. "Harvey's still in there," he explains. "Nobody's gone in or come out."

"And what's . . . what's in there?" Mistral asks, sitting down next to Ermete.

The engineer from Rome jerks his thumb at the brasserie. "I tried asking them if they knew."

"And . . . ?"

"All they did was ask me if I'd ever heard of Materazzi."

"I don't understand. . . ."

"He's an Italian soccer player. To make a long story short, there's a little hostility between Italy and France. I think it was a friendly way to tell me they don't want to talk to me."

"They sound nice," Mistral remarks.

Ermete tells her everything he's seen. Then he nods at the restaurant and asks, "So you've never seen the place before?"

"No, I live on the other side of town."

"Right," Ermete says with a sigh. "Of course."

Ermete's cell phone rings and vibrates. It's a French number. "This must be the airport calling to ask if I want them to donate my luggage to charity," he explains as he answers. "Yes, hello?" A moment later, he cups his hand over the receiver and looks at Mistral. "They're asking if I speak French."

"Well, do you?"

"No!"

"Then give me the phone. . . . Hello, who's speaking?"

A woman's snobbish voice is on the other end. "I can't believe my ears! Is this the voice of a sweet young girl? Of a sweet young girl? Are you Mistral, by any chance?"

"Who is this?" the girl replies, jumping to her feet. "How do you know my name?"

"Goodness gracious, my little Parisienne! Who was I talking to a second ago? Your little Chinese friend? No, no . . . it can't be. He must still be on the train."

"Who is this?" Mistral insists, almost shouting. She starts to pace nervously down the street. Seeing that she's headed toward the restaurant, Ermete darts after her, grabs her by the shoulders and guides her in the other direction.

"It isn't important who you're talking to, my little Parisienne," Mademoiselle Cybel continues, her voice oozing like molasses. "I think you know that your friend Harvey Miller is here with me . . . and he isn't having any fun at all."

"Let him go this instant!"

"Of course, my dear! Of course! That's exactly what we'd like to do. But first we need the things we're looking for. You know what I'm talking about. . . ."

"No, I don't. Why don't you tell me?"

"As you like. We need four more tops, a wooden map and some ancient objects you found here and there. Am I forgetting anything?"

Mistral silently mouths a desperate "They know everything!" to Ermete.

The engineer waves his hands around, telling her to stall.

"We don't have any of those things," Mistral lies.

"Well, I think you do. Here's my proposal: Harvey in exchange for a few trifles. What do you say? Let's meet in an hour and be done with it."

Mistral covers the phone with her hand and tells Ermete.

"Someplace with lots of people," he whispers.

"Up in the Eiffel Tower," Mistral says. "On the nine hundred and ninety-ninth step."

"Very well," Mademoiselle Cybel replies. "We'll see you *à la Tour* in one hour, then."

"We'll be there."

The conversation comes to an end.

"They know everything!" Mistral tells Ermete again. "And this time we don't have a chance! They know absolutely everything . . . even that Elettra and Sheng are coming here by train!"

"We need to warn them," Ermete says, taking his cell phone back. He gives Mistral a warm hug and jerks his thumb at the faux crocodile backpack slung over his shoulder. "There's still hope. We haven't given them anything yet."

"If you don't mind, Mr. Miller Junior, I'll need your word you won't leave," Mademoiselle Cybel tells Harvey as she takes him back into the green room.

Harvey raises his right hand. "Scout's honor."

"Goodness gracious, no! I detest Boy Scouts. With those horrible knee-length shorts and those kerchiefs around their necks? I detest Boy Scouts! So it seems your word won't be enough."

"Well, aren't I going with you to the Eiffel Tower for the swap anyway?" Harvey asks, confused, having overheard Mademoiselle Cybel's conversation with Mistral.

"Oh, certainly not! After all, what if something goes wrong? You'd better stay here and wait. Stay here and wait. It'll just take a few hours, you'll see." Mademoiselle Cybel hands him the phone. "But first, call home and tell them you got to Paris safe and sound."

"Forget it."

"I have a recording of your voice. I could do it for you, if you like. This is your home phone number, isn't it?"

Harvey rolls his eyes and grabs the phone. He gets voice mail and leaves a very short message.

"Well done, Mr. Miller Junior. Very well done. You're clearly an intelligent boy. But now, just to be sure you don't do anything foolish . . ." With amazing swiftness, Mademoiselle Cybel reaches down into the leaves carpeting the room, snatches up something black and plunks it down on Harvey's arm. Before the boy even has the chance to pull his arm back, he sees the spider and feels a sharp sting.

"Ow!" he cries, more from fear than pain. "It bit me!"

The old woman straightens out the shoulders of her silk gown. "Exactly. He bit you." A small, transparent vial appears in her clawlike fingers. "And this is the antidote for the poison my little dearie just sent into your bloodstream."

Harvey tries to grab the vial from her, but once again the woman proves to be faster than he ever would have imagined.

"A word of advice," she adds. "Friendly advice. The more you move around, the faster the poison circulates . . . and the less time you have left to live."

"Witch!" Harvey shouts, clenching his fists but stopping in his tracks.

"Yes, that's right." Mademoiselle Cybel glides across the grass and reaches the door. "You finally understand. Now be a good boy and nothing will happen to you. If our little meeting at the Eiffel Tower goes well, I'll come back with the antidote. I'll come back and you'll be free. On the other hand, if things don't go well . . ." She waves the vial in her fingertips.

Totally powerless, Harvey watches her from the center of the green room. "It doesn't end here!"

"How should it end, hmm? How should it end?" Mademoiselle Cybel asks, gliding away. "If you get bored, feel free to feed the plants. The insects are behind the counter. But do it slowly. Very slowly . . ."

8
THE PLOT

◯

THE MOUNTAINS OUTSIDE THE WINDOW GROW TALLER AND TALLER
as the TGV zips past Exilles and its giant fortress, which peers
down over the valley like a giant stone mammoth. Finally, it's hidden from view by an endless series of tunnels.

Elettra and Sheng stare out the dining car window, check
their cell phones and shake their heads.

Finally, another text message from Mistral arrives. "They're
going to make the trade up in the Eiffel Tower," says Sheng.

"When?"

"In an hour."

"Oh, no!"

Sheng looks at his watch. "It'll take us at least six more hours
to get there."

Elettra stomps her foot. "This is the last time I'm ever taking
the train! The very last time! I can't believe it! They kidnapped
Harvey and I . . . we . . . we can't do anything about it!" she says,
waving her hands in the air and feeling helpless.

"Mistral says the woman she talked to knows we're coming
by train."

Sunlight bursts in through the window, and the curtains flap wildly in the wind. Then the train is engulfed by the darkness of yet another tunnel.

"But how?" Elettra asks in a whisper, peering around the dining car, which is illuminated by electric lights.

"I don't know. We paid for our tickets in cash. No debit card, no credit card . . . We didn't talk about it to anyone on the phone."

"Except Mistral."

"Maybe they're listening in on her phone calls."

"Or someone gave us away."

"Gave us away? But who?"

"How should I know?"

"Your aunt Irene, maybe," says Sheng, "or your dad. I mean, they're the only people who knew about this trip, except us."

"You're forgetting Ermete."

"It might as well be you, then."

"Be serious!" Elettra bites her lip.

The dining car is half empty, and the waitress seems to be keeping her eye on them.

"What's she looking at?" Elettra whispers.

"*Hao!* She's looking at me."

"But why?"

"My Asian charm?" Sheng says, laughing and flashing his big white teeth.

"She might be spying on us." Elettra scoops up her long, curly locks in both hands and says, "The first thing I'm doing when I get off this train is cutting my hair and dyeing it blond."

"What should I do, then? Get a perm?"

63

Despite the tension, the thought of Sheng with a head full of fluffy curls makes Elettra laugh out loud.

The train comes out of the tunnel and starts to slow down. A voice over the loudspeaker announces that they're arriving at the Oulx station. The next stop will be Bardonecchia, and then, once they've reached the other side of the Fréjus Tunnel, France.

"This train isn't safe," Elettra says, frowning.

"So what's your plan?"

"I'm not sure yet, but I'll keep thinking. Meanwhile, come with me."

When they get back to their compartment, Fernando is looking through some novels, underlining things here and there. When he sees them walk in, he's caught off guard. He quickly stashes the books beneath a mountain of papers. "Oh, kids, it's you. . . ."

"What were you reading?" Elettra asks suspiciously.

"Oh, nothing. Nothing important."

The train stops in the little station in Oulx, just two tracks surrounded by wooded mountains.

Elettra peeks under her father's papers. The first book is *The Da Vinci Code*, the mystery of all mysteries. The second is *The Crossroads*, by Chris Grabenstein.

"I'm just getting inspiration," Fernando says, trying to brush it off.

Some people get on board and drag their suitcases down the corridor, reading their reservation numbers aloud.

"Hey, Dad," Elettra says when the TGV shuts its doors with a groan and sets off toward Bardonecchia. "I came up with an idea for the first part of your novel. Listen to this: four main characters from four different cities around the world . . ."

Fernando taps his pencil on the corner of his mouth. "Mm-hmm, keep going. . . ."

"They meet by some bizarre coincidence, which even they don't really understand, on a dark and stormy night in . . . um . . . why not in Rome?"

"Excellent, yes. I know the city well. Then what?"

"Then the four of them . . . cross a bridge . . . like the one that goes to Tiber Island. . . ." As she's speaking, Elettra opens her suitcase and takes out the Ring of Fire, a small, ancient mirror, which is bundled up in a cloth. Trying to act casual, she passes it to Sheng, who tucks it into his ever-present backpack.

"While they're crossing the bridge . . . they run into an old professor, who seems a little crazy. He gives them a briefcase and begs them to keep it for just one night."

"Wow . . . ," Fernando murmurs, twirling his pencil around in his fingers.

"But the next day . . . ," Elettra continues, passing Sheng a wooden top.

"The next day," Fernando continues for her, "the professor shows up, takes the briefcase back and disappears!"

The perfect way to ruin a plot.

"That's a great start," Fernando admits. "It would even fit in well with the second part I've written." That said, Elettra's father dives into his papers again and starts frantically jotting down ideas.

Elettra motions to Sheng to follow her out of the compartment and points at his backpack. The Chinese boy frowns, but only for a second.

"Hey, Dad, we're going."

"Yes, yes, go right ahead."

Elettra shuts the door behind them, satisfied.

"Well, at least we told him."

"Told him what?"

"That we're going."

The train starts slowing down.

"You mean . . . we're getting off the train?"

"Exactly, even if it means I have to make it stop."

"But how? Do you know how to drive this thing?"

"No." Elettra raises her hands, which are full of energy. "But it's electric."

9
THE DOOR

Harvey has the gift of making plants grow and hearing the voice of the earth, but there isn't much earth in the green room. There's a layer of soil only thick enough to make short grass crop up on the floor. The roots of the vines on the walls grow from pots hidden in the corners of the room. It's simply a greenhouse built as a home for rare animals.

Harvey's arm itches like crazy, but he's determined not to scratch it. A small, puffy, reddish bruise has formed around the spider bite. Moving around slowly so that the poison won't circulate through his bloodstream faster, the boy has only one thought on his mind: He has to find a way out of there.

The room's only external window is thicker than bulletproof glass. They clearly want to keep Marcel from sneaking off to visit the neighbors. Harvey peers outside and sees that he's on the top of the three floors above the restaurant.

"Don't scratch it, Harvey," he repeats to himself. "Don't scratch it."

Out of the corner of his eye, he sees something move. Maybe it's Marcel. Maybe it's another snake or a spider or a creeping carnivorous plant. And Harvey wants to use the plants to his advantage somehow. If he can make them grow faster, maybe their roots will burst through the wall and let him escape.

Not knowing how else to go about it, Harvey grabs some of the thicker branches and vines and rubs them between his fingers.

"Come on, guys, grow!" he whispers, squeezing his eyes shut as he tries to work his gift. "Grow and knock everything down."

He concentrates as hard as he can, but nothing happens.

He's just about to give up when he hears something moving on the other side of one of the walls. At the same time, a noise rises up from the street. A horn, someone yelling.

Harvey lets go of the vines. The noise gets louder. Then he hears someone running and a female voice calling out, "Harvey? Harvey Miller?"

"I'm in here!" the boy shouts, going over to the wall where the voice came from. He rests his ear against it and hears muffled footsteps.

"Talk to me! Keep talking! Here *where*?" the voice asks.

"Over here!" Harvey hollers, banging his fists on the wall.

The footsteps draw closer, as does the voice. "Behind this?" she asks, just a few centimeters away from Harvey's ear.

"Yeah! Yeah! I'm right here!"

Pounding on the other side of the wall.

"Darn it!" the woman snaps. "There must be a way in, but I can't find one! What is there over on your side?"

"A room completely covered with plants!" Harvey yells. "There are snakes, too, and spiders . . . poisonous ones!"

Strange sounds come from behind the wall. Things being shoved aside. Hands groping around.

"I can't find the door!"

"Get me out of here, please!"

"I'm trying, Miller. I'm trying! See anything that might be a keyhole?"

Harvey searches around and sees a tiny opening. "Yeah!" he shouts. "There's one right here!"

"Where, exactly?"

The boy takes a few steps back, grabs a vine, leans over the keyhole and slips it through. Nothing blocks it. "See it?" he asks. Without thinking, he scratches his spider bite.

"Yes!" the woman on the other side yells.

In a matter of seconds, there's a click and a section of the wall swings open.

Harvey takes a step back. Standing in the doorway is a middle-aged woman with very short, lustrous black hair. A stunningly beautiful middle-aged woman.

"Harvey Miller?" she asks, looking over her shoulder.

"Yeah."

"We don't have much time for introductions," she explains, holding out her hand. "I'm Zoe, your father's friend. We need to get out of here, and fast."

"I can't leave," Harvey replies, showing her the bite mark. "A spider bit me, and I need the antidote."

She quickly studies his arm. "What did the spider look like? Was it black? Hairy? About this big?"

"Yeah, exactly."

"Does it itch?"

"Totally."

The woman grabs him by the hand. "Perfect!"

"What are you doing?"

"A *Lycosa tarantula* is what bit you. It's less poisonous than a bumblebee," Zoe says, "but it looks a whole lot scarier, doesn't it?"

10

THE TOWER

"Eight hundred and two, eight hundred and three, eight hundred and four, eight hundred and five," Ermete counts, panting as he climbs the seemingly endless stairs of the Eiffel Tower, which will lead them to the meeting place. Finally, he leans against the iron guardrail, notices how high up they are and recoils. "*Mamma mia!* Why'd you have to choose the nine hundred and ninety-ninth step, of all places?"

Mistral's skirt with black, white and red circles flutters in the breeze, which is also pushing her hair forward onto her face, forming two crescent moons.

"Couldn't we have just met at the elevator?" Ermete moans. He nods at the yellow panoramic elevator car, which has just stopped below them on the restaurant floor. "Or have gone up in the elevator and taken the stairs down?"

"I'm sorry," Mistral says. "It all happened so fast. I said the first thing that came to mind. We can turn back, if you want."

Ermete rests his hands on the tower's boiling-hot black railing and stares dismally up at the two hundred steps they have yet to climb. "No, let's keep going," he says, brushing his hand almost reverentially over one of the two and a half million rivets used to build the tower. "Ten thousand tons of iron and it still looks so airy."

Around Ermete and Mistral, pure white shafts of sunlight stream through the reticulated iron structure, casting the tower's grill-like shadow onto the gardens below.

"Long ago," says Ermete, "they used to construct important buildings on particularly receptive locations on the Earth, places that were full of energy."

"Like the ones where Harvey can . . . hear voices?"

"Exactly."

As they're talking, one of the hydraulic elevator's thick metal cables groans and goes taut, signaling that one of the cars is about to ascend.

"The Earth is crisscrossed by energy lines, and they used to establish cities where the biggest ones intersected. They planted roots there so they could tap into all that energy, and—"

"Your pocket's glowing," Mistral points out.

Ermete stops talking, takes out his phone and answers it. "Hello? Harvey? *Harvey?* How'd you manage to—? You escaped? Way to go! Of course! Hey, that's great! Yeah. Sure. No, no, no. We aren't there yet. We're leaving. Of course! We're going down these stupid stairs and leaving . . . and just in time, if you ask me. Yeah! Great! See you there."

"Great!" he cheers, slipping the cell phone back into his pocket. "Harvey managed to escape. Let's get out of here!"

Below them, the yellow elevator slowly starts to ascend.

"Where are we going?" Mistral asks, her silver sandals clattering against the steps.

"Away from here!"

"We could go to my place," the girl suggests.

"And pick up my suitcases!"

When the elevator reaches their level, the two stop, holding on to the railing. They silently wait as the yellow car, which is full of visitors, passes by. Through its windows, Ermete and Mistral can see sunglasses, sunburned arms, cameras hanging from straps.

"Oh, no!" gasps Mistral.

"What is it? What's wrong?" asks Ermete. He notices that the girl is still gaping at one of the windows, even though the car's already passed them by.

Mistral sinks down onto the steps.

"What did you see?" Ermete asks.

"It can't be. . . ."

"What?"

Mistral feels like the whole tower is trembling beneath her like a house of cards. "I just saw Jacob Mahler . . . ," she whispers.

"Where? In the elevator?"

"Yes."

"So he isn't dead after all! He's after us again!" Ermete bursts out. He grabs Mistral's arm and pulls her down the stairs behind him. "Well, we aren't going to let him mess around with us!"

As the yellow elevator climbs even farther up, Mistral feels as wobbly as a water balloon. "I'm telling you, he died in Rome. Beatrice shot him. I saw it for myself," she insists. "She called the police, and then . . . then the house . . . caught fire. That can't have been him. . . . It isn't possible. . . ."

She feels cold. It's an icy cold that neither the hot June sun nor the city's stifling air can warm. The birds' calls sound like chains being dragged through the sky, creaking and groaning.

* * *

"*Hao!* What a great idea!" exclaims Sheng when the last car of the TGV disappears around the bend. "So what now?"

Elettra turns around and walks through the little Bardonecchia train station. Once outside, she looks around. A steep, straight road leads up to the heart of the quaint little town nestled among the mountains.

"Via Medail," says Elettra, reading the street sign.

"Medal Street? Oh, that's perfect! Because they should give you a medal for coming up with this brilliant plan!" Sheng grumbles. "What's your dad going to do when he realizes we got off the train?"

"He won't notice until he's in Paris," Elettra replies, "which means we've still got six hours before the catastrophe." She spots a little café with a wooden pergola and a sign announcing an upcoming bocce tournament. "Let's go get something to eat at the Café Medail."

"Sure, why not? Hello, Mr. Melodia? We just wanted to tell you we got off at Bardonecchia to grab some ice cream! See you tomorrow!"

"Would you cut it out?" snaps Elettra. "If you didn't think it was a good idea, you could've said so!"

"First of all, calm down before you melt all the TVs in a two-mile radius," Sheng snaps back. "And secondly, I spent fifteen whole minutes telling you it was a bad idea, but you wouldn't listen to me!" he says, looking her straight in the eye. "The only reason I got off the train was so you wouldn't be all alone. You should be thanking me!"

Sheng's right, Elettra thinks. She has to admit that when she's convinced she's doing the right thing, there's no talking her out of it. She simply shuts herself off from the outside world until she's reached her objective.

"I'm burning up," she says, walking into the café with the pergola.

"I'll wait for you here," Sheng mutters. "Call me when you've made their freezers explode."

"Why are you acting like such an idiot?"

"Um, because my friend the genius from Rome just got me stranded in a little town in the mountains hundreds of miles away from Paris?"

"There were people on that train who wanted to kidnap us!" Elettra reminds him.

"You don't know that for sure."

"In any case, we need to eat."

"Let's just hope the owner of the café doesn't look at us funny," Sheng grumbles. "You might think she's a kidnapper, too."

Elettra stops in the doorway. "Since you're being so nice, Sheng, you know what I say?"

"No, what do you say?"

"I say you go in and order for us."

"Meanwhile, what are you going to do? Rent a missile that'll fly us to Paris?"

"I might surprise you."

"Please, no!" Sheng groans. But then his cheerful disposition finally wins out. "Okay, what should I get you?"

"Whatever you're having," Elettra replies, tweaking his cheek.

"No cuddles for me, thanks. Save them for Harvey."

*   *   *

Ten minutes later, Sheng's beaming triumphantly.

"Here," he chimes, handing Elettra a gigantic sandwich. "So, come up with any ideas yet?"

"Uh-huh," the girl replies, pointing across the street. "Today is the town's open market day, and lots of French merchants will be here. It shouldn't be so hard to find a ride."

"A ride? A ride where?"

"As far as they're willing to take us. At that point, we can ask around for another one."

Sheng gapes at her as if he's seeing King Tut's mummy rising up from its tomb. "You're crazy!"

"Trust me. It'll work. So, what'd you get me?"

"The same thing I got for myself."

Elettra looks warily at the piping hot sandwich bundled up in waxed paper that Sheng's holding out to her.

"What's in it?"

"Brie, arugula, French fries and spicy salami."

"And you're calling *me* crazy?"

Sheng pulls the sandwich back. "Did you want ketchup on yours?"

Bardonecchia's open market is held in a sunny little square. It's almost over for the day. The various stand owners are packing up their unsold goods and loading everything onto their trucks.

"A ride? Why not?" says one of the first merchants they ask, half gruff, half amused. "Where is it you want to go, exactly?"

"That way," Sheng replies, pointing, a whitish Brie mustache on his upper lip.

76

"I'm going to Chambéry," the man says, scratching his beard.

"Chambéry!" exclaims Elettra, who has absolutely no idea where that is. "Perfect!"

"Then climb aboard. Clear some of the junk off the front seat and make yourselves comfortable."

Sheng crosses his arms over his chest and glares at Elettra until she finally gives in. "Chambéry's on the way to Paris, right?" she asks before opening the door to the van.

The man laughs. "Yes, of course it's on the way. In France, all roads lead to Paris!"

"See?"

Sheng wipes his mouth off on his sleeve. "Don't look at me. You decide."

When they get in, Sheng sniffs the air suspiciously but keeps quiet, not wanting to be rude.

They head off.

When they reach the Fréjus Tunnel, the merchant tells the kids they need to roll up all the windows.

After ten minutes driving through the tunnel, the smell inside the van is overwhelming. "Sorry, but what are you carrying?" Sheng finally blurts out.

The man laughs. "You smell that, do you?"

"Do I ever! What is it?"

"Aged goat cheese!"

11

THE CAFÉ

Zoe and Harvey's escape from Cybel's restaurant is a quick one. They run down the stairs and outside through a back door. Once they're out on the street, they rush over to the Sorbonne Métro station. The woman hands Harvey a ticket. "This end down," she explains, showing him how to feed the ticket into the slot and pick it up again before stepping through the gate.

"Where are we going?"

"Someplace quiet," Zoe says, smiling.

The quiet place is three stops and one line change away. It's a café with lots of outdoor tables surrounded by leafy trees bathed in sunlight. An old barrel organ is playing a melancholy tune. The name of the café, Les Deux Magots, is printed on the green canopy shading the tables. Zoe picks one of them, puts her purse down on a wicker chair beside it and motions to Harvey to take a seat. Then, as though she were looking at him for the first time, she says, "I'm so, so sorry about what happened to you. I don't know what to say."

"Actually, neither do I," Harvey replies, still standing. "And to be honest, I still can't figure out how she managed to find me in the first place." He checks the bite mark on his arm.

"It was entirely my fault," Zoe explains. "I wasn't thinking. Honestly, I never imagined it would all be so dangerous."

When a waiter wearing a black tie appears, Zoe orders a mocha. "What about you, Harvey?"

He asks for a Coca-Cola and finally sits down. "Don't say my name around waiters. They're her informers."

Zoe nods. "I know." She rests both hands on the table. Hands with dark, tiny freckles, like an old woman's, far different from her bright, lively eyes. Her perfume is both old-fashioned and fresh, springlike, and her hairstyle is exquisitely French. "Sometimes when I'm excited I just don't think straight. When I called your father last month and he sent me the samples of your stone for analysis—"

"Wait, you got in touch with my dad?"

"Yes, because I hadn't heard from him in a long time. We were in graduate school together."

"So he wasn't the one to contact you, Miss . . . um, Mrs. . . ."

"Harvey, please," she says, smiling, "just call me Zoe. I'm a friend, okay?"

"Okay."

"As I was saying, when I saw your samples, keeping the news a secret didn't even cross my mind."

"What news?"

"The possibility that we'd found another one."

"Another what?"

"Another matrix stone."

When their order arrives, Zoe starts talking again. "It's all very simple. I'm an archaeologist. I did my postgraduate work ages ago, studying fossils and other incredibly boring things like that. Six years ago, a colleague of mine in Iceland stumbled upon a major discovery, the kind we all dream about. He was in the bay of Stykkishólmur, which is famous for its seal population. While my friend was observing them, he noticed them going to nap in a partially submerged cavern that you could wade into if you crouched down. The cavern was covered with a strange reddish marble with unknown properties. It was a place no other human had ever stepped foot in before: the inside of a meteorite that fell to Earth millions of years ago."

Harvey gapes. "So what'd your friend do?" he asks, taking another sip of Coca-Cola.

"He collected some samples and analyzed them under a microscope. When he enlarged the details twenty thousand times, he noticed a whitish grain, a sort of concretion that wasn't part of the marble. It was something deposited. Confined. Protected."

Zoe smiles, waiting for Harvey to ask the inevitable question. "So what was it?"

"A fragment of human DNA. A fragment of the DNA of a man of infinitesimal proportions. A tiny, minuscule man who, in order to get out of his stone shell, needed one essential component. A component that, by sheer luck, he'd fallen right into."

"Water . . . ," whispers Harvey.

"Exactly. Water. The stone shell is currently undergoing scientific analysis in laboratories in three different universities around the world. If the discovery's confirmed, it'll disprove centuries of theories. It'll mean mankind didn't descend from the apes but from the stars, like the ancients believed, including Anaxagoras, Seneca and many others. We might've come here in crystal cribs, in meteorites that crashed to Earth millions of years ago containing our miniature-sized ancestors. Little men made of silicon and carbon who grew . . . until they became us."

"What about my stone?"

"It's the same kind of stone, Harvey. The same kind as the one found in Iceland. It might be incredibly important. That's why Cybel kidnapped you. She wanted to get her hands on it."

A number of pieces in the puzzle start fitting together in Harvey's mind: Professor Van Der Berger studying the stars, Seneca's book on comets, the underground room in New York with depictions of men and gods being born from stone. . . . Their search is suddenly starting to make sense.

Harvey shakes his head, dazed. "If you only knew how I wound up finding that stone . . ."

Zoe leans back in her wicker chair with a satisfied smile. "Actually, I think I do." She reaches into her purse and pulls out a wooden top with a whirlpool engraved on it. It's the one Harvey was forced to give Cybel. She hands it to him. "Unless I'm mistaken, this is yours."

12

THE PERFUME

○

"Dad, don't worry! We're fine!" Elettra yells into the phone.

"*Hao!* We're great!" echoes Sheng, who's right beside her, trying to keep his balance through the curve. It isn't easy, given that he's standing in the back of a truck with two hundred honking geese in just as many cages. "Shut up, you dumb birds! Shut up!"

"What? I can't hear you!" Elettra continues. "No, we aren't running away from home! I can't explain it over the phone. It might be tapped. . . . You need to trust me, Dad! You have to learn my number by heart! If you have it written down somewhere, rip it up. And once you get to Paris, change hotels. No, this isn't a joke! I'm sure someone's following us! What, that? Oh, they're geese. Yeah, geese. Don't ask me to explain!"

"Like he'd believe you anyway," Sheng remarks, holding on to some cages so that he won't fall. A goose nips his finger. "Ow!" he shouts. "That hurt, you stupid ball of feathers!"

"Would *you* be quiet, at least?" Elettra groans, covering the receiver for a moment before saying goodbye to her father.

The truck bounces as it drives over a pothole. "We should be there pretty soon," the girl says.

Sheng checks his notes. "Yeah, in Vézelay. From there, we get onto the mustard truck that'll take us to Dijon, and then to Fontainebleau with the wine delivery guy. At that point, we'll only be sixty-five kilometers away from Mistral's place."

"You have goose feathers in your hair."

"I'm going to keep them as a memento, if you don't mind."

Elettra groans and thinks, *I'm coming, Harvey!* But she'll have to slip in through the back door and hide once she's there.

As night falls like a cool mantle over Paris, the city switches on its thousand lights, turning the buildings on the twisty little roads into fairy homes adorned with garlands of twinkling stars. A million little cafés turn on their lights, and a million little kitchens start mixing together spices and onions, oysters and escargot. People, music and laughter fill the sidewalks, the squares, the *bateaux mouches* that glide down the Seine accompanied by notes from accordions. Flocks of nocturnal birds fly across the sky. Others, perched atop domed buildings, peer down at the dark, ghostlike figures passing by. The lights of the Louvre remain on, as if someone were still there contemplating works of art, preferring not to mix with the crowds of tourists. The Palais-Royal is lit up as if it were daytime. The Eiffel Tower is like a precious brooch pinned to the jardin du Trocadéro.

In the Latin Quarter, which is swarming with students, Cybel's restaurant is open. Her network of waiters and waitresses wearing black ties is combing every last café and restaurant. In their pockets are descriptions of the four kids to be found.

*　*　*

Back at her house, Mistral is pacing across the parquet, too nervous to stand still. Ermete's sitting at the table in the living room, looking through the book from Agatha. They wait.

Her hands are trembling with anxiousness and doubt. She checks the clock for the hundredth time. Harvey should be showing up any minute now with his new friend, Zoe.

The engineer flips through her book. "How to summon stray dogs . . . Squeals that drive away mice . . . Have you tried using this stuff?" he asks Mistral.

"No," she answers.

"'Argot' is a word of unclear origins," Ermete explains, "meaning 'secret language' or 'coded language.' The French term 'art gothique,' or 'Gothic art,' derives from the word 'argot,' because most of the people who built churches were French, and they had secret construction techniques they wouldn't reveal to anyone. Still today, every Gothic church has its mysteries."

Mistral nods distractedly.

"Did you know," Ermete goes on, "that the major cathedrals dedicated to the Virgin Mary all over France are arranged exactly like the stars in the constellation of Virgo, the Virgin? Paris, Chartres, Evreux, Bayeux, Rouen, Amiens, Laon, Reims . . ."

Mistral isn't listening to him. She double-checks the bourguignonne fondue pot, counts the colored dipping forks again and makes sure there's enough meat and sauce for everyone. While Ermete's talking, expounding on theories that Harvey and Sheng might find sensational, Mistral looks at the clock one last time, wondering how much longer it's going to take Harvey to show up,

Elettra and Sheng to reach Paris, and her mother to get home for dinner.

Then she hides away in the bathroom. She leans against the door, overwhelmed, a world of thoughts whirling through her head. She turns on the tap and rubs her hands together under the cool water. She stares at her reflection in the mirror. Her eyes are still big and bright, but they almost look misted over.

She wishes she could fog up the mirror, wipe her hand over it and erase everything. Go back to seeing herself like she was before. Before Rome, the professor, his briefcase and the wooden tops.

"We have five tops . . . ," she murmurs, touching the mirror with her fingertip five times. Five tiny wet splotches remain on the glass. Mistral shakes her head. Something doesn't make sense. She adds two more.

Fifteen minutes later, Harvey and Zoe buzz Mistral's apartment and start climbing the stairs. The moment Harvey's uncombed hair appears at the end of her landing, Mistral runs over to hug him.

"It's over. Everything's okay," he says, smiling and returning the hug. They walk into the apartment, where Ermete and Harvey exchange a manlier high five. The American boy shows them his swollen spider bite and then makes the introductions. "This is Zoe."

Ermete looks at her suspiciously at first, but with his second glance his eyes meet the woman's and all his distrust vanishes instantly. Although the engineer's outfit isn't exactly stylish, he introduces himself with the air of an accomplished actor. "It's very nice to meet you, Zoe. I'm Ermete. Harvey's told me so much about you."

Then he thinks, *Very attractive woman. Thirty-eight years old? Forty? Forty-two, maybe?*

"I made fondue for everyone," Mistral says. "If you like, we can have something to eat while we're waiting for . . . for the others. And my mom."

Everyone thinks it's a great idea. They all sit down at the dinner table and help themselves to the cubed meat and different sauces. As they wait for the oil to get hot enough to put in their dipping forks, they start to recap everything that happened to them that day.

"So get this," Harvey says. "Zoe isn't just a friend of my dad's. She knows about the tops, too!" He rests the one with the whirlpool on the table. "All thanks to a mutual friend of ours . . ."

"Alfred Van Der Berger," Zoe adds.

"You knew the professor?"

The woman nods. "I met him for the first time five years ago," she lies.

Five years ago, Mistral notes. *That's when the professor left New York.* She tells her guests to start eating, and within moments the pot has become a spiny porcupine, its quills tipped with chunks of meat.

"How did you two happen to meet?" Ermete asks.

"Nothing in this whole thing happens by coincidence," Harvey replies. "Wait until you hear the rest."

Ermete raises his dipping fork so clumsily that his chunk of meat drops back into the pot.

"The professor needed an archaeologist who knew Paris well. But not just any archaeologist. He needed someone a little out of the ordinary. . . ."

"What do you mean?"

"We met five years ago at the Paris Observatory, where I was doing my doctorate on the astronomical knowledge of ancient civilizations. They knew almost as much as we do today," Zoe adds, skewering her fourth morsel of meat.

"They sure did!" Ermete remarks, grabbing his dipping fork again. "Did you guys know that the Gothic cathedrals in France are arranged—" He stops midsentence when he notices that nothing's on his fork. Faced with the loss of yet another mouthful of food, he doesn't feel like continuing his explanation. He hasn't managed to eat a single thing yet. "Is one of you stealing my dinner?"

"Alfred needed someone who could accept all his odd notions without asking too many questions," the archaeologist continues. "I often had to do research for him that seemed like nonsense to me."

Harvey raises an eyebrow, as if to say, "Here comes the good part."

Mistral, on the other hand, is following Zoe's movements and words with a certain detachment. Something about the woman's story doesn't entirely convince her.

"Alfred Van Der Berger was obsessed with the idea that a special object was hidden in Paris. A very important object that could help reveal one of nature's best-kept secrets of all time."

"We know something about that," Ermete says, "although we don't know what secret they're supposed to lead to."

87

"They?" asks Zoe.

"We found objects in Rome and New York," Harvey explains, "but we still haven't figured out how they're connected or how to use them. All we know is that the thing we found in Rome helped us track down the thing hidden in New York. We found them by following a string of clues. And the professor left the first clue for us."

Zoe waits a few seconds. Realizing Harvey isn't about to add anything else, she goes on. "The professor was convinced that the clues led to Paris . . . to something hidden in this city."

"So he wasn't the one who hid it?" asks Mistral.

The woman shakes her head. "No, the professor was looking for it. He knew how to start out and where to end up, but he didn't know how to go about it. Whenever he saw a map of Paris, he'd say, 'It's like a board game, you see? We're the playing pieces, the clues are the dice and the neighborhoods are the squares.' He thought the final square in the game was somewhere near the Seine."

"Why?"

"Because water is Paris's natural element," Zoe says, sounding perfectly sure of herself.

Mistral detects a hint of resentment in her tone. Toward whom, the girl has no idea. It's just a hunch, a nagging doubt, like she smells the faint scent of a rat. However, everyone else seems perfectly won over by both Zoe's explanation and her perfume.

"Paris even owes its name to water," the woman explains. "It derives from the words 'par île,' that is, 'around the island,' because it was founded around île de la Cité, the island in the middle of the Seine."

The third city and the third island, thinks Mistral. *After Tiber Island in Rome and Roosevelt Island in New York . . .*

"Alfred believed the object he wanted to find was hidden right there on île de la Cité, in the heart of Paris. He thought it was a boat."

"Which you obviously never found . . ."

Zoe shakes her head. "No, despite years of research, we never found anything. He kept insisting it had to be there, but . . . no luck."

They pass the platter of meat around the table again.

Mistral stares at the woman, wondering how close she and the professor were, and whether he left New York and Agatha to be in Paris with Zoe. But she doesn't ask. Instead, she asks, "Are you from Paris?"

"No, no," the woman replies. "I came here to study and I liked it, so I stayed."

"Where are you from originally?" Ermete asks her.

"Istanbul."

"Could you show them the clues the professor left you?"

"He left them with you? But why?" Mistral asks.

Zoe laughs uncomfortably, as if she's not sure how to answer. She dips another chunk of meat in the hot oil and eats it practically raw. "He told me you'd all show up one day. I didn't know when, but in a way I was expecting you. I knew your names: Elettra from Rome, Mistral from Paris, Harvey from New York and . . . and . . ."

"Sheng," Mistral says, before she can stop herself.

"Sheng from Shanghai," Zoe continues.

"What did he tell you about us?" Harvey asks curiously.

"He said you'd know how to use this," the woman replies. She riffles through her purse and pulls out a flashy, gaudy gold clock that's as big and as bulky as an ancient nautical instrument.

When he sees the old clock, Ermete's eyes light up with fascination.

"This is known as Napoléon's Clock," Zoe explains. "It's a mechanical wonder built by a Venetian clock maker by the name of Peter Dedalus. The clock face is divided into five sections, see? They form a sort of five-pointed star. If you press it here, it marks the hours, minutes and seconds. This button starts a chronometer, and this one stops it. If you press it harder, the date appears. Flip this tiny switch to the left and a drop of perfume comes out. Flip it to the right and it plays 'La Marseillaise.'"

She hands it to the kids, who turn it over in their hands, amazed. One of the five sections of the clock face has a picture on it, but before they have the chance to look at it carefully, Zoe continues. "Then there's this. . . ."

It's a small white and red coat of arms depicting a white ship at sea, its sail billowing in the wind, its prow pointing toward a star in the sky. Above the ship and the star, in the fiery red sky, are three bees.

"This is a reproduction of the Parisian coat of arms Napoléon Bonaparte commissioned when he became emperor. The original one from 1811 is at the Bibliothèque Nationale." Zoe taps her finger on the ship. "And this . . . this is the ship we're looking for."

After dinner, Ermete and Zoe get up to leave. Harvey, on the other hand, is going to sleep in Mistral's guest room. If Cybel's network of informers is as vast as the woman claims, it isn't a good idea for him to check into a hotel. Besides, Zoe hasn't offered to let him stay at her place.

They say a quick, cordial goodbye and agree to meet up tomorrow morning, along with Elettra and Sheng. Ermete's voice slowly fades away down the stairwell, as does Zoe's strange perfume.

A few minutes later, Mistral can finally shut the door behind her.

"So, what do you think?" Harvey asks her the moment they're alone.

"It's a real stroke of luck," the girl replies. "But . . ."

"But what?"

"It's almost too good to be true."

The two friends walk back to the table, where a place is still set for Mistral's mother.

"While we're waiting, I'll get your room ready."

The girl pulls open a few drawers, takes out a clean set of sheets and some towels and shows her friend to the guest room.

"There's something strange about her," she says as she's making the bed. "Something I can't put my finger on."

"Really?" Harvey asks. "I mean, she's a friend of my dad's. She knew Professor Van Der Berger. He left her the clock and the coat of arms so she'd give them to us and—"

"And she helped you escape from Cybel's. Don't you see? It's all too . . . too *perfect*."

"She told me some important things about the Star of Stone," Harvey says. As he helps Mistral make the bed, he tells her about the discovery of the cavern in Iceland and the human DNA fingerprint found inside the meteorite.

"The professor was right, then," Mistral concludes. "We're pawns in a game. White versus black. It's us against Jacob Mahler, Egon Nose, those women who worked for him . . . and now, Mademoiselle Cybel."

"The bad guys."

"Sent by the man from Shanghai."

"Yeah . . ."

Harvey and Mistral go back to the table and sit down.

"Did you catch what she said about the elements?" the American boy asks.

They're interrupted by the sound of the apartment door being unlocked. It's Mistral's mother, Cecile, who walks in carrying a mountain of boxes and packages. "Mmm . . . that smells wonderful! You've made dinner, already?"

"It's almost ten o'clock, Mom."

The woman puts her packages down on a couch and shakes her head. "Oh, of course. Sorry I'm so late." She walks up to her daughter, who's about her height, and plants a kiss on her forehead. Then she notices Harvey.

"You remember Harvey, don't you, Mom?"

"Why, certainly! How are you, Harvey?"

Firm handshake.

"Just fine, ma'am, and you?"

"Busy, as always." She quickly rinses off her hands and sits down at the dinner table.

"Harvey just got to Paris today. He had some trouble with the hotel and asked if he could stay at our place for a few days."

"We have terrible luck with hotels, don't we?" Madame Blanchard jokes, referring to the confusion with their New Year's Eve reservations in Rome.

"Sure seems that way."

Cecile Blanchard picks up a dipping fork and skewers a few chunks of meat. Suddenly, she sniffs the air, an amused smile on her face. "How strange . . ."

"What?"

"Was someone else here tonight?"

"Yes, a couple friends of ours," Mistral admits.

"One of them was female." Cecile stands up and slowly walks halfway around the table. "And she was sitting right here!" she says, resting her hand on Zoe's chair.

"How did you know that?"

"Her perfume. I haven't smelled this for years . . . but I could never forget it. . . ." Madame Blanchard sniffs the air one last time. Smiling, she concludes, "There's no doubt about it: It's Air du Temps!" She laughs. "It's the very first perfume I ever designed. I didn't think anyone wore it anymore. Oh, I'm so pleased! I like this friend of yours already!"

Mistral and Harvey look at each other, thinking the same thing: *This can't be a coincidence.*

"Back then, I was a real nobody, without any self-confidence . . . ," Mistral's mother tells them. "You hadn't even been born yet. I was so young and so scared. . . . But then I created Air du Temps for a small firm in Provence. It was sold in a bottle shaped like a boat. . . ."

"A boat?" Mistral says, jumping in her seat. "What kind of boat?"

Madame Blanchard blinks. "Just . . . a boat."

"Do you have any bottles of it left?"

"No," Cecile says. "It sold out in no time. It was such an incredible success that I ended up in all the leading trade magazines virtually overnight. From inexperienced young woman to guru perfume designer!"

"I'd love to see a bottle of it. . . ."

"We could go shopping for it tomorrow," Harvey suggests.

"I doubt you'll find any. After all, Air du Temps was Air du Temps . . . my first, one-in-a-million perfume. Still, I suppose a few bottles might be out there somewhere. . . ."

Like a good omen, a gust of wind makes the curtains billow.

Across the street, a gray-haired man is watching them through the military binoculars he bought at the open market. He's listening to them thanks to a bug he planted in their home phone a month ago, passing himself off as a repairman from France Télécom.

The man is borrowing an apartment whose owner is away on vacation. He's covered it all with sheets of clear plastic so that he won't leave behind any trace of having been there. Beside him is a concert artist's musical case with a handmade violin inside of it. It isn't the original violin, which was destroyed in Rome. Nevertheless, it's a fine copy that was made based on his own designs by a stringed-instruments shop in Cremona. The shop was paid handsomely for its work. And for its discretion . . .

Discretion. That's been a key word for him ever since he was forced into hiding. First he hid in a small town just outside Rome to recover from his injuries following the explosion in the house in the city's Coppedè district. Then he hid in the woods to avoid Egon Nose's henchwomen. Finally, he hid in Paris, where he did everything in his power to track down the girl he once kidnapped. And now he's waiting for just the right time to make his move.

His violin bow glimmers like the blade of a knife.

The man patiently watches and listens. He drinks mineral water, which he buys in the shop next door. He eats very little. The only thing he makes on his own is strong, black coffee. It helps him stay alert.

Many blocks away, Ermete De Panfilis drops Zoe off at the front door of what is probably the city's narrowest building, at 22 rue Saint-Séverin. He doesn't realize they aren't very far away from Cybel's restaurant.

Tired after his long day, he finds the closest inconspicuous-looking hotel he can and checks in under a false name. The room he's given has faded blue carpeting and wallpaper that reeks of pipe tobacco. The engineer fills the bathtub with hot water, sinks down into it, exhausted, and calls his mother one last time.

Fifteen minutes after Ermete walks away from the tall, narrow front door to the building, Zoe comes out again and peers around. Then she steals past the shuttered shop windows and over to the little square on rue Galande. She enters Cybel's restaurant through the back door, climbs the stairs and, without knocking, goes into the room with the aquarium under the floor.

Mademoiselle Cybel is flipping through a glossy magazine. She looks up and stares at the woman with her watery eyes, a little smile on her face.

"I found out where the Parisian girl lives," Zoe tells her, "and I know the Chinese boy's name. We need to keep an eye on someone else, too. His name is Ermete De Panfilis. He probably checked into a hotel in this neighborhood."

"Do they trust you, my dear? Do they trust you?"

"Yes. In fact, I'm going to meet them tomorrow morning, just as soon as the other two arrive."

"Ah, yes, the ones who got off the train!" Mademoiselle Cybel says, interlocking her fingers like Shanghai chopsticks. "There's no news about them yet, but I have people at the hotel Le Saint-Grégorie, where the girl's father is staying. They'll meet up eventually. And if they don't, I'll take care of it."

Zoe sits down. The piranhas are snapping away beneath her sandals. "I need to use the phone."

"Certainly, my dear, certainly. But I should warn you that since it's so late—"

"He never sleeps."

"As you wish. You're the one calling. . . ."

Mademoiselle Cybel hands her a satellite cell phone.

It can only be used to dial a single three-digit number: 666.

After a few crackling noises, a voice replies. It's as sharp as a razor blade. "Heremit."

"It's Zoe. I found them."

"Did you give them the clues?"

"Yes. All we need to do now is help them. And wait."

"Fine."

Zoe speaks with a faint, faint voice, like someone who's incredibly weary.

Mademoiselle Cybel peers at the woman through her interlaced fingers, enviously staring at her young features. She claims she's over a hundred years old. That she was born in Istanbul in 1896.

Zoe smells good. It's her perfume. She bought up every last bottle of this perfume, stashing it away in an anonymous garage in Paris. It had to be done, as did many other little things, so that young Cecile Blanchard could start working. So she'd have a successful career. So she'd keep her baby.

It had to be done so that everything that was supposed to happen ultimately happened.

SECOND STASIMON

"Irene?"

"Hello, Vladimir. We have a bad connection. I hear static."

"I talked to Zoe. She's in Paris. With the kids, I think."

"I don't know if that's good news or bad news."

"Neither do I."

"She can't just disappear like that. Not the year when everything begins."

"You don't trust her?"

"Not even Alfred trusted her. After we failed in Paris, he started keeping his eye on her. He never said our search failed because of her . . . but maybe he always thought it."

"So did I."

"That's why we kept Sheng's identity a secret from her, remember?"

"Yes. And she disappeared right after we met in Iceland. She said she was going to the Blue Lagoon to relax . . . but five years have passed since then. Five years. And she only came back just now. Right at the beginning of summer."

"Well, at least she's punctual. Did she tell you what she was doing all that time?"

"She was somewhere in China and Siberia."

"But why?"

"She claims she was doing research, but I think she actually went back to Tunguska."

"How can we know for sure?"

"There's only one way. One of us has to go there to find out."

"It's dangerous. I can't do it. Not with my legs, you know."

"Do you have any better ideas?"

13

THE CLOCK

THE MILKY GRAY MOONLIGHT SEEPS IN THROUGH THE PARTIALLY closed shutters in Mistral's room, forming pale stripes and squares on her bedspread. The girl can't fall sleep. She stares at the bookshelves on the far wall, trying to make out the titles through the darkness.

She closes her eyes, but at the slightest creak from the furniture or the roof, she opens them wide, afraid she might see Jacob Mahler's evil face again at any moment.

When she checks her alarm clock for the millionth time, it's three in the morning. Sheng and Elettra haven't been in touch, and she can't get through to their cell phones. *Something's wrong,* Mistral thinks. *Something's seriously wrong.*

She gropes around for the light switch on her nightstand and flicks it on with a sigh. The butterfly shapes cut into her lamp shade cast a glowing pattern on the walls and ceiling.

Mistral nimbly rolls over and picks up the three objects resting on the trunk at the foot of her bed. Then she curls up on top of the sheets with Agatha's book, Napoléon's golden clock and the Parisian coat of arms.

The book is such a kind gift. For a few moments, it takes her mind off her frightening situation.

The clock, on the other hand, is puzzling. It's heavy, it's bulky and it has a big letter "N" etched on the back of it. "N" for "Napoléon." To the right of the "N" is a star. The bottom compartment is wobbly and feels like it might even fall off. It's held in place by a large retractable button. When she presses it, the compartment juts out a few millimeters and lazily gyrates halfway around.

Mistral looks at the clock from the side. It's a centimeter thick and has three hands that can be adjusted with metal rings. There's a tiny opening that, Zoe explained, dispenses a drop of perfume at the flip of a switch.

The clock's face is magnificent. It's pure white and divided into five sections, the hours written all around it in Roman numerals. In one of the sections is a painting of a woman with a veil covering her face. She's sitting on a throne and wears a long white gown with tiny animals printed on it. Clasped in the woman's hand is an ancient musical instrument. Between her feet is writing so tiny that Mistral can't read it. She does a backward somersault, reaches over, opens her nightstand drawer and pulls out her old magnifying glass. Then, with another somersault, she goes back to her original position and examines the writing. NATURE LOVES TO HIDE, she reads.

Mistral passes the magnifying glass over the whole clock face, pausing on its three hands. The first has a sun engraved on it, the second has a moon and the third has a star.

Once the girl is done studying both the clock and the Parisian coat of arms, she picks up a sketchbook to draw their most striking features. She really likes the three golden bees hovering in the sky over the star indicating the route. The ship's sail is full and taut with wind. There's a tiny detail on the ship she didn't notice before: At the prow is a woman sitting on a throne.

"Find anything?" a voice suddenly whispers, making her jump.

It's Harvey, who's looking at her from the crack in the door.

Mistral rests a hand over her heart. "You scared me," she admits.

"Sorry about that. I couldn't sleep," the boy says. "When I saw your light on, I figured you couldn't, either. Can I come in?"

"Of course. Have a seat." Mistral scooches over and pulls her nightgown down over her long legs. "I was just taking another look at the things we got today."

"See anything interesting?"

"Both the clock and the coat of arms show a woman sitting on a throne."

"What, like a figurehead?"

"Not exactly. She looks more like . . . like the commander of the ship."

"Why would Napoléon Bonaparte want a woman in charge of his ship?" Harvey wonders, taking a look for himself. "Hmm . . . Still, you're right."

The alarm clock on her nightstand reads three-thirty. Harvey and Mistral are sitting there, side by side. Neither of them can sleep, and for the same reason: They're both worried about Elettra and Sheng.

"Any news from them?"

Mistral shakes her head. "No," she whispers.

* * *

"Help! Enough! Please!" Sheng screams into Elettra's ear. He starts poking her in the side. "I mean it! I want off! I can't take it anymore!"

"Stop it! You'll make me lose control!"

"Go ahead! Let's crash! Just get me off this thing!" The two kids are riding down a dirt road on a rickety old motor scooter from the 1950s. Its engine sounds like a trumpeting elephant, and its overheated exhaust pipe is belching out thick, black smoke like a coal plant. Elettra's driving it, with Sheng hanging on for dear life behind her.

The girl finally gives in and loosens her grip on the throttle. The bike slows down, lurching and sputtering. Soon, the two are surrounded by a cloud of dust and exhaust fumes that blocks their view of the countryside around them. Paris is a wall of lights that looms on the horizon.

"Turn off the engine!" Sheng yells once they've stopped.

"No!" Elettra yells back, resting her feet on the ground and gently revving the engine. "If I do, it might not start up again!"

"Suit yourself. I'm getting off," Sheng grumbles, but rather than climbing off, he ends up practically falling off the bike. He takes a few staggering steps, rubs his back and hurls his backpack to the ground, yelling, "Mercy!" While patting the seat of his jeans to make sure it's still in one piece, he looks down and discovers that a whole section of his sneaker, the one that was next to the exhaust pipe, is warped. "Aw, man! Look at this! No wonder my ankle hurt! My shoe was melting!" He tries to straighten his back. "Ow! Ow! Ow!" he yelps.

"We should get going," Elettra says, still astride the rickety old scooter. "We only have a few more kilometers to go."

"You think I'm getting back on that thing? Forget it!" Sheng snaps. "Just forget it!"

"Sheng, this is the only way we can get to Paris!"

"Over my dead body. Hear that? *Over my dead body!* My behind is burning up, my back's as stiff as a board and I feel numb everywhere else." Sheng coughs as the dust settles around him. "Sixty-five kilometers riding down dirt roads sitting on a burning-hot pincushion that'll blow up if it goes over fifty an hour! Without a helmet! At night! With a headlight about as bright as a firefly!" he wails between one cough and the next. "And all because the *high-speed TGV* might've been dangerous!"

Elettra revs the engine. "What difference does it make which road you follow as you seek the truth? Such a great secret is not to be reached by a single path," she says, quoting something the four kids found written in the professor's notebook.

"Funny! Very funny!"

"We can't stay here all night, Sheng. What do you say we do?"

"I don't know!" The boy pulls his cell phone out of his backpack. "Oh, of course! No signal! What a surprise!" He points at the illuminated highway off in the distance. "We're a kilometer away from civilization!"

"I'm going," Elettra warns him, zipping forward a meter on the motorbike. "Are you coming with me or aren't you?"

"Okay . . . but I'm driving."

"Have you ever driven a scooter before?"

Sheng rakes his fingers through his hair. "What do you take me for? *Of course* I've driven a scooter before!"

"Fair enough, then." Elettra slides back on the seat. "But we need to trade places fast or it'll stall. And like I said, I'm not sure it'll start up again."

Sheng walks up to the bike warily. He looks at it, looks at Elettra and looks at the throttle grip. "Right."

"Hand me your backpack. . . . Well, you ready?"

"Yeah."

"Okay, then. On my three. One . . ."

Sheng looks at the throttle grip again.

"Two . . . Three!"

Elettra quickly slides her hand off the grip, which Sheng is supposed to grab. The boy climbs onto the seat as nimbly as an astronaut wearing a space suit, grabs the throttle and cranks it hard, but without touching the brakes.

"Careful!" she shouts.

It's too late. With a roar of the engine, the scooter zooms forward five meters, making Elettra fall off the seat, while Sheng ends up clinging to the handlebars like he's riding a bucking bronco.

"Let go of the throttle! Let go!" Elettra yells.

Sheng does what she says, quickly pulling his hand off of it. The scooter stops dead in its tracks, and the engine drops to zero, dying with a sputter.

All they hear now are crickets chirping and cars racing down the highway in the distance.

"No! Darn it!" Elettra hollers, getting up to her feet. "You let the engine die!"

"I'm sorry," Sheng says. "I . . . I don't know how it happened. . . ."

Elettra tries to get the engine running again, but all it does is whimper pitifully. "It happened because you have no idea how to drive this thing."

Sheng scratches his head. "What do we do now?" he asks, changing the subject.

"It looks like there's a bit of a downhill up ahead," Elettra says. "Maybe we can get it going again." They trudge along with the scooter until they come to the top of the slope.

"Push," Elettra orders him, tilting the scooter so that he can grab one of the handlebars.

"It's outrageous! Absolutely outrageous!" Linda exclaims, climbing the stairs of the Domus Quintilia, a towel wrapped around her head like a turban. As she passes by a doorway, she slows down and repeats, "Outrageous!"

"What's outrageous?" her sister asks from inside the room.

Linda whirls around. "My exam results won't be ready for two whole weeks!" she replies. "I could be dead by then!"

"But didn't you say you felt perfectly fine?"

"Of course I feel perfectly fine," her sister retorts, "but after they kept me in the hospital for a month—"

"Three days, Linda. They only kept you there three days."

"So what? It *felt* like a month! Oh, I'm sick! And I'm tired! Just imagine: I'm sick and tired!" She walks in, sinks down onto the couch and closes her eyes for a moment. Then she opens them and scrutinizes the cushions. "Hmm . . ."

"Whatever you're going to say about that couch, it isn't my fault," her sister quickly points out. "I've never even sat on it."

106

"These cushions need to be fluffed. All of them! It looks like an elephant rolled around on them!" With clinical precision, Linda plucks a hair from the edge of a cushion and examines it against the light. "Short, black, straight . . . I'd say it was a Chinese elephant!"

Irene chuckles as she rolls her wheelchair onto the rug. "Nothing gets past you."

Linda carries the hair out onto the terrace and tosses it into the courtyard.

"If you keep this up, the kids will be too terrified to even step foot in the house."

"Well, good, given those shoes they wear! All rubber and plastic, all muddy and sweaty. In my day, we—" The woman breaks off when she hears someone buzzing. "Are we expecting customers? Weren't they supposed to get here tomorrow?"

Irene wheels herself over to the intercom panel on the wall and buzzes the front door open. "Oh, of course. That must be Assunta."

"Assunta?" her sister says, stiffening. "Who's Assunta?"

"She's a woman I hired to help out around the hotel for the next few days."

"A maid? You hired a maid?" Linda asks, looking insulted.

"Well, yes," Irene admits. "I wasn't sure when you'd be discharged from the hospital or—"

"You shouldn't have let Fernando and Elettra leave town, then!"

"Or how you'd be feeling once you got back home. Didn't you just tell me you were sick *and* tired?"

"So what?"

"So Assunta can help you. Let her do the things you don't enjoy doing and—"

"But I can't let her do things around here! Believe me, it would be a total disaster! Where's she from, anyway? You said her name was Assunta? Is she from Naples?"

"She's Sinhalese."

"Sinha-*what?*"

"She's from Sri Lanka."

"Heavens!" Linda cries, rushing out of the room. "How will we understand each other?"

14

THE MUSIC

AT 8:18 THE NEXT MORNING, A BREATHLESS CECILE BLANCHARD rushes out of 22 rue de l'Abreuvoir with one question on her mind: *Where did I park the car last night?*

She looks both ways down the street. The other parked cars don't help her remember, nor do the nearby buildings, which she's seen day after day, night after night for fourteen years now.

Left or right? Trusting her instinct, she chooses a direction randomly and is hurrying down the sidewalk when she hears a voice. "Hello, Madame Blanchard."

For a moment, she keeps walking, distractedly zipping up the apple-shaped purse Mistral brought her from New York. Then she's forced to stop, because the person who just greeted her is blocking her way. She looks up, surprised.

It's a man with a baseball cap pulled down over his gray hair and a violin case in his hand. "Hello, Madame Blanchard," he repeats.

The woman brushes the hair out of her eyes, stalling as she tries to remember if and where she's seen him before. "Hello," she finally says. "I'm sorry, but—"

"Don't worry," he replies. "I'm running late myself. I just wanted to give you something for your daughter."

"My daughter?" Cecile thinks as hard as she can, but she has absolutely no idea who the man is. And there's something cold about the way he talks and moves, which is making her a little uneasy.

The man's holding some sheet music out to her. When she sees it, Cecile instantly relaxes. He's probably the father of one of Mistral's friends, someone she met at Madame Cocot's music school. Or maybe he's one of the people who wants her daughter to study at the conservatory. Whatever the case may be, she decides not to ask any embarrassing questions. She has the reputation of being a scatterbrained mother, which is already bad enough. Why make things worse by admitting she doesn't remember him?

"Oh, of course . . . ," Madame Blanchard says, taking the score from him.

The man smiles. "Tell her not to be fooled by appearances."

Cecile turns back toward the front door of their building. "If you want to talk to her in person, we live right there, see? You can—"

"I know where you live, Madame Blanchard," he says from behind her.

When she turns back, the man's gone.

She looks around, astonished. *How is that possible?* she wonders. *Did I just dream it?*

She's tempted to peek down under the cars to see if the man's hiding there, but self-respect stops her from doing it. Instead, she sets off down the sidewalk in search of her car again. She tucks the sheet music into her purse, casting only a quick glance at the frontispiece:

GUSTAV MAHLER

KINDERTOTENLIEDER

(SONGS ON THE DEATH OF CHILDREN)

"Wow," the woman says to herself. "Sounds pretty morbid."

Circled in red on the front page is the year of the work's publication: 1907. Written at the bottom of the page are three letters: "Z-O-E."

As soon as she reaches the corner, Cecile Blanchard realizes she's made a mistake. Her car is nowhere to be seen. It's 8:25. She's terribly late. Maybe she should run over and take the Métro.

"Hello, Madame Blanchard!" a second voice exclaims.

Who could it be now? she wonders.

It's an Asian boy who's pushing an old motor scooter, his face and clothes covered with dust. Beside him is a girl with curly black hair whose face is just as dirty. She has a backpack slung over her shoulders and two baguettes tucked under her arm. Wafting out of the paper bag they've brought with them is the irresistible aroma of freshly baked *pains au chocolat.*

"How are you, ma'am?" the black-haired girl greets the woman, staring at her with eyes that seem to sparkle with electricity.

This time, Madame Blanchard doesn't have any doubts. "Mistral's friends from Rome!" she exclaims, shaking their hands.

"We brought breakfast!" Elettra smiles, holding up the paper bag. "Would you like to join us?"

She shakes her head. "I'd love to, but I can't. I'm incredibly late. It's the same thing every morning. I'm sleepy and late."

"Boy, do I know what you mean!" Sheng replies, leaning against the scooter and yawning.

"Mistral and Harvey are upstairs. They've been expecting you," the woman says.

"Harvey's here already?" Elettra asks.

"Yes, he slept over last night."

When she hears the news, the girl visibly stiffens.

Madame Blanchard points the front door out to them and makes a hasty goodbye.

"How silly of me," she says a moment later with a sigh, knowing it's too late to turn back now. She could've given them the sheet music for Mistral.

15
THE BREAKFAST

WHEN SHE HEARS THE BUZZER, MISTRAL LETS OUT A HAPPY CRY. She calls through the bathroom door to let Harvey know and goes down the stairs in her nightgown. The three friends hug on the landing, their laughter and questions echoing through the stairwell. Mistral walks them up to the top floor and into the apartment. "That smells wonderful!"

"Freshly baked *pains au chocolat* and baguettes," Sheng says, smiling. "And in case you feel like something salty, we brought *pâté de foie gras*, Dijon mustard and a dozen chunks of goat cheese."

"Tell me everything! How did you get here?"

"We rode . . . no, we *pushed* a motor scooter somebody lent us in Fontainebleau."

"Elettra! Sheng!" Harvey exclaims, coming into the room in his pajama bottoms. His hair and torso are still damp from the shower. He walks over to Elettra to hug her, but she dodges him and follows Mistral into the kitchen.

Harvey stands there, stunned.

"*Hao!* You can hug me if you want," Sheng offers, grinning.

The two boys slap each other on the shoulder. "What the heck's up with her?" asks Harvey.

"Girl stuff," Sheng says, shrugging. "She'll get over it."

"Don't tell me she's jealous. . . ."

"Okay, I won't. So, ready for an awesome breakfast?"

At nine o'clock on the dot, someone else buzzes up to Mistral's.

"*Et voilà! Petit déjeuner* for everyone!" Ermete exclaims a minute later, holding up a bag full of fresh croissants. When he sees Elettra and Sheng, he waves his arms happily, almost tossing the bag into the air. His new Hawaiian shirt is as colorful as a junkyard.

"Great minds think alike!" Sheng cheers, grabbing the bag of croissants before letting out an incredibly loud yawn. "Oh, man, am I beat!"

Ermete takes a seat at the table and asks the kids to tell him about their trip. While they're explaining, Harvey keeps glancing over at Elettra, but she ignores him completely. Mistral has put on a knee-length aquamarine dress and a pair of flats with green, blue and pink flowers. Sheng is pacing back and forth in his half-melted gym shoes, grumbling about the heat. When Harvey hands him some flip-flops, he finally relaxes.

While Harvey's slipping on a Che Guevara T-shirt, Mistral shows the others the two objects Zoe gave them and explains everything she and Harvey discovered during their sleepless night. Just then, Elettra gets up from the table and walks toward the bathroom. She runs into Harvey in the hallway.

He smiles at her. "I'm happy you—"

"Nice shirt," she says coldly, cutting him off.

"You think?"

She shrugs. "Let me through. I need the bathroom."

"What's wrong?"

"Nothing. Are you going to let me through?"

"Would you tell me why you're mad at me?"

"I'm not mad at you. I just need to go to the bathroom."

"You're jealous," Harvey says, laughing.

Elettra looks down, her hair tumbling over her eyes. She tries to squeeze past Harvey and get through the doorway. "Leave me alone!"

"I can't believe it! You're jealous of Mistral?"

"Let me through, now!" she insists.

"Or what?" Harvey teases her. "You going to electrocute me?"

"*Hao!* Oh, man!" Sheng shouts from the other room. "It's her!" he cries, looking at the picture on Napoléon's Clock. "I don't believe it! It's really her!"

"Who, Sheng?" Mistral asks.

"That woman I keep dreaming about! This is her! The dress with all the animals, the veil covering her face . . . It's her! I mean, in my dreams she's always standing on a beach, but this is definitely her!"

The clock is passed from hand to hand.

"We all swim over to an island, where she's waiting for us, and . . ."

"And . . . ?" Ermete asks, anxiously.

"She's holding something different every time, but I wake up the second she shows it to me."

Harvey peeks into the room. "What's up?"

"Are you two done fighting?" Sheng asks.

"Sheng has recurring dreams about the goddess Isis," Ermete says, giving Harvey a recap.

"Huh?"

The engineer/radio ham/archaeologist/comics reader/gaming master Ermete De Panfilis turns the clock over in his hands. "This woman depicted on the clock is Isis, the goddess of nature, wife of Osiris and mother of Horus. The goddess also known as the white lady, the lady of magic, the moon spirit or, more simply, the goddess of a thousand names."

"What else do you know about her?"

Ermete shakes his head. "Not much, to tell you the truth. She's the supreme goddess of nature worshipped by countless civilizations in countless ways. She has a long, mysterious history. She was passed down from the Egyptians to the Greeks, from the Greeks to the Romans and from the Romans to all of Europe."

"Kind of like Mithra?"

"Mithra was Persian. Isis was Egyptian," Ermete points out.

"Mithra was the god of the sun, and Isis was the goddess of the moon," Sheng adds.

"That's because she loves to hide," Ermete continues, "just like the moon, one side of which is always dark." He puts the clock down on the table. "Like Mithra, Isis also had a mystery cult that was reserved for a small number of initiates who protected the secret."

"What secret?"

"How should I know?"

"Isn't she called the Black Madonna, too?" Elettra breaks in

CENTURY

ARIA

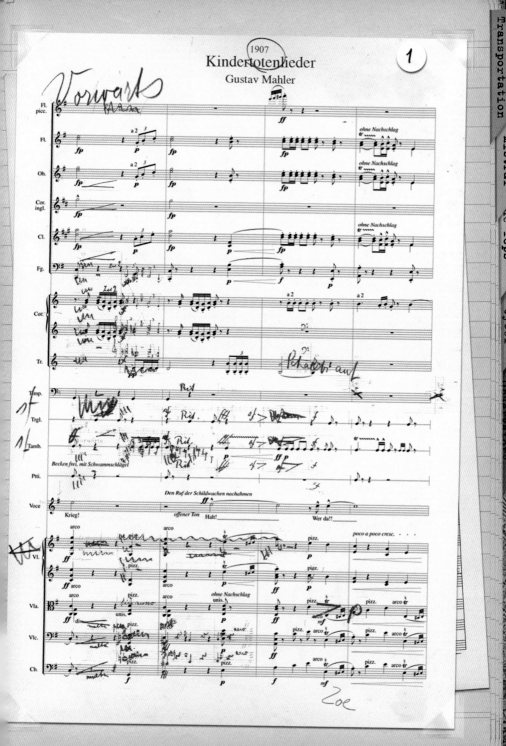

6

7

8

9

10

11

TARIF APPLICABLES	A	B	C
	10 h à 17 h lundi au samedi	17 h à 10 h lundi au samedi 7 h à 24 h les dimanches et jours fériés	00 h à 07 h dimanches et dimanches fériés
ZONE URBAINE Paris, Boulevard périphérique compris			19 h à 19 h lundi au samedi
ZONE SUBURBAINE	7 h à 19 h lundi au samedi 0 h à 24 h dimanches et jours fériés		

TARIF A : 0,82 € par Km.
TARIF B : 1,10 € par Km.
TARIF C : 1,33 € par Km.

Tarif horaire A : 26,2
Tarif horaire B : 29,9
Tarif horaire C : 27,80 €

TAXIS

J.BONSERGENT
A4 16-A 5126 6423
13:43:50

∞ PAIEMENT PAR MONNAIE

Carnet 10 tickets t Métro
NOMBRE DE TITRES : 02
PRIX UNITAIRE: 11.10EUR
TOTAL TTC: 22.20EUR
TVA:5.50%
HT:21.04EUR
NUMERO STV : 0002979.8

from:
Agatha — 122 East 42nd Street
Chanin Building — New York NY

INTERNATIONAL AIRPORT
18
PM
11430

USA 12

AIR FRANCE

RY W
NY

Mistral Blanchard
Rue de l'Abreuvoir 22
18ème arrondissement
Paris

n° F.BVFF et F.BTSC
VBF AF 4150 via CDG
Cdt de bord : MM. Leclerc et Lortsch

Entier philatélique voyagé à bord

16

Madame Cocot
SEPT NOTES ET SEPT PAS

École de Musique   Avenue de l'Opéra - Paris

17

GINKGO BILOBA

18

19

20

Air du Temps

PARFUM

PROVENCE

3 fl. oz.

26

27

28

29

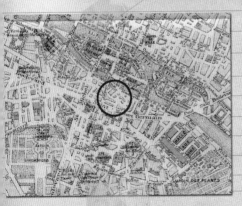

31

32

Cybel

Suggestions

Œufs brouillés aux Épices
Escalope de Saumon au Beurre
Sardines marinées en Papillote
Chester mariné à l'Ail
Terrine de Rouget à la Provençale & Tapenade
Filets de Grondin à l'Escabèce à l'Huile pure au Thym
L'Avocat grillée au Jambon
Tagliatelles aux Cèpes

Spécialités

Pâté d'Huître & Truite
Cuisses rouge d'Autruche marinée
Entrecôte Poivre au chèvre chaud
Cocktail de Crevettes à l'Andalouse
Salade Mélangée Gourmande

Petits Plats

Quenelle de Brochet à l'Ancienne
Dodu bouilloté du Saumon
Tagliatelles au Ganache
Assiette Végétarienne
Cuisses de Grenouilles Provençale

Pièces de Bœuf

Grillé, beurre Maître d'Hôtel
Grillé, Sauce Béarnaise
Grillé, Sauce au Poivre Vert
Grillé, au Bleu d'Auvergne
Grillé, Sauce aux Épices

Desserts

Tarte chaud aux Pommes, cannelle & glace vanille
Tarte au Citron ou à l'Orange ou au Beurre
Baba Lorrain
Crème au Chocolat
Profiterolles au Chocolat
Flambé au Sherbet, sauce Café
Glace Pommes à la Crème fraiche
Nougat Glacé & son Coulis de framboise
Sabité au Glace
Île Flottante
Charlote Poire au Gingembre
Crème Brûlée à l'Orangette
Poire au Vin à l'Alsacienne, glace Vanille
Salade de Fraises ou Macaron

Entrées

Salade de Lentilles à l'échalote
Crudités Maraichère
Salade Maraichère
Herring, pomme à l'Huile
Salade Niçoise
Frisée aux Lardons & Œuf poché
Chèvre chaud en Salade
Assiette de Charcuterie
Tomate à la Mozzarella
Bloc de foie gras & Toasts
Lardons au Bleu & son toast

Poissons

Filet de Saumon grillé
Brochette de Lotte
Truite aux amandes

le Filet de Canard

Grillé, sauce Provençale
Poêlé, sauce aux Écrevis
Poêlé, sauce au Poivre vert
Poêlé, sauce aux Épices

l'Entrecôte

Grillée aux herbes
Grillée, Bordelaise
Grillée pour deux personnes, sauce Bercy

Plats de nos Régions

Franc-Fêlé Campagnard
Boudin aux Pommes
Andouillette sauce Moutarde
Bœuf Bourguignon
Confit à l'Échalote
Blanquette de Veau à l'Ancienne
Côte d'Agneau à la Provençale

Fromages

Le Fromage en Bloc
L'Assiette de Fromages
Le Fromage Blanc à la Crème

prix en euro

33

PARIS.— Notre-Dame, vue d'ensemble

37. PARIS
e de la Bastille

PARIS. — L'ARC-DE-TRIOMPHE DE L'ÉTOILE

Fig. 3.— The Universal Exposition of 1889.— Champ de Mars at the Eiffel Tower, Paris.

LES DEUX MAGOTS

LES DEUX MAGOTS

INDEX

1	Sheet music for Kindertotenlieder by Gustav Mahler	18	Swarm of bees over Paris	35	Ticket from the Louvre
2	Charles de Gaulle airport	19	Madame Cocot's Music School	36	Room 12 bis
3	Tunguska	20	Air du Temps perfume	37	Japanese guidebook to the Louvre
4	Bardonecchia station	21	TOWER Avenue de l'Opéra	38	Astronomical observatory
5	Motor scooter	22	WHIRLPOOL Rue de l'Abreuvoir 22	39	The Paris meridian
6	Citroën 2CV—car	23	RAINBOW Passage du Perron	40	Notre Dame
7	TGV—train	24	EYE Rue de Montmorency	41	Place de la Bastille
8	The white hot-air balloon	25	DOG Louvre	42	Arc de Triomphe
9	Taxi receipt	26	Cybel's restaurant	43	Eiffel Tower
10	Paris Métro	27	Piranha	44	
11	Ticket for the Paris Métro	28	White-collared pitcher plant	45	
12	Letter for Mistral	29	Drosera	46	
13	Mistral's house	30	Mademoiselle Cybel's maison secrète	47	
14	Mistral's drawing of bee	31	Micrurus fulvius	48	
15	Mistral's bedroom window	32	Menu from Cybel's restaurant		
16	Madame Cocot's business card	33	Rue Galande		
17	Ginkgo biloba seed	34	The Zodiac of Dendera		

once she gets back from the bathroom, her face still red from her talk with Harvey.

Ermete nods. "Yes. With the introduction of Christianity, certain elements of the Isis cult were transferred to the Madonna. The same thing happened with the cult of Mithra, who was celebrated on December twenty-fifth, our Christmas. Since a lot of the statues of Isis were black, you can still find a Black Madonna in some churches. First Isis, then Mary."

"That doesn't explain why I keep dreaming about her," Sheng insists.

"It doesn't explain anything," Harvey says, shaking his head.

"That's not true," snaps Elettra.

"So what do you think it explains?"

"If Mithra was hiding the Ring of Fire in Rome, then the goddess Isis is hiding . . . well, *something* here in Paris."

"The ship," Harvey adds.

"The one following the star."

"With three bees over it."

"And Isis at the helm."

The five of them fall silent for a few seconds.

"Pretty confusing, isn't it?" Sheng finally concludes, saying what all the others are thinking. "Well, I think I know what we can do. . . ."

Mistral gets the map of the Chaldeans from under her bed and puts it in the center of the kitchen table. It's a wooden box with an endless series of engravings and drawings on its outer surface. There are markings and signatures reminding them of the many hands through which it's passed: the Magi, Christopher Columbus, Marco Polo, Pythagoras, Plato, Seneca, Leonardo da

Vinci . . . the many people who've used the concentric furrows on its wooden surface, seeking answers and guidance. On top of it, the kids spread out a map of Paris, which is divided into concentric subdivisions.

"These are called arrondissements," Mistral explains, "which are Paris's districts. They spiral out, going from number one in the center of town up to number twenty on the periphery."

"The professor said this kind of search was like a board game," Harvey says.

"Well, then . . . let's play!" Elettra declares, holding up her wooden top. It's the one with the engraving of a tower, which symbolizes a safe place.

Actually, the kids realize the tops aren't a game. They're sacred instruments that spin in harmony with the universe. In New York, the antiques dealer Vladimir Askenazy explained to them that each of the wooden casings contains a golden sphere, which, in turn, contains a gem.

"I'm going first," Elettra declares, casting her top onto the map of Paris. As it begins to spin, with its slow, steady movement, the kids look at each other inquisitively. The top makes its way through the arrondissements on the north side of the city, the area where Mistral lives, and slowly descends toward the Seine. Finally, it comes to rest on a large street.

"Avenue de l'Opéra."

"What's there?"

"Why would it be a safe place?"

"That's the street leading to the Paris opera house," Mistral replies. "My music school's right here, on the corner where the top stopped."

"Okay, music school," Sheng says, making a mental note of it. "I'm going next."

"Why you?"

"Because I'd better do it while I'm still awake." With this, the boy spins his top, the one with the eye on it. It quickly makes its way around the map.

"*Rient ne va ploo,*" Sheng remarks. "*Le jeus son fay!*"

Mistral giggles at his French. "You didn't get a single word of that right!"

"Who cares? Just tell me where I landed."

"In the historical heart of the city," Mistral tells him. "But I don't know what's on that street."

Sheng is so tired that he doesn't even try to pronounce the name on the map.

"Rue de Montmorency," Harvey says, reading it for him.

"Rue de Montmorency," Elettra repeats. "We'd better go there and take a look. The eye top points to something unusual we need to discover."

"Thanks, but we knew that already," Harvey grumbles.

"Watch it!" Elettra says threateningly.

"My turn," says Mistral, smoothing down her aquamarine dress and going to stand between the two. She picks up the dog top and gently rests it on the map. Almost reluctantly, she lets go of it with a flick of her wrist. The top that indicates something being guarded whirls around eerily and angrily, quickly reaching the center of the map and stopping on a corner of the Louvre's Cour Carrée courtyard.

"The Louvre?" Mistral sighs. "That's like saying the whole world. All sorts of things are on display there."

"Then let's write down exactly where it stopped in the museum," Ermete suggests.

"Well, what have we got left?"

"Mine," the engineer replies, picking up the bridge top, the one that seems to indicate a place connecting two others. Last time, it showed them a bridge between Siberia and Paris, although they still haven't figured out what it means. "Mine and Harvey's, that is."

"Go ahead," Harvey says. "I'll go last."

"As always," Elettra says sourly.

"Cut it out."

"*You* cut it out!"

"Cut it out, *both of you!*" Mistral shouts. "We've all had it with you two!"

It's so unlike Mistral to lose her temper that Elettra's and Harvey's jaws drop.

"You're both being perfectly ridiculous!" the French girl continues. "After all these months and everything we've been through, I don't think we should sit around acting like children!"

"But she—" Harvey grumbles.

"He—" Elettra murmurs.

"I don't care," Mistral snaps. "And I'm particularly amazed at you, Elettra. Are you actually jealous? Why, for heaven's sake? Because he slept over at my house? That's ridiculous. R-I-D-I-C-U-L-O-U-S! I should feel totally offended! But I'm not, because we have more important things to think about right now. If you have anything to say to each other, you can go outside and say it. Then, when you come back, come back as Harvey and Elettra. Because that's what we need right now, not two . . .

two . . . grr! I can't even find the words for it!" Mistral rests both her hands on the table. "Cast your top, Ermete."

In the awkward silence following Mistral's outburst, the bridge top spins around over the city's streets and parks, passing from one bank of the Seine to the other. Finally, it slows down once it's reached the Louvre.

"The Louvre again."

"No, wait . . ."

It passes the museum and the nearby rue de Rivoli. Then it starts to whirl around the Palais-Royal, where it spins more and more slowly, almost ready to stop.

"The Palais-Royal."

Just then, the top makes a little bounce and comes to a halt on the street right behind the palace, rue de Beaujolais.

Mistral nods. "Of course . . . a connection between the Palais-Royal and rue de Beaujolais! I know what it is. That's Passage du Perron."

"What is it?"

"A *passage* is a kind of covered passageway. There are lots of them here in Paris. They come in very handy on rainy days. Some of them have glass ceilings, and others, like this one, are just tunnels."

Ermete writes down the name. "I'll go check it out."

"That just leaves me," says Harvey, picking up the whirlpool top, the one indicating danger. Rather than just casting it, he hurls it onto the map. The top darts off with an eerie-sounding hiss, heading straight up to the north side of Paris. Everyone is shocked when they see it stop right on Mistral's house.

* * *

Standing at the bottom of the stairs, Linda Melodia watches as the maid whom her sister hired moves the plants from in front of the door leading down to the basement. "One of the leaves fell," she says when the woman is finished.

Assunta picks it up and giggles. She's a tiny, smiling woman with a tea-colored complexion. "I down, go," she says, holding up some rags and a bucket.

"Yes, yes . . . You down go. I down go soon," Linda says slowly, mimicking the woman to make sure she's understood. The moment Assunta disappears through the doorway, she quickly climbs the stairs and walks back into her sister's room.

"Well?" Irene asks. "What do you think of her?"

"She's tiny!"

"Yes, but apart from that?"

Linda peeks down the stairs to make sure they're alone. "She seems awfully cheerful. She's always giggling."

"Good. We could use a little laughter around here, don't you think?"

Elettra's Aunt Linda groans. "I'm tired of your criticism! Tired of it, you hear?"

"What did you ask her to do?" says Irene.

"Clean the basement."

"What do you mean, clean the basement? We haven't touched those rooms for years!"

"Exactly."

"But, Linda! I hired Assunta to help you with the kitchen, the dining room, the guest rooms. . . ."

"Are you joking? A stranger tidying our rooms? With all the

filth down there in the basement? Trust me, she has enough work cut out for her down there to keep her busy for weeks!"

"But you can't—"

Suddenly, they hear a crash.

"Oh, no!" exclaims Linda, rushing down the stairs. "I knew it! Who knows what she's destroyed!"

16

THE FLOWERS

It's almost noon when Harvey and Elettra get off at the Rambuteau Métro station, carrying a map of Paris.

"Just stay calm," he says softly, walking up to the street level and looking around.

"I *am* calm," snaps Elettra.

"I wasn't talking to you. I was talking to myself."

"Crazy people normally do that."

"Well, I must be a little crazy to hang around with you."

They're surrounded by a maze of little streets, and there's no trace of the rue de Montmorency shown by the eye top.

Harvey turns the map around one way and then the other. He walks down one street and then a second. He retraces his steps and walks down a third one.

"Why don't we just ask for directions?" Elettra finally says.

"No, we'd better not." The boy looks around, more determined than ever to figure all this out. But it isn't easy.

The small, reddish bump where the tarantula bit him still itches. He scratches it furiously, making the thin scab on it glisten.

Elettra grumbles. She stops a woman passing by, and the two start to communicate in gestures. Then Elettra walks back to Harvey, a smug smile on her face. "We go straight until we reach the museum, turn down rue du Temple and take the second left."

"You sure?"

"You're lucky I'm so tired, Harvey. Otherwise I think I'd strangle you."

Elettra turns around and walks down the street the woman pointed out to her while Harvey broods. "Welcome to Paris. The city of romance . . ."

"What'd you say?" she asks, turning around, annoyed.

Suddenly, her eyes open wide. Harvey's grabbed her by the shoulder. Without giving her the chance to react, he kisses her on the lips. "Nothing," he says a moment later, laughing as he runs down rue du Temple.

"If only this were just a nightmare!" Sheng moans, standing in line outside the glass pyramid through which visitors enter the Louvre. "That way, at least I could fall out of bed and wake up."

Mistral shakes her head, staring impatiently at the hundreds of people lined up in two rows in front of them. One line is for people with purses and backpacks to be passed through scanners, and the other is for people who aren't carrying anything. The glass pyramid sparkles in front of them like a crystal greenhouse.

Their line moves a step forward. "Man, at this rate, it'll take us hours," Sheng says.

"It's always like this. After all, it's the world's most famous museum."

"They could cut the line in half if they just stuck the *Mona Lisa* someplace else," he grumbles.

"Since when have you been so whiny?"

"Since when have you been so edgy?"

"Since I saw that last top . . . ," she says.

"The one that landed on your house?"

"Yes. I just can't get over it."

To play it safe, the four friends split up all the objects and took them with them. The map and the tops are with Elettra and Harvey; Napoléon's Clock and the coat of arms are with Sheng and Mistral.

As he takes another step forward, Sheng lets out a massive yawn.

"Mind your manners," Mistral teases him, giggling.

"Oh, please. You didn't spend the whole night pushing a buns-burning motor scooter from the suburbs all the way to your house. You didn't hitch a ride with hundreds of honking geese, either." A second colossal yawn. And then another one.

"Maybe you should've stayed at my house."

"The place of danger? No, thanks! But . . . But . . ." Yet another yawn. "I can barely stay on my feet," Sheng says. He pretends to pass out, but when he leans over toward Mistral, she jumps aside.

"Hey, you would've let me fall?"

"You weren't really going to fall."

"But what if I did?"

"Oh, stop it," Mistral says, laughing.

Sheng smiles. *I really like this,* he thinks. *I really like making Mistral laugh.*

*   *   *

Once he breaks free from the swarm of tourists strolling down the steep streets of Montmartre, Ermete De Panfilis sprays on tons of cologne and rushes over to the Marais district in search of the Mille Feuilles flower shop.

"Are you sure it's the best one, Mom?" he asks over the phone before walking in. "All right, all right. I'll take your word for it."

Twelve minutes later, he comes back out looking satisfied and carrying a giant bouquet of flowers so perfect they look like silk. He heads toward the gardens of the Palais-Royal. There, he stops on the main boulevard, which is lined by a row of identically pruned trees, not far from the central fountain, its misty aura casting rainbows against the sunlight.

He feels like a total idiot.

"I'm not giving them to her," he thinks out loud. He sits down on a bench next to a toweringly tall black street lamp. "Or maybe I will. Like it's no big deal. I could say something like, 'Oh, I was just walking around and I came across this bouquet of flowers . . . at the city's most famous flower shop.'"

As he's talking, he gesticulates like an actor going over his lines right before walking onstage. He rehearses it and re-rehearses it until he finally makes up his mind. "No, I'm not giving them to her."

He plunks the flowers down next to him on the bench and stares at them. Fifty-eight euro and fifty cents abandoned at the Palais-Royal. Maybe he should try to get his money back. He checks his watch. Too late. Zoe should be here any minute now.

They agreed to meet and take a look at Passage du Perron,

127

which leads into the short side of the gardens and may be hiding something that has to do with a bridge.

"A bridge connects two sides . . . and two people . . . ," Ermete murmurs. "Maybe it's a sign."

He whirls around as if he's sensed someone behind him, but it's only his overpowering cologne, which hangs thick in the air. He sits there for a few minutes, basking in the sunlight. When he checks his watch again, he discovers it's noon.

"Hello, Ermete," Zoe greets him, eerily punctual. She's wearing a smoke-gray suit that makes her look like a UN official.

Enchanted, the engineer forgets everything else and jumps up from the bench. "Oh, Zoe. You're here. Perfect. Come on. Let's go."

She casts a dubious glance at the bench. "Something serious must've happened here," she muses.

"Huh?"

"People don't leave behind a beautiful bouquet of flowers like that for no reason."

"Oh, right, the flowers!" Ermete exclaims. He leans over to pick them up, but Zoe's inquisitive look makes him stop in his tracks.

"What are you doing? You don't mean to steal them, I hope?"

Ermete smiles sheepishly. "Oh, no. No, no. Of course not. They might . . ." He looks around. "They might come back to get them any minute now."

"You're right. Shall we go?"

Ermete follows her uncomfortably.

"It's going to rain," says Zoe, leading the engineer toward the entrance to the passage.

"You think?"

"Can't you smell the mildew in the air? That's what the Seine smells like when it's about to rain."

Ermete takes a step back, hoping Zoe doesn't realize that the smell of mildew is actually his cologne.

17
THE ALCHEMIST

"THIS IS IT," HARVEY ANNOUNCES, TURNING ONTO THE
anonymous-looking rue de Montmorency. Elettra follows him
without complaint. Since their kiss, things seem to have gone
back to normal.

They hold hands as they cross rue Beaubourg and continue
down the one-way street, surrounded by an unusual silence that
muffles all the capital's other sounds.

"Where do we need to look?" she asks.

Rue de Montmorency is narrow and gray, the parked cars leaving them barely any room to pass.

"Hang on," Harvey says, checking the map. "Straight ahead
until we get down there."

The spot indicated by the top with the eye on it is located on
the far end of the street, just before the intersection with the
busier rue Saint-Martin.

"It should be up here on the left," Harvey says once they're
almost there.

In the spot shown to them by the top, they find a gray, three-
story house. Most of it is hidden behind scaffolding, but they can

still make out parts of the old, austere-looking building behind it. A sign points to the door of a little inn, which has been kept clear. It reads:

AUBERGE

NICOLAS FLAMEL

They also see a faded plaque on a gray stone architrave on the facade.

"How's your French?" asks Harvey.

"About as good as my Chinese."

"Then we'll need a translator," he says, taking out his cell phone.

"Mistral?" he asks a moment later. "What does '*Maison de Nicolas Flamel et de Pernelle sa femme*' mean?"

"The home of Nicolas Flamel and his wife Pernelle," Mistral translates. Then, when he reads the rest of it to her, she goes on. "'To commemorate their charitable works, in 1900 the city of Paris restored the original inscription of 1407.'"

"Bring anything to mind?" Harvey asks into the phone.

"Maybe . . . ," Mistral replies. "I think it's the oldest house in Paris. And Flamel . . . Wait a moment. What did you say, Sheng?" Mistral covers the receiver for a moment and then comes back on the line. "Have you read Harry Potter?"

"I saw the movies."

"Sheng says they mention Flamel in the Harry Potter books. They say Flamel was an alchemist."

"An alchemist's house, huh? Great place to take a look around."

"If it makes you nervous, don't go inside. Just keep safe."

"You guys, too. How's it going over there?"

"We've almost reached the escalator."

Harvey ends the call.

"I'll go in and try to ask a few questions," Elettra says.

"I'll take some pictures." He steps back so that he can get a shot of the building with Sheng's camera, but it isn't easy, given the scaffolding on all three floors. The left side is receding, with big iron tie-rods supporting the facade. The walls are freshly painted, and the window frames are brand-new.

Meanwhile, Elettra reads the menu written on a blackboard in the window. "Wow! Whatever these dishes are, they sound great. *Coquillages et crustacés, baignés d'un aigo boulido, fleurs épicées, gigot d'agneau de sept heures, purée de céleri rave, lingot choc-or de Flamel . . .*"

Through the window facing the street, she can see two small rooms with white tables and chairs.

Harvey zooms in on the building's architraves and posts, discovering several inscriptions and bas-reliefs, all faded and worn with time. There are incomprehensible figures, including a man with a turban, sorcerers wearing capes and pointy hats, and four angels playing music. Maybe Ermete will be able to decipher a few of them. The only thing the boy clearly recognizes are two letters repeated here and there: "N" and "F."

" 'N' and 'F' are written all over the place," says Harvey, snapping more pictures.

"Maybe they stand for 'Nicolas Flamel.' "

"Or the rule of the house," a voice exclaims. "No foreigners."

Harvey lowers his camera. Standing in the doorway of the inn is a man with a round nose, a pointy mustache, close-set eyes and the belly of someone who loves good food. He's wearing a ruffled bow tie, a red-and-white-checkered apron and a pair of light-colored wooden Dutch clogs.

"Oh, sorry . . . ," the boy says, hoping he isn't one of Cybel's men.

"I'm only joking. It's just that so many strange people have come to see this house that—"

"Strange people?"

"Ones who are looking for the philosophers' stone, the fountain of youth or some other bizarre secret. But you two don't look like aspiring alchemists to me. Where are you from?"

"Spain," Elettra replies, looking Harvey straight in the eye.

Good idea, Harvey thinks. "Canada," he says.

"If you'd like to come in for a bite to eat, we have a special menu today: June twentieth, twenty euro," the man explains. "Plus an interesting story . . . free of charge."

When Sheng and Mistral finally manage to get into the Louvre, they leave the large underground ticket hall and head straight for their first stop, the Sully Wing, which is dedicated to ancient art. They make their way down a long, dark, spectacular passageway that winds around the museum's medieval foundations. Finally, they reach the stairs leading up into the Egyptian antiquities halls.

"*Hao!*" Sheng exclaims in front of the Crypt of the Sphinx, and then again, a moment later, beside the statue of Nakhthorheb.

They pass through halls with curved white ceilings, rows of display cases and reconstructions of everyday life in ancient

Egypt, including agriculture, activities in the home, games, fishing, accounting and writing techniques.

"Sheng? Are you still with me?" Mistral asks when she notices her friend has lagged behind and is staring blankly at a sphinx.

"Give me a sarcophagus and I'll take a thousand-year-long nap," he mumbles.

Mistral walks over to him and looks around with fascination. This must be her tenth visit to the Louvre, and, just like the other times, her heart's racing with excitement. "We need to look for the guard dog," she says.

"Think it might be one of these monkeys?" wonders Sheng, yawning in front of a row of baboon sculptures in light-colored stone.

"Maybe," Mistral says, pausing to read a few panels. "Oh. See this?"

"What?"

"It says here that Isis made the first mummy."

"I thought my math teacher was the first one," Sheng says, yawning again.

"Very funny. When her husband, Osiris, was murdered and chopped into fourteen pieces, she went out, found them all and put them back together again."

"I'm falling to pieces right now," Sheng grumbles, staggering. "Somebody bandage me up!"

The next hall has cathedral ceilings and spectacular pillars. It almost looks like it was designed specifically to make people feel small and isolated. Mistral checks the museum map to see where they are. They're very close to the area pointed out by the top.

"I have some bad news, Sheng. . . ."

"Lay it on me."

"If I'm reading this map correctly, the guard dog could be in one of the six or seven halls up ahead . . . or above them, on the floors upstairs. Or downstairs."

"There are more floors upstairs?"

"Yes, at least three of them."

"And downstairs?"

"At least one."

"I think I'm gonna faint."

"We can split up to make this faster, if you want."

"Mm-hmm."

"I'll go downstairs . . . and then upstairs."

"Mm-hmm."

"You check this floor, okay?"

"Mm-hmm."

Yawning, Sheng waits until Mistral has gone down the stairs. Staggering from exhaustion, he steps back from the two wooden ships on display by the window and looks around groggily.

"A guard dog?" he asks himself.

Behind him is a small side room overlooked by the many visitors. Sheng walks in and finds himself all alone in the dimly lit room.

He yawns.

He yawns again.

He checks the room number. Twelve *bis*. It's a long, very narrow room with only two items on display. On one side are the ruins of something that might have been part of a temple. On the other side, a square slab of stone covered with hieroglyphs is affixed to the ceiling. But most important, there's a black leather armchair by the wall. It looks irresistibly comfortable.

Sheng peers around.

Nobody's there.

Heaving a sigh of relief, he sits down on the chair. A moment later, he sinks back against the backrest, fast asleep.

Passage du Perron is a narrow gallery with a whitewashed ceiling, connecting the Palais-Royal gardens and rue de Beaujolais. It's slightly lower than street level, making it quite dark. Ermete's a little disappointed. Given Mistral's description of it and its proximity to the Palais-Royal, he was expecting something entirely different. Besides, there's absolutely nothing to discover. Both walls are simply lined with shops.

"Here we are," he says.

"What is it we're supposed to be looking for?" Zoe asks.

The engineer scratches his head. "To tell you the truth, I don't know."

She shrugs. "So how do the tops work, exactly?"

"Each one points to a place, but it doesn't tell you why that place is important. You need to figure that out based on what's engraved on the top."

"In this case, a bridge," says Zoe, pausing by a charming little shop selling handmade music boxes, the Maison Anna Joliet.

"Exactly," says Ermete. "That is, a symbol that in ancient times—"

"Varro, *De lingua Latina V*, eighty-three," Zoe recites by heart. "In ancient times, pontiffs were those in charge of building bridges. Their trade was considered sacred, and bridge builders became priests."

Ermete gapes at her, impressed.

"Genesis nine-thirteen. The covenant between man and God is shaped like a rainbow, a bridge connecting Heaven and Earth."

"That's . . . that's exactly right," the engineer stammers. He almost forgot he was talking to such a learned scholar.

"In the Middle Ages, they had the custom of walling up a living person inside a bridge's foundation, making him its guardian. Even today, similar rites are carried out in various corners of the world. I could add a few more archaeological facts, if you like, but I don't think they'll help us with this."

"Probably not."

The two continue down the passage, looking unenthusiastically into the shop windows. Finally, they reach the other end and step outside into the sunshine. "Maybe the top was wrong," Ermete is forced to admit.

"Or maybe we need to take a closer look," Zoe suggests, shading her eyes with her hand. "Can I ask you a question, Ermete?"

"Of course."

"How'd you end up getting involved in all this? I mean, was it the kids' idea, or Alfred's, or . . ."

Ermete doesn't answer. He's been keeping this all a secret with Elettra, Harvey, Sheng and Mistral for months now, and he's not entirely sure he should tell her about it. "It's a long story" is all he says.

"Feel like a coffee?" Zoe offers, pointing at the bright green door of the Café Pistache. "A pale, watery, completely flavorless coffee compared to your Italian espresso?"

Ermete laughs and accepts. The moment they sit down at the table, he gives in. "They came to see me. At my shop."

"You have a shop?"

"I used to. It was called the Regno del Dado," Ermete says, sighing.

"Cute name." Zoe orders two coffees from a waiter wearing a black tie. "What about Alfred? When did you meet him?"

"A couple of years ago."

18

THE GUARDIAN

Lunch at the alchemist Flamel's restaurant is delicious. Sitting on white wooden chairs, like a real couple, Elettra and Harvey enjoy a peppery, spicy shrimp soup, roast lamb with fresh plums and, for dessert, a small slab of dark chocolate covered with vanilla icing and garnished with giant strawberries.

The maître d' comes over to sit down at their table, bringing with him a little glass of aromatic wine and the story he promised to tell them. "Everything we know about Flamel is shrouded in legend," he starts out. "In fact, even the notion that this was his house is a legend. They say he was born somewhere around the year 1330 in Pontoise, which is far away from here, and that he was a scrivener, someone who would write letters by dictation. He and Pernelle married, the two of them spent a few years in Spain and then they returned to Paris, very wealthy. No one knew how they made their fortune, but they became one of the city's most important couples. They used their money for good causes: They built hospitals, houses for invalids and several chapels. In the church of Saint-Jacques-de-la-Boucherie, most of which is gone today, mass was said in their honor until 1789."

"The year the French Revolution started."

"Yes. That same year, the church was destroyed and one of Flamel's tombs was opened."

"*One* of them?"

"Both Flamel's life and death were shrouded in mystery. They say he died in 1418 and had asked that his great secret be buried in that church, sealed in a cedar case along with seven tablets of gold."

"What kind of secret?"

"It was a book with brass binding, written with a lead pencil on thick sheets of finely illuminated bark. On the first page, in gold lettering, the mysterious author warned the reader not to use the book's secrets unless they were a rabbi or a scribe. The book had been compiled with the sole purpose of giving the Jews of France a way to pay their taxes to the empire. Basically, it contained instructions on how to turn iron into pure gold."

"The philosophers' stone!"

"Call it what you will. The book was known as the Book of Abraham, or the Book of the White Lady, and—"

"Hear that, Harvey?" Elettra interjects. "The white lady! Didn't Ermete say that the white lady was one of the names used for Isis?"

The boy nods.

"The book contained the great secrets of the universe and mankind," the maître d' continues. "How to become immortal and make gold . . . all in ten easy steps."

"I'd love to take a look at that!" Harvey says, laughing.

"As would millions of other people." The man stands up. "But no one ever has. In any case, Flamel's riches were all spent on charitable works. As for immortality, who can say? Some claimed they saw Flamel at the Opéra de Paris in the late 1700s, while others said he had a traditional burial in Paris's Cemetery of the Innocents, like it says on his tombstone, which is mysterious in itself."

"We could go check it out," Elettra suggests.

"That won't be easy," the maître d' remarks before walking away. "Right after the revolution, all the bodies in the cemetery were moved and Flamel's tombstone was donated to a museum."

Harvey drums his fingers on the table. "The church is gone, the cemetery's gone . . . ," he grumbles. "Our search is getting pretty tough, if you ask me. What do we do now?"

"I say we go to the cemetery."

"But it's not there anymore!"

"We can still go to the place where it was." Elettra rests her napkin beside her plate, gets up from the table and looks at Harvey, grinning. "Thanks for lunch."

"My pleasure," Harvey replies, like a perfect gentleman. He walks over to the register to ask for the check. As he leans against the counter, he sees a big book with brass studs.

"What's this?" he asks the maître d'.

"Our guest book."

"Can I look in it?"

"Certainly. You can even write something in it, if you like."

At the Louvre, a booming voice suddenly exclaims, "I see we're having fun here!"

Sheng wakes up with a start. He sees a cane and two massive

legs in front of him. The boy looks around, dazed, not recognizing the bare walls, the white ceiling, the temple ruins. "Where am I?"

"Just outside dreamland, I'd say," replies the voice from a moment ago. It belongs to a giant, corpulent man with a boxy head and a bristly, gray beard. He's dressed in an elegant, double-breasted blue jacket and has both hands clasped on top of his cane, carved into which are two intertwined snakes.

"I—um—" Sheng stammers, struggling to wake up completely. "I'm sorry. I didn't mean to—to fall asleep."

"What are you doing here?" the man bellows, thumping his cane on the ground to emphasize his irritation.

Sheng takes a better look at him, but he can't tell whether the man's bristly beard is hiding a ferocious sneer or a good-natured smile. Just to be on the safe side, he tries to stand up, but when he does, he feels pins and needles all the way down his leg. "Aaaah!" he gasps, falling back into the chair.

"It just so happens that that's my seat," the big man in front of him roars, "and I want it back!"

"Aaah, aaah . . . I'm sorry," Sheng moans, stomping his foot on the floor, trying to wake up his leg.

"Pins and needles?"

"Exactly."

"You need to stretch it out, then," the man orders, grabbing Sheng's foot.

"Aaaaaah, no!" the boy howls, but the man's grip is so strong that it could hold a crocodile still.

"Don't make such a fuss! In ten seconds, it'll all be over."

Sheng holds his breath as the fiery red sensation of pins and needles crawls up his leg and creeps all the way up to his brain. But after ten seconds, as promised, the tingling sensation disappears as if it's never been there at all.

The man lets go of his foot. "Is that better?"

Sheng gets up and tries to walk. "Wow, yeah . . . Thanks."

"At last!" the big man says, chuckling as he takes Sheng's place in the chair. "At least you kept it warm for me."

Even sitting down, the man is still taller than Sheng. But now the Chinese boy can read the name tag clipped to his pocket. JEAN TURIE.

"Are you a museum attendant?" Sheng asks him.

The man nods. "Actually, I prefer the term 'guard.' In any case, yes, I am. And who are you?" The man's every sentence snaps in the air like a whip.

"My name's Sheng."

"So what are you doing here, Sheng, sleeping in the Louvre museum's most important Egyptian antiquities room?"

The boy looks around, convinced he's joking. "I was looking for someplace quiet."

The guard nods with understanding. "And you found it: the one room in which you can contemplate our entire universe."

"Yeah," Sheng says, laughing. "The whole thing . . ."

"The room where the real treasure of the Louvre is hidden," the man continues.

"Hao!" Sheng exclaims, going along with the joke.

"The room in which the world's greatest story is there for all to see: the explanation of the great circle of life and death," the guard adds, moving his hands around in front of him.

143

This time, Sheng doesn't make a comeback. The guard doesn't seem to be kidding at all. "Are you joking? I really can't tell . . ." the boy admits, smiling sheepishly.

The man leans back in his seat, grinning. "What do you think?"

"The truth is . . . Well, I came here to the museum looking for something really precious."

"Everything's very precious here."

"But you just said that . . . that the real treasure of the Louvre is in this room."

"I said it and I meant it. You just need to have the eyes to see it."

Sheng looks around. "Is it those ruins over there?"

The guard lets out a loud chuckle. "No, no. Not the ruins. Try focusing your attention on that. . . ." He raises his cane and points at the stone slab hanging three meters overhead on the other side of the room. "They brought that bas-relief here in January 1907," the man says in a low voice. "My grandfather used to guard it. Then my father took his place. Now it's my turn."

"You come from a whole family of guards?"

"Exactly," the big man replies, his eyes gleaming.

It finally dawns on Sheng. *The guard dog,* he thinks. *He's the guard dog we've been looking for!*

"And the bas-relief . . . What . . . what's on it?" he asks, almost breathless.

"The Zodiac of Dendera," the guard replies, as if that explains everything.

* * *

144

"Oh, hi, Harvey," Ermete says, answering the phone. It's one-thirty. Chatting with Zoe has made him lose all track of time. "I didn't realize . . . With Zoe, yeah. What about you guys?" The engineer listens to Harvey's excited voice. "Okay, let's meet there." Then he asks Zoe, "Do you know where the Cemetery of the Innocents is?"

"I know where it *was*. It's been gone for over two hundred years."

"So where did it used to be?"

"The place where they set up Les Halles open market," the woman replies. "But that's gone now, too. It was taken down on February twenty-seventh, 1969," she adds with mechanical precision. "Les Halles is an ultramodern, useless place these days."

"Can we go there? The kids will be waiting for us," Ermete explains.

"Sure. It's not far from here."

"Good."

"Is something the matter? You seem a little tense."

Ermete looks around, trying to hide his nervousness. "Not at all. Shall we go?"

"Just give me a sec." Zoe disappears inside the café, slips a note to a waiter wearing a black tie and comes back out to Ermete.

"I already paid," the engineer says, smiling.

"Thanks!"

Zoe's note is for Cybel. It reads:

Going to Les Halles with the idiot engineer. Send someone to the Louvre.

* * *

145

Fernando Melodia throws open the windows of his hotel room and looks through the perfectly still tree branches at the coming and going of cars on the boulevard below. The sky is clear and cloudless. The heat is stifling.

On his cell phone is Elettra's latest message and notification that he missed a call from Irene and Linda. Nothing out of the ordinary.

"Why doesn't anything ever happen?" the man grumbles, stretching. The room service breakfast tray is lying at the foot of the bed, not a scrap of food left on it.

My life is so monotonous, Fernando thinks. *No wonder it's taking me so long to find inspiration for my book.* He could use a little excitement, an unexpected adventure, which doesn't include his daughter missing their train at the border.

"Who knows what she was doing in a truck full of geese?" Fernando wonders aloud, smiling.

He quickly gets dressed and grabs his things to go. But go where?

On the nightstand are the books he's been reading. He picks up the world's most famous thriller and thumbs through its first pages for the millionth time. The novel is full of yellow sticky notes, which he's using to mark references to locations that actually exist. It all starts in the Louvre. . . .

"A beginning like any other," Fernando reflects as he walks out of the room.

A moment later, he comes back in. He grabs a pen and a notebook and leaves again.

He walks back into the room a second time to get his cell phone.

* * *

On the other side of the ocean, Professor Miller walks into the kitchen, looking grim.

"Have you heard from Harvey, dear?" his wife asks.

"No, you?"

This brief exchange is enough for her to understand something's the matter.

Her husband sits down wearily, rests his elbows on the table and rakes his fingers through his hair. "It's more serious than I thought."

"What's wrong?"

"What's wrong is that I can't make heads or tails of anything anymore."

Mrs. Miller instantly calms down. He's obviously talking about work, about some crisis that has nothing to do with their family.

"Why don't you try to explain it to me?"

"You know why the civilization on Easter Island went extinct?"

"No, dear."

"What about the one on Crete? Or Greenland? Or the Maya?"

"Because they were killed off?"

"Because of eight fundamental reasons: deforestation, overexploitation of the soil, poor water management, excess hunting, excess fishing, the introduction of new plant and animals species, wars with neighboring peoples and staggeringly high population growth. And you know what's happening to our civilization today?"

"No, dear."

"All of the above, with four things to make matters even worse: the accumulation of chemicals and toxins in the environment, depletion of energy resources, reduction of the Earth's capacity for photosynthesis, and climactic changes caused by man's intervention."

Professor Miller tosses a thick book onto the table. It's entitled *Collapse: How Societies Choose to Fail or Succeed*.

"That doesn't sound very cheery," his wife states calmly.

"The data we're collecting from the Pacific Ocean doesn't make sense. It's heating up more than it should, more than is even possible. The fish on the surface are dying. The ones living in the depths can't find enough food, so they're migrating. And when they migrate, they start to disrupt other ecosystems . . . triggering a chain of disasters." Professor Miller shakes his head gloomily. "And nobody cares. Most people are happy enough if their gas stoves are working. . . ."

"Ours is electric."

"Same difference. We're using up too much energy!"

"Don't you think you're being a little catastrophic?"

"The most optimistic experts believe the Polynesian islands will disappear within the next fifty years. At least ten of the world's most important cities will become ghost towns. Venice will sink down into the sea, along with Banjul, the capital of the Gambia. Meanwhile, Tokyo, San Francisco and São Paulo all have earthquakes in store. Naples will be wiped out by the next eruption."

Mrs. Miller switches off the burners on the stove. "My mother always used to say that people get what they deserve."

"She was right. We deserve to go extinct." George Miller jumps up from his chair to leave the room.

"What about dinner?"

"I'm not hungry," he says, stopping in the doorway. "Listen . . . I need to do something about this."

"But how?"

"I'm leaving town."

"Where are you going?"

"I'm meeting up with my colleagues on a ship in the Pacific. I want to figure out what's going on. It's abnormal. Everything's way off the charts. The sea can't behave like this. It simply . . . *can't*."

"At least wait until Harvey gets back from France."

"Harvey already knows. He's fine with it."

"Very well, then. You're a man of science. You'll find an explanation for all this, you'll see."

Professor Miller chuckles. "Just like the moon . . ."

"What does the moon have to do with it?"

"Quite simply," Professor Miller says, "there isn't a single valid scientific theory about how our moon was born. So how can we expect to find one for why our planet's dying?"

19
THE ZODIAC

IN A HALL INSIDE THE LOUVRE, SHENG CATCHES UP WITH MISTRAL and grabs her by the wrist. "Come with me, quick! I found it!" he pants.

"Where?"

"Downstairs in room twelve *bis* of the Sully section."

"Are you sure?"

"Yeah! It's a treasure and it's protected by a guard!"

Sheng and Mistral hurry down the stairs.

"So what is it?"

"An Egyptian zodiac. The guard explained some of it to me, but I'm not sure I understand it all. They hung it really high up, so it's hard to see. And they did it intentionally, the guard said. They wanted the zodiac to go unnoticed."

"*They . . . ?*"

"Yeah, *them*. He says they're everywhere. Even here in the museum. Anyway, he said we could get a poster with the reproduction of the whole zodiac in the bookstore. We've definitely got to pick one up."

"What's so important about the zodiac?"

"It's the oldest one in the world that shows the Egyptian and the Chaldean constellations."

"Are you kidding?"

"No. It's got everything! The Egyptian gods and the signs of the zodiac. Pisces, Aries, Capricorn, Cancer, Taurus . . . all twelve of them. You can see all the planets, too. There's even an extra one: a hobbling planet that goes around the sun with a cane. Like the guard! Mithra's on it. Isis is on it. . . . *We're* even on it!"

"Sheng, what are you talking about?"

"I'm telling you, the four of us are on it! The guard explained it to me!"

"So who's the guard, anyway?"

"His name's Jean Turie and—" When they run into room 12 *bis*, Sheng stops in his tracks. It's empty. "Darn it! He's gone."

"Are you sure this is the right room?" Mistral whispers, peering around.

Sheng shows her the armchair he dozed off in. "Of course I am. I sat down right there and fell asleep."

"You *fell asleep?*"

"Yeah, but only for a minute! Then the guard showed up and explained everything to me. He had this funny-looking cane, and he used it to point up at the things sculpted on the zodiac. He told me the zodiac was made in fifty-one BC, a really unusual year, when there were four eclipses. Four of them, get it?"

"Actually, no."

"Four, just like us!"

"Well, then what?"

"Then nothing! I showed him the clock and—"

"*You showed him the clock?*"

151

"Sure. He told me the woman on the clock is Isis. Then he showed me where she is on the zodiac, too. Look, that's her! Professor Van Der Berger wrote in his journal that nature loves to hide, remember? Well, Isis is hiding right there on the zodiac. Her back's turned toward us, and she's the only figure doing that!"

Mistral listens to his river of rambling words, horrified. Finally, she says, "Listen, Sheng. I don't see any of that up there, and quite honestly I don't understand a single word you've said. Do you want to go to the museum bookshop to look for the poster?"

"The real treasure of the Louvre . . . ," Sheng murmurs.

"What?" Mistral asks.

Sheng stands there, stock-still, below the stone zodiac. "He said this zodiac is fundamental but that it's aligned wrong, that it shouldn't be facing this direction."

"Then why did they put it this way?"

"So we wouldn't understand it. It was *them*."

"Who are *they*?"

"The people who know the secret behind this zodiac."

"But who are they, Sheng? And what secret?"

"I don't know, Mistral! Maybe that's what we're really looking for! The zodiac points to a path. The path leading to the secret. Maybe the answer's right here in this room. The stars, the planets, the signs of the zodiac . . . Think about it!"

"I *am* thinking about it, but—"

"So far, we've followed clues that helped us find the Ring of Fire and the Star of Stone, but what good are they to us? They aren't. They aren't . . . *magical*. They're just things!"

"That's not true. When Elettra looked into the mirror in Rome—"

"Elettra! You said it yourself! Elettra. It wasn't the mirror, it was her. This search . . . We . . . We don't need to find a bunch of things. We need to find ourselves!"

"Sheng, listen—"

"And the stone from New York? What's so magical about that? Harvey said it might have fragments of human DNA in it. DNA, the most scientific thing there is!"

"Sheng, please, not so loud . . . ," Mistral begs him. "You're scaring me."

"It's not that they're magical! It's just that we don't understand them! And now we need to start figuring things out!" Overcome with excitement, he grabs Mistral's hands. "It's like it's all around us and we aren't even noticing it."

"Stop it, Sheng." Mistral pulls her hands free and finds they're trembling. She takes her cell phone out of her pocket.

"You don't believe me, do you?"

"I never said I didn't believe you," the girl replies. "I just don't understand a word you're saying."

"But I saw it!" Sheng insists, pointing first at the stone zodiac hanging from the ceiling and then at his eyes. "For a moment, everything was so clear!"

"Sheng!"

"What?" he asks, instantly lowering his voice, frightened by his friend's terrified expression.

Mistral runs her hands over his face. "Your eyes are yellow again."

20
THE MESSAGE

IT'S THREE. HARVEY AND ELETTRA ARE WALKING FROM THE alchemist Flamel's house to the large cluster of modern buildings of Les Halles shopping center, where the Cemetery of the Innocents used to be.

"We can't trust her," Elettra repeats for the millionth time.

"No, and it's more complicated than we thought. If I hadn't looked at that book, we probably never would've realized it. . . ."

Flipping through the pages of the Auberge Nicolas Flamel guest book, Harvey noticed a message written in familiar handwriting. Not by coincidence, it was right beside the date of February 29, their thirteenth birthday. It read:

To Mistral, Elettra, Harvey or Sheng,

   This is a special message wishing a happy birthday to four young friends. If you're reading this, it means I died before my time and that the secret is in jeopardy. It means that not only were we unable to fully discover it but we weren't even able to protect it. Stay close to each other. Help each other. Use the tops and try to learn how the clock works. Don't tell anyone what you know unless you're sure they'll help you. And among those who'll offer to help you, beware of the archaeologist. She can't be trusted.

May the stars smile upon you, kids.

Alfred Van Der Berger

"The professor wrote 'we,'" Elettra points out as she rereads the message, which she's copied down onto a piece of paper. "*We were unable to discover it. We weren't able to protect it. . . .*"

"He was looking for the secret himself, but he left it up to us to actually find it."

"But why us?"

"Because we're special," Harvey replies. "The professor was a Star of Stone, like me. He could hear the voice of the earth. Maybe the others . . . were like you."

"They made mirrors go dull?"

"And radiated energy."

"Then Sheng and Mistral must be special, too."

"You remember back in Rome, when Sheng's eyes turned yellow? Maybe that was . . . well, a sign. We've got to do what the professor says and help each other. And not talk to anybody."

They pass by the tube-covered Centre Pompidou building. In the square surrounding it, Gypsies are hounding people for change outside the cafés.

All that's left of the Cemetery of the Innocents is a square fountain surrounded by trees. Farther on, the area that was once home to the city's biggest open-air market has made way for odd buildings that look like ship hatches and parts of giant electrical appliances sticking up out of the ground. Rounded and curved, in white aluminum and glass, the buildings are home to an underground shopping center that clashes with the harmonious rooftops of the buildings and the spires of the Gothic church nearby. Beside the complex is a big, green park with a thousand bicycles and an amphitheater square built around the statue of a face and a large hand. Just before that is the entrance to the Métro station, which roars belowground. On the street level, a wood and brass carousel revolves lazily next to two hot-air balloons offering sightseeing tours in the skies over Paris.

"Doesn't that look like fun?" Elettra chimes. "If we have time, I'd love to go up in one of those. . . ."

"You got it," Harvey says, smiling. "Which one?"

The first is a gaudy red balloon with the picture of a dragon on it. The second is pure white and decorated with a big bear.

"The white one," Elettra says.

"Okay, we can go for a ride, but let's get Zoe out of our hair first."

"I can't even picture her," says Elettra.

"Well, that's her, over there."

They exchange a quick hello. Harvey introduces Zoe to Elettra, who immediately takes the woman aside, asking her what she knows about the area, all to give Harvey the chance to pass the professor's message on to Ermete.

"The cemetery was closed not long before the revolution," the archaeologist explains, "when the bodies started to smell so bad that it made the air in Paris reek. It was in that era that they started producing really strong perfume."

To cover up the smell of death, thinks Elettra. *So what's your perfume covering up?*

"But what did they do with the bodies?" the girl asks, turning to look at the surviving fountain.

"Massive catacombs were dug below the city, even right here, under our feet," Zoe explains. "There are millions of bodies below Paris. You can visit them, if you want," she adds with a laugh.

Just then, Harvey shoots out his hand and slips the note into Ermete's pants pocket, but his friend doesn't notice.

"Let me see if I can hear their voices," Harvey suggests. He kneels down, rests his hands on the ground and looks up at Zoe. "Alfred taught me," he adds.

The woman stiffens.

"Everybody, put your hands in your pockets," Harvey orders them, pretending to concentrate.

The others do as he says. Ermete notices the slip of paper, pulls it out and reads it.

Harvey smiles.

"Do you hear them?" Elettra asks him.

Harvey closes his eyes and, after a few seconds, opens them. "Oh, yeah . . . I heard them all right."

"What did they say?" Zoe asks tensely.

"Unfortunately, I didn't understand them," he says, smiling. "They were speaking French."

The intercontinental phone call is relayed by a satellite locked into Earth's orbit.

"Heremit," replies the man from Shanghai.

157

"Goodness gracious! I'm very happy to hear your voice," exclaims Mademoiselle Cybel. "Very happy!"

"Have you done it?" the icy voice on the other end of the line asks.

"Not yet, Heremit, my dear, not yet. But we're on the right path."

"There are no right paths."

"It's just an expression, my dear, just an expression. My kids are following your kids. Goodness gracious, pardon my little joke! I have a young man watching Fernando Melodia and another one at the Louvre following Mistral and the Chinese boy."

"Sheng," Heremit points out. "We learned his name is Sheng."

"Yes, of course. Sheng. Mistral's house is being watched, as is the hotel of a certain . . . let me see . . . Ermete De Panfilis."

"He's a small fish."

Mademoiselle Cybel taps her foot on the aquarium floor. "At times, small fish bite worse than big fish."

"Zoe?"

"She's with them now. She says it will all be taken care of in due time."

"Tomorrow is June twenty-first. I can't wait."

"What difference does it make, my dear . . . just one day?"

"Tell Zoe I don't intend to wait. Tell her I've waited long enough."

"But Heremit, Heremit, my dear! Your friend believes the kids can solve whatever it is that she wasn't able to solve herself."

"She's not my friend. Tell her I can't wait."

"And if she insists?"

"We can do without her now."

Fernando Melodia is waiting in the relentless sun outside the Louvre. He's wearing a paper hat to protect his head from the glare reflected off the pyramid's panes of glass. By the time he finally manages to buy a ticket, he doesn't feel like going in. His interest in seeing the *Mona Lisa* has been replaced by the more practical idea of grabbing a bite to eat. He walks over to the Grand Café, where he's lucky enough to find an empty seat at one of the few tables facing the ticket offices. He orders a delicious baguette and a glass of sparkling white wine.

That's better, he thinks, once he's done eating. Now that his stomach is full, he's ready to go in.

Fernando starts out his visit in the Greek section, where he's captivated by the *Winged Victory of Samothrace* at the top of the stairway, his heart filling with the echoes of ancient conquest and a vague longing for triumph.

But after a while, having seen his hundredth urn, he decides to visit another part of the museum before his enthusiasm dwindles to nothing. He considers his many options and chooses the area that sounds the most legendary.

"Egyptian antiquities!"

Around him, the Louvre itself is like a fascinating character, like an adventurous uncle who's full of surprises, the kind who always has an exciting new story to tell you when he comes to visit. However, quite like that sort of character, it's a museum that you need to take in small doses to avoid being overwhelmed. Hall after hall, stairway after stairway, through the underground levels and up steep ramps, Fernando Melodia walks through the Egyptian antiquities halls that overlook the museum's large courtyard.

Having crossed through a room with giant pillars, he sees two kids who seem to be having some trouble. One of them looks like he's fainted. He sits on a windowsill with a damp cloth covering his eyes. The poor boy is being helped by a tall girl as slender as a reed, who moves quite gracefully. Looking at her, Fernando has the funny feeling he's seen her before. But where?

When he stops a few steps away from her, she looks over at him, worried.

"Mr. Melodia?" the girl asks in a tiny voice.

Being recognized in the Louvre museum in Paris makes Fernando shiver with excitement, the kind of excitement famous authors must feel when they're spotted on the street by one of their fans.

"Have we met?"

"I'm Mistral, Mr. Melodia. Remember me?"

"How foolish of me! Elettra's French friend! Hello! What's wrong? What happened?"

Mistral shakes her head. "Sheng isn't feeling very good."

"Hello," the Chinese boy says without taking the cloth off his eyes.

"Sheng? I'm so happy to see you again, at last! Where's Elettra?"

"In Les Halles."

"What's she doing in Les Halles?"

"Um, sightseeing?"

"So what happened to you, anyway?"

"My eyes turned yellow."

"That happens to him sometimes," Mistral explains, "but we don't know why."

These kids are getting stranger every day, thinks Fernando. "Do they hurt when that happens?" he asks.

"Only if there's too much sunlight."

"Maybe we should call a doctor," Elettra's father suggests.

"No, no!" Sheng says. "Just let me rest for a few minutes. I'll be fine."

Fernando turns to Mistral and quietly asks her if they can speak in private.

The girl nods. "Sheng, we're going over to the bookshop to pick up that poster of the zodiac you wanted. Will you wait for us here?"

"You think I'm going anywhere in this condition?" he replies.

Mistral and Fernando go up and down the stairways, following the signs for the entrance. A man wearing a black tie watches them out of the corner of his eye, pretending to consult a map of the museum. Then he starts following them from a distance.

"I don't want to be nosy," Fernando Melodia says, "but are you kids thinking of keeping up this game of spies and secret agents for very much longer? I'm asking you because you seem like the most mature one in the whole group."

"Mr. Melodia, you're p-putting me in a difficult position," Mistral stammers, not sure what to say.

"What's my daughter doing in Les Halles?"

"She's . . . looking for something."

"Looking for something? That's all you have to say?"

"Yes."

"Are you sure there's nothing else I should know?"

"I think you should talk to Elettra about it. If I told you everything—"

"You'd be betraying her, of course. I understand. She's your friend. But your mother . . . Does she know?"

"I've told her a little about it."

"But don't you think this is all a bit childish? Don't get me wrong, I'm happy you're traveling the world and visiting each other, but I think you're going a little too far."

"You're right, Mr. Melodia," Mistral replies, nodding.

"Talk to the others and then explain everything to us . . . to me, to Professor and Mrs. Miller, and to your mother."

"I will."

"Good. So, what is it you need to get at the bookshop?"

The cloth resting over Sheng's eyes has such a soothing effect that before he knows it he nods off again. And once again, he's awoken by a booming voice and a thumping cane. "What's going on, son?"

Even with his eyes covered, Sheng knows it's the guard of room 12 *bis*. "Oh, you're back! Where've you been?"

"I went to the restroom. What about you? Why are your eyes covered?"

"They ache."

The guard sits down on the windowsill beside him. "The eyes often deceive. You're convinced you're seeing something, but it's just them fooling you."

"You're right."

"The ancients realized that, which is why they used symbols when they needed to write down something important. Those who didn't know how to read the symbols didn't see anything, while others . . ."

"Others understood."

"Take the pyramids, for example. Do they make any sense at all? No. At least, not until you realize that they were built in exactly those spots and with exactly those dimensions to mimic the stars."

"French cathedrals were built that way, too!"

"Very good! And you know why? Because Paris is actually an Egyptian city. It has pyramids, sphinxes, statues . . . and even the Luxor obelisk."

"Like the one in New York?"

"New York has an obelisk, but it isn't from Luxor. Here in Paris, they did things right. They brought all of Egypt here, including its gods. . . ." The museum guard chuckles. "They worshipped the sun, and we had our Sun King. They worshipped Isis, and we put her all around the city. She's even here at the Louvre, outside on a wall. She's facing east, but she isn't looking at the rising sun. No sir! The goddess of the night doesn't care one bit about the sun."

"What's she looking at, then?"

"Her guiding star. Paris means *par Isis*. 'Around Isis.' What Isis does, we do."

"And what's Isis doing?"

"What she's always done. She's sailing off toward her star."

Isis, sail, star.

So Isis is on a ship, thinks Sheng. *Ship, Isis, star. Ship, Isis, star . . .*

"Napoléon's coat of arms!" the boy shouts, pulling the cloth off his eyes.

All he sees is Mistral, standing in the doorway.

"Sheng? Is everything okay?"

163

"Where were you? Did you see him?"

"See who? Here, I got you that poster of the zodiac."

Sheng looks around for the guard with the cane, but he's nowhere to be seen. Then he kneels on the floor and excitedly unzips his backpack. He pulls out the gold clock, Napoléon's coat of arms and the map of Paris they used when they cast the tops. "Quick! Give me the poster!" he orders Mistral.

"What about your eyes?"

"I can see fine! Everything's clear now!" Sheng shouts.

21
ZOE

WHEN HARVEY STANDS UP AGAIN, HE HUGS ELETTRA AND BURIES his face in her hair.

"Hey!" the girl exclaims, caught off guard by his display of affection.

But Harvey doesn't let go of her. He pulls her closer and whispers in her ear, "I lied when I said I didn't hear voices. I heard them, all right."

Elettra smiles at Ermete, who's standing there rigidly, his hands in his pockets.

"They kept saying, 'Traitor! Traitor!'" the American boy continues. He pulls away from Elettra and stares into her eyes.

"Well," Zoe says. "What do we do now? Should we meet up with the others?"

Elettra looks at the hot-air balloons moored nearby, their round, fabric tops swaying. Suddenly, she has an idea. She knows how they can get away from the woman, at least for a little while. "I say we go for a ride in one of those hot-air balloons!"

After all, there didn't seem to be anything particular in the place where the Cemetery of the Innocents used to be, and she and Harvey have managed to do the most important thing: They've let Ermete know that Zoe can't be trusted.

"Sounds great," Harvey agrees. "Ermete, you coming? Zoe?"

The archaeologist shrinks back a step. "No, I don't think so."

"Okay, then. See you later."

"You're just wasting time," the woman blurts out.

"What do you mean?"

"I mean you haven't gotten much accomplished today."

"Were we supposed to?"

"I thought so, yes. I gave you what Alfred told me to give you, the clock and the coat of arms, and I thought you'd . . ."

"We'd what?"

"Nothing," Zoe says with a smile, giving up. "I guess I just got all caught up in your search . . . a bit like Ermete."

Elettra smiles at her. "Well, right now, Ermete and the two of us feel like going for a ride in a hot-air balloon."

"Yeah, Paris must look beautiful from up there," the engineer adds.

"In that case," Zoe says with a sigh, "I'd be happy to come along."

The little group slowly heads over to the two balloons. Harvey takes out his cell phone and looks at Elettra. She reads his mind. Making sure Zoe doesn't see her, she dials his number.

"Dad?" Harvey answers, pretending to speak to Professor Miller. "Hey, Dad. What's up? Yeah, in Paris. With your friend. Uh-huh. Sure . . . Yeah, she's really nice. Want to talk to her?"

Harvey holds the phone out to Zoe, who shakes her head and waves her hands.

"She can't. She's busy," Harvey continues. "What's that? Sure.

I will. Okay. Bye, Dad . . . He says hi," he tells Elettra and Ermete. Turning to Zoe, he adds, "He told me to thank you and to give Randolph his best."

"I'll do that," Zoe replies.

Harvey nods grimly. "So . . ." He stops a few feet away from the hot-air balloons. A woman dressed in blue is explaining to a small group of people how safe and easy they are to fly. "Who the heck's Randolph?"

"What?" Zoe gasps.

"I wasn't talking to my dad," Harvey says, holding up his cell phone.

Elettra holds up hers. "And there is no Randolph. So who are you, really?"

Back in the Louvre, Sheng spreads out the reproduction of the Egyptian zodiac in front of Mistral. "Look! Right here, above the boat! See the figure that looks like a cow?"

The girl nods. "Yes . . ."

"She's turned around. She's the only one looking the other way. You know why?"

"Because she's shy?"

"Because she loves to hide! The guard explained to me that this is Isis. She's holding a star in her horns. Her star."

Sheng moves on to Napoléon's coat of arms. "Now check this out. There's the boat, there's Isis sitting at the prow and there's the star, the same star, showing her the way. It can only mean one thing: To find the boat, we need to find the star . . . and to find the star, we need to ask Isis where to look."

"How do we do that?"

Sheng lays the poster of the zodiac over the map of Paris. "The guard told me this was facing the wrong direction," he says, turning the poster around.

"How do you know it needs to go that way?"

"There's a little bear right in the middle of the zodiac. See it?"

Mistral looks closely and nods.

"The bear's tail," the Chinese boy explains, "is Polaris, the North Star. So it points north. That way . . ." He grabs the map of Paris. "Now, if the center of Paris is île de la Cité . . ." He shifts the zodiac so the bear is positioned right over the island. "We'll find Isis . . ."

"Right here in the Louvre," says Mistral.

Sheng bites his lip. "Let me see the clock," he tells her. Once it's in his hands, he looks at the depiction of Isis sitting on the throne. "Five sections. The star has five points. Isis is sitting. . . ." He turns the clock over. Engraved on the lower section are the letter "N," for "Napoléon," and a star. "There's a star here, too," Sheng murmurs.

A few curious passersby stop to stare at the kids kneeling on the floor. A Japanese man takes a picture of them.

"Why's the bottom of the clock wobbly?" Sheng wonders. He notices the retractable button in the center of its lower section. "What happens if I push this?" The section juts out from the rest of the device and gyrates back and forth slowly for a couple of seconds before coming to a halt.

"Now I understand!" Mistral gasps. "It isn't a clock. . . ."

"No," Sheng agrees. "It's a compass."

"North!" the girl cries. "The 'N' stands for 'north,' not 'Napoléon.'"

"But the star . . . It doesn't point south. . . ."

"Where does it point, then?" asks Mistral.

Her face is very close to Sheng's. So close, in fact, that when he notices, he instantly stops breathing. "I think it's pointing east."

"Meaning . . . ?"

Sheng jumps to his feet. "The guard told me the museum has an Isis facing east, but she isn't looking at the sun. . . ."

"But the Louvre is huge, Sheng, and there are thousands of statues!"

"No!" he exclaims. "He said that Isis is on a wall outside. Hmm . . . And she's facing east." He checks the museum map. "Isis must be here, on this outer wall. Or here," he says, pointing at the internal courtyard called the Cour Carrée.

The two friends quickly gather up their things from the floor.

"Can I you ask something?" Sheng says as they're racing to the courtyard.

"What?"

"Mr. Melodia . . . Did we really run into him here?"

"Yes, why?"

"I was thinking about the guard."

"What about him?"

"You think I might've just dreamed him?"

"There she is," Mistral exclaims a few minutes later.

Looking in the direction of the pyramid from the center of the Cour Carrée, they see a bas-relief of Isis on the second floor, beside the first window to the right of the way in. She's sitting on a throne, a sun disc held up in her bull's horns, just like she's depicted on the zodiac.

"Yes!" cries Sheng. "That's her! She's the one who needs to guide us!" He looks at Mistral and adds, "The woman of my dreams."

"How is she going to guide us?" asks Mistral, still staring up at the wall of the museum.

Sheng shakes his head and pulls out the clock again. "Maybe . . . maybe we need to use this. I just don't get how."

"Well, sailors used to find their way by looking at the stars with instruments called sextants," Mistral says, her heart racing. "Maybe this is some kind of sextant." She pushes the clock a little closer to Sheng and points at it. "When I studied it last night, I noticed something strange about its hands. . . ."

"You mean the fact that they never move?"

She laughs. "That too. But most important, they're all the same length. What good is a clock if you can't tell the difference between the hour hand and the minute hand?"

"Keep going. . . ."

"I don't know. Maybe . . . maybe they aren't really clock hands. Maybe they're something else. In any of your books, have you ever read that you can use a watch to find out which way is north?"

"Yeah . . ."

"You need to point one hand toward the sun and the other hand at the twelve. And then . . ." Mistral shakes her head. "I can never remember what to do next."

"Let me try, then. I turn the clock so the twelve is pointing north. Now let's point the hand with the sun over it toward the sun. . . ." Sheng positions the hand at around nine o'clock, since the sun is partially hidden behind the museum's rooftop. "What do we do with the other two?" he asks.

Mistral giggles. "I don't know! I can't see the moon or any stars."

Sheng looks up at the statue of Isis. "You might not," he says, remembering what the guard told him, "but that doesn't mean their symbols aren't here." That said, he adjusts the hand with the moon over it so that it's pointing at Isis, and the hand with the star over it so that it's pointing east.

Suddenly, the clock's gears start to whir and tick. A moment later, the section of the clock face with the picture of Isis disappears.

"It worked!" exclaims Mistral, giving Sheng a sideways hug.

With a metallic click, a different image appears in the second section of the clock.

"There's another picture!"

The kids look at each other, baffled. The new picture depicts a woman kneeling at the feet of a majestic-looking man with rays of sunlight all around his head. Both of them are surrounded by a giant blazing star.

22

THE BALLOON

MISTRAL'S CALL TO ERMETE'S CELL PHONE SHATTERS THE LONG, ICY silence that has fallen among the three of them and Zoe.

"Answer it," the woman snaps at the engineer.

"Who are you?" Harvey asks again. "And what do you want from us?"

"Do you work for the man in Shanghai?" Elettra adds.

Behind them, her voice loud and shrill, the woman dressed in blue continues to demonstrate how the hot-air balloon works by firing up the burners.

"Answer it," Zoe repeats.

She slips a hand into her purse.

Ermete gapes at her. "Zoe? What . . . ?"

The archaeologist is holding a gun. "You two stay where you are. Ermete, answer the phone."

"Let's all keep calm," the engineer says, holding his hands in front of him. "I'll answer it, and you put the gun down."

"You aren't a friend of my father's, and you weren't a friend of Professor Van Der Berger's, either."

"You're wrong about that, kid," Zoe snaps. "I was a very close friend of Alfred's. And now answer the phone," she adds, turning to Ermete.

The engineer stiffly holds the cell phone up to his ear. "Oh, hello, Mistral."

A long silence follows.

"Great. Really. You can tell me all about it later. Yeah, yeah. Sure I'm excited. What? No, I have no idea. Maybe . . . maybe we should—"

"You idiot!" Zoe snarls, ripping the phone out of his hand. "Mistral? Hi, it's Zoe! What do you want to know?" she asks, keeping her purse pointed at all three of them.

Harvey clenches his fists, looking like a caged lion, Ermete shifts nervously from one foot to the other and Elettra glares at the woman with all the hatred she has inside of her.

"Oh, so you've discovered how the clock works?" Zoe says with a laugh. "Wonderful! That's absolutely wonderful!"

The cell phone, Elettra thinks. *The cell phone.* If only she could touch it . . . but she can't. Her fingers start tingling, and her skin slowly grows hotter.

"A man with rays of sunlight around his head?" Zoe says, repeating Mistral's words to needle the three of them. "That must be the Sun King. Where are you two?"

I can do it, Elettra thinks, closing her eyes. *I can do it, I can do it, I can do it.*

"There's a statue of the Sun King at the Louvre, right next to the glass pyramid, and—"

Zoe shrieks as the cell phone explodes in her hand with a muffled bang.

"Run!" shouts Elettra. She grabs Harvey's arm and drags

him toward the wicker basket of the hot-air balloon nearest them.

"No!" Zoe screams the moment she gets over her shock. The explosion has scorched some of her hair. She raises her purse and aims it at the two kids, but just as she's firing the gun, Ermete kicks the purse out of her hand, changing the bullet's trajectory.

"Are you crazy?" the engineer yells.

"You idiot!" Zoe shrieks.

The instant they hear the gunshot, the people around them break into a panic. They start running in every direction, including the young woman from the balloon service, even though she's noticed that Harvey and Elettra have clambered into the wicker basket and are undoing the mooring ropes.

Zoe leans over to pick up her purse, but Ermete tackles her a moment before she reaches it. They both tumble to the ground.

Zoe kicks Ermete in the mouth. "Do you really think you can stop me?"

People scream and run away as Ermete curls up on the ground, covering his bleeding lip with his hands. A second later, he bolts to his feet. "That's it!" he shouts furiously. "I've had it with women beating me up! Got it?" He towers over Zoe and shoves her back down to the ground when she tries to stand up.

Ten meters away, the white balloon lifts up off the ground. When Zoe notices, she starts kicking out at Ermete.

"You're just an amateur!" the engineer yells, remembering his frightening experience back in New York with Egon Nose's henchwomen. He grabs her by the ankle and stills his mind, analyzing the situation with mathematical coolness. He's got Zoe

174

pinned, but he knows he'll only be able to keep her down for a few seconds.

People are screaming and running away in every direction.

Harvey and Elettra are heating up the balloon with the burners, making it rise higher and higher.

"Ermete! Quick!" Elettra calls out to him, leaning out from the basket and holding out her hands. But they're too far away, and the balloon is ascending too quickly. With her free foot, Zoe kicks Ermete in the shoulder.

"Would you stay put?" Ermete fumes just before a third kick hits him full in the cheek. He falls down on the grass, losing his grip on her ankle.

Zoe grabs her purse.

Ermete gets up to his knees, ready to make a break for it.

"You haven't got a chance!" the woman growls.

The engineer notices something glimmering in the grass beside him. He reaches out his hand and, for the first time in his life, finds himself holding a gun. It must've fallen out of Zoe's purse. He points it at her. "What do you say now, huh?"

"You're pathetic," Zoe hisses. "Just drop it! You don't get it, do you? This is serious business! It's way out of your league!"

"Don't move, Zoe . . . or whatever the heck your name is! Stay right where you are!" Ermete says threateningly.

She scowls at him like a ferocious beast that someone's trying to put in a cage. She's clearly not willing to be bossed around. "Go to hell," she mutters, turning her back on him.

"Freeze!"

"You'll never shoot me," the woman exclaims, waving her hand dismissively.

Ermete aims the gun at her back.

Then he shakes his head. Zoe's right. He can't shoot her. He isn't a murderer. He just can't do it.

He watches her walk away through the screaming crowd. Then he staggers to his feet and looks up at the balloon, which is now thirty meters off the ground.

"Darn it," he grumbles, touching his mouth. "She busted my lip."

He dumps the gun in the first trash can he sees and hobbles over to a nearby taxi stand, where the cabbies have gotten out of their cars to see what's going on.

The hot-air balloon is drifting off to the west.

"Darn it! Darn it!"

Despite all the confusion, he suddenly remembers one of his mother's countless warnings: Never trust a woman who wears too much perfume. She has something to hide. Something unpleasant.

"Follow that balloon!" he yells as he climbs into the taxi at the front of the line. When he realizes there's no cabby behind the wheel, he leans out of the window and shouts, "Well? Are you going to drive me, or do I have to do everything myself? Follow that balloon!"

23

THE KING

Mistral is euphoric when they come out from the Louvre's glass pyramid in search of the statue of the Sun King. Beside her, Sheng isn't tired anymore.

Mistral's phone rings. Her battery is almost dead.

With a river of words, Elettra tells her about their escape in the hot-air balloon.

"Oh, I can see you!" Mistral exclaims, spotting the big white ball high up in the sky.

"There it is!" Sheng cries at the same time, seeing the statue of the Sun King sitting on a horse.

Just as Mistral finishes the call, her battery dies. "Sheng! Sheng! Wait!"

"But I found the Sun King!"

"We need to go, and fast!" she explains, giving him a quick update.

"You were right about her," the Chinese boy says. Then he looks at the clock. "But then why'd she give us this?"

"Maybe she doesn't know how to use it."

"We need to keep going," Sheng insists, standing in front of the statue of the king.

"No, we need to leave! Zoe could show up any moment now!"

"This'll only take a second."

"Sheng!"

"Less than a second!" he says stubbornly. He walks around the statue and points the clock north. He searches for anything that looks like the kneeling woman in the picture but finds nothing. Then he looks up. The sun is slowly sinking toward the horizon, descending right over the statue. In a while, it will set at the end of the long Champs-Elysées. Behind the statue of the Sun King, they can see the Egyptian obelisk in place de la Concorde, Napoléon's Arc de Triomphe and far, far away in the distance, the Grande Arche. It can't be a coincidence. Or a mistake. Paris really was designed to mimic the sky.

Sheng quickly adjusts the clock hands.

"We need to go, right now!" Mistral says breathlessly, standing beside him. She looks around nervously.

"Just a sec."

Clock pointing north. Sun hand pointing toward the sun. Star hand pointing to the east . . .

Two men run out of the Louvre exit.

"Sheng!"

Moon hand toward the statue of the king . . .

"Wait, wait!"

Sheng waits. Nothing happens. His smile freezes on his face. "It can't be," he says.

"Sheng, it didn't work!" Mistral cries. "And there are two men running toward us!" She grabs him by the hand. "Let's go!"

Sheng reluctantly lets her drag him away. "Maybe it's the wrong statue. Maybe this isn't the Sun King after all." He peers around like a lion in search of a gazelle. He breaks free from Mistral's grip, rushes over to two tourists looking through a guidebook of Paris and rips it out of their hands. "Sorry!" he exclaims, ignoring their protests. "This'll just take a minute!"

He flips through the guide until he finds what he's looking for. "The Louvre Carrousel . . . yeah . . . glass pyramid by I. M. Pei . . . whatever . . . in 1989 . . . ticket office . . . how to avoid long lines . . . statue of the Sun King! All right! Here we go! The statue of the Sun King . . ." But the next lines in the guide make Sheng's cheers turn into a cry of frustration. "No way!"

Mistral sees that the two men who ran out of the museum are only a few dozen yards away from them. "Come on, Sheng! Let's go!"

He throws the book to the ground and they start running.

"The statue was put outside the Louvre in 1981. The Japanese architect who designed the glass pyramid wanted it there so that it'd be kissed by the setting sun on the summer solstice. *Hao!*"

"Run!"

"It wasn't here! It was at Versailles!"

Mistral looks over her shoulder. The two men seem to have disappeared among the crowd in the square. But she doesn't slow down.

"No wonder it didn't work," Sheng says, panting. "The clock was made in the time of Napoléon, and back then the statue of the Sun King wasn't there yet!"

The two reach rue de Rivoli, where they slow down and blend

in with the people walking down the sidewalk. Behind them, a waiter wearing a black tie rests a tray of soft drinks on a table and starts to follow them.

"Oh, man! Oh, man!" Elettra exclaims, looking down. "We're really flying."

"Well, I promised you we'd go on a balloon ride," replies Harvey, who's working the burners mounted beneath the mouth of the round fabric envelope.

"Can you steer this thing?"

"No, it goes wherever it wants to. All I can do is make it go up or down." Harvey cranks the handle on the burner set, which lets out a blue flame.

"Nothing's happening," Elettra points out.

"Just wait." Around twenty seconds later, the balloon ascends. "If I put more hot air in it, it goes up," Harvey summarizes. "And if I don't do anything, it goes down."

Elettra looks at the streets racing by below them. She sees the Seine, the Eiffel Tower, the towers of Notre Dame and the white cupolas of other churches. "Where are we headed?"

"I have no idea."

"Well, let's just hope we keep away from Mistral and Sheng. At least we can create a diversion for them."

"Take over," Harvey tells her.

Walking around inside a wicker basket fifty meters above the ground feels strange.

"What are you doing?"

"Calling my dad. I want to try to figure out what happened."

"It's simple. Zoe definitely isn't a friend of your father's like she said she was."

"That's what I think, too," says Harvey. "Maybe Zoe just called him up and he pretended to remember her. He does that all the time."

"Or maybe . . . maybe they did something to your dad's real friend. Didn't he tell you what her name was?"

Harvey shrugs. "Of course he told me. It was the right name, but we can't be sure it's really the same person. Besides, in any case, if my dad's friend isn't the same person anymore . . . who knows what happened to her?"

Whatever it is that happened to her, Professor Miller's phone is switched off.

24

THE SQUARE

MISTRAL IS PULLING SHENG ALONG BY THE HAND LIKE A LITTLE BOY. He keeps shaking his head and repeating, "That wasn't what we needed to make the clock work! That wasn't it!"

The girl is thinking about Elettra and Harvey. She's thinking about Zoe. She's thinking about the men who ran out of the Louvre and started chasing them. She's thinking that although she's pretty sure they lost them, someone else is bound to be following them. She's so afraid as she weaves through the people on the sidewalk that she envies how concentrated Sheng is. He's completely lost in thought.

"What could it be, Mistral?"

"I have no idea."

On rue de Rivoli is an orderly row of magnificent buildings that overlook the green expanses of the jardin des Tuileries. The smell of horses hangs in the air. Haute couture is on display in the shop windows. To their left, the Eiffel Tower pierces the sky like a perforated knife.

"Where are we going?"

Once again, Mistral has no idea. *They're heading toward place de la Concorde,* she thinks, looking up at the hot-air balloon. In the middle of the square is the Luxor obelisk. There are fountains there. . . .

"We need to take another look at the zodiac," Sheng suddenly says.

"We can't stop," Mistral protests, looking over her shoulder. A river of people is behind them. "Let's go to place de la Concorde," she pants. "There are fountains there. Lots of them. Maybe one of the fountains has a kneeling woman."

Place de la Concorde is a magnificent square with a dazzling display of shimmering waterworks.

"How old is this thing?" Sheng asks, staring up at the slab of stone from Luxor.

"Thousands of years old," Mistral replies. "It was definitely around back in the times of Napoléon."

"In Luxor, yeah, but when was it brought here to Paris?"

The girl shakes her head. "I don't know . . . a hundred years ago? Two hundred, maybe?"

"A hundred or two hundred? When did Napoléon die?"

"In 1821," Mistral replies confidently.

"Excuse me!" Sheng says to the first person who passes by. "Do you know when this obelisk was brought here?"

The only reply he receives is an annoyed glare.

When they look up, they can still see the white balloon, which is drifting over the Champs-Elysées.

"They certainly chose a great way to escape without attracting attention," Mistral remarks.

Sheng notices a tourist stand surrounded by little flags.

"Come to the music festival!" repeats a young woman roller-skating around it. "Get the full program! Tomorrow, June twenty-first, la Fête de la Musique!"

Without thinking twice, Sheng runs over to the stand and asks, "Do you have a Paris guidebook?"

"Come to the music festival!" the woman repeats.

"A guidebook! A guidebook! For tourists!" Sheng says, almost yelling. "Do you have a guidebook?" He spots one, grabs it and slams some money down on the counter. He flips through the pages. "This isn't it, either!" he exclaims angrily a moment later. "They put the obelisk here in 1836, after Napoléon died. We're on the wrong track." He spreads the poster of the zodiac out on the ground and studies it. "I don't see a guy with sunbeams around his head or a woman kneeling."

"Here's one," Mistral points out, her finger resting on the lower edge of the zodiac.

"That isn't a woman."

"It isn't?"

"No! She's got a lioness's head."

"So what?"

"I don't know!"

Hearing sirens, Mistral gives a start. Several police cars come racing through the traffic, their lights flashing. They zoom around the square and head west down the city's historic axis toward the large square named place de Gaulle, also called place de l'Étoile, "Star Square," because of the ten streets that branch out from it in all directions.

Mistral looks up at the hot-air balloon.

The police are chasing after it.

Sheng, on the other hand, seems completely oblivious to what's going on around them. He's already spread the zodiac out on top of the map of Paris again. "What's this, right here?"

"What does it matter? We need to go help Elettra and Harvey! The police are chasing them!"

Sheng grabs her by the wrist. "Tell me what's there!"

Mistral looks at the map. "Nothing. There's . . ." Once again, she looks up nervously, seeing even more police cars weaving through the traffic on the Champs-Elysées.

In front of her, Napoléon Bonaparte's Arc de Triomphe looks like a big upside-down "U" in the middle of place de Gaulle. The girl stares at it for a second. "Oh, wow . . . ," she says. Her gaze lingers on the arch. The sun is slowly setting over it. In a few more hours, it'll be right behind it. "Napoléon's arch . . . ," she murmurs. "Napoléon's arch was there back in the times of Napoléon."

"So what?" asks Sheng.

"There are figures sculpted on the arch. They're all around Napoléon. And the sun is right over the arch's head."

"Keep talking. . . . ," Sheng says encouragingly.

"The arch is in place de Gaulle, but everyone calls it place de l'Étoile . . . and 'étoile' is the French word for 'star.'"

"Hao!" Sheng exclaims, rolling up the map and the zodiac poster. "Why didn't you think of this before?"

The two kids start running.

Behind them, three other people start running, too.

25

THE COIN

On the pediment of the Arc de Triomphe, Isis is kneeling at Napoléon Bonaparte's feet. Around the monument is place de l'Étoile, with ten streets that radiate from it like rays of light. Because of the nonstop stream of noisy traffic, visitors reach it through an underpass.

Standing below the arch, Sheng adjusts the clock hands.

The moment he's positioned the one with the star, the clock activates a second time.

"Yes!" the two kids exclaim, hugging.

In the third section of the clock face, the goddess of nature is still kneeling. But this time her hands are sunk down into a lush meadow divided in two by a line of little stars that lead to something that looks like a castle atop a hill in the distance.

"After Isis and the sun . . . Isis and the earth," Mistral murmurs.

"Fire, earth . . . ," Sheng says, nodding. "Where to next?"

"This one is easy," Mistral answers, smiling. "This one is very easy."

"Feel like sharing?"

"I think it's the gardens of the Paris astronomical observatory."

"The place where the professor and Zoe met?"

"Yes . . . that is, if she was telling the truth about how they met."

Sheng feverishly flips through his guidebook, looking for more information. "The Sun King ordered the construction of the observatory, which was founded in 1667. . . . On June twenty-first, the summer solstice, the academy's mathematicians marked out the meridian line on the ground, along with the other directions needed to determine the building's alignment. With this, they established the Paris Meridian, the prime meridian that was later replaced by the one in Greenwich."

"In Paris, the meridian line is still marked by little stars on the sidewalks," explains Mistral, who's now as excited about the search as Sheng is.

"Then it's easy!" Sheng cheers. "We just need to follow the stars again! Come on!"

"What about Harvey and Elettra?"

"They'll manage! They just need to find a way to get that thing back down to the ground, right?"

The two are about to walk down into the underpass leading to the Métro when Mistral recognizes one of the men she saw run out of the Louvre on the other side of the roundabout. She nods in his direction. "They're still following us."

"You sure?"

"Yes. See that man over there? He was in the square outside the museum."

Out of the corner of his eye, Sheng tries to spot the man she's talking about, but he keeps walking, pretending like nothing's happening. "Is there any other way out of here?"

"The underpass's other exits, for the Champs-Elysées."

"Let's give it a shot."

"What if they follow us?"

"Let's try not to worry about that," Sheng says, starting down the stairs. "I mean, after all, the only thing we can do is run."

"A coin, please . . . ," a beggar pleads just outside the Arc de Triomphe's underpass.

"Get lost!" the waiter wearing a black tie replies, walking past him.

Trying to walk past him, that is.

The beggar's hand whips out as fast as lightning and grabs him by the shoulder. "A coin . . . ," he repeats.

The waiter whirls around, but what he sees in front of him isn't the customary sad, dirty, pleading face of a beggar. It's a stern face with piercing eyes so pale they look like ice. The man who's stopped him has short, gray hair, most of it hidden under a baseball cap. In his free hand, he's holding a violin case.

"What the devil do you want?" the young man with the black tie asks, trying to break free from the man's grip.

"Leave them alone . . . ," Jacob Mahler hisses at the waiter.

Crowds of indifferent tourists pass by them.

"Who are you?"

"Tell the person who sent you that the chase is over" is Mahler's answer.

"Don't hold your breath!"

Mahler takes a step toward him.

The waiter kicks out at the phony beggar, but his foot hits empty air. The man with the violin has already dodged to the side

188

with the speed of thought, then is instantly standing in front of him again.

"A coin . . . ," Jacob Mahler says again, tossing a fifty-cent piece down the waiter's throat.

The man coughs and spits it out. The beggar hits him with the violin case and gives him a kick that sends him sliding down to the ground. Then he disappears into the indifferent crowd.

It's five o'clock in the evening when the man who's come from Siberia finally walks down the platform at Paris's Gare de Lyon. He's sweating. The station is like an upside-down basin with boiling-hot stones inside it, a basin trapping clouds of bluish steam. Dozens of colorful trains are lined up one beside the other. The shiny rails winding away into the distance outside look like glowing neon tubes. The man is walking, perspiring and looking around, dazed. This is the first time he's ever seen this city, but his eyes find no joy in it. They're red from exhaustion and have deep, dark bags under them.

The man is very tired. He's been traveling for weeks. He traveled all day long on a second-class train from Berlin. And before Berlin he was in a number of stations full of black metal, cement, broken windows and dim lighting. Warsaw, St. Petersburg, Moscow, Yekaterinburg . . . all the way back to Tunguska, the tiny station he started out from. A station that isn't even really a station. A nameless town in the middle of Siberia.

He traveled nonstop just to come here to Paris, the City of Wind, where there isn't even a trace of wind.

He didn't expect it to be like this. He expected to feel cool air on his face. He expected to see kites and whirling clouds. He expected it to be just like it's described in the old guidebook with yellowed pages that he bought for a few coins at a book stand in Moscow. The City of Wind. Of handkerchiefs. Of perfume. That's how it was described to him by the old woman, the Seer, whose amber-colored eyes scrutinize the past and the future with the same meticulous tranquility. That's how she convinced him to come here.

Instead, the city is perfectly still, as parched and dry as a sponge far from the sea. But it isn't Paris's fault. The whole world is changing. The whole climate is going berserk. The seasons are wallowing, the oceans are rising, the ice breaking, the water receding.

And it's only June.

His head bowed, the man walks along in his wool jacket and trousers, his coarse shirt, thick socks and big, black shoes. He also has a wide, red hat that feels like it's stuck to his head. His hands are puffy, his nails dirty and black. With him he's brought an old guidebook written in Cyrillic, and an endless imagination.

A river of commuters is moving in the opposite direction. The man weaves through them like a silver-scaled salmon determined to make it upstream. He finally steps outside, under the Paris sky.

He has no luggage.

They stole it from him in Warsaw.

In his pocket are a few strange banknotes in bright colors. They explained to him that they were called euro. He used them in Berlin, and now he's using them in France. He has 369 euro. He has no idea if that's a lot or a little, or even if it's enough to get him back home.

He slides his right index finger down the middle of the old

Paris guidebook. The city he sees before him has a thousand colors.

The wind hasn't disappeared, the man thinks. *It's only hibernating.*

The thought of hibernation makes him smile, because the reason he's in Paris is to find the Children of the Bear and give them the object tucked away in his pocket. A wooden top with a small bleeding heart engraved on it.

The man has no idea how to find the Children of the Bear.

He sighs, weary and sweating. He takes off his hat and looks up at the sky.

He can't believe his eyes.

He smiles. Then he laughs, making the commuters passing by stare at him like he's crazy. And maybe he is. But you need special eyes to see things as they really are, to see the signs.

He's looking for the Children of the Bear. And drifting across the sky over Paris is a hot-air balloon with a big bear on it.

"They're chasing us!" Elettra says, looking down at the flashing lights of the police cars on the street below.

"Oh, great! Just what we needed . . ."

"What do we do?"

Standing before them is a large, shiny building called the Grande Arche.

"I've never flown one of these things before," Harvey says, "but I think it's going down too fast." He crouches beneath the burners and peers up into the top of the balloon. "I knew it."

"What?"

"We've got a leak."

"What do you mean we've got a leak?"

"There's a hole."

"How could there be a hole?"

"Take a wild guess."

"Zoe's gun?"

"Exactly. I think she shot it."

Elettra stares at the police cars below them nervously. "Just what we needed."

"Uh-huh."

Harvey paces back and forth inside the wicker basket. Finally, he makes up his mind. He fires up the burners, adding more heat. After a moment, the balloon drifts up a dozen meters.

"What are you doing?"

"I'm making us go higher."

"What good will that do?"

"It'll keep us up in the air longer."

It also moves them right into an air current that starts pushing them back toward the Seine.

"Turn around!" shouts Ermete, leaning halfway out of the cab window. "C'mon! Turn around!"

In the sky, the hot-air balloon has completely changed course. On the street below, the police cars start making U-turns and driving in the opposite direction. Ermete grabs hold of the handle over the door as the taxi swerves, avoiding them by an inch.

"Wow! This is like being in an American movie!" the cabbie cheers, driving up onto the sidewalk, turning the car around and resuming their chase after the balloon.

26
THE OBSERVATORY

FROM THE DENFERT-ROCHEREAU EXIT TO THE PARIS OBSERVATORY, it's two hundred paces down a tree-lined lane. A faded medallion on the sidewalk directs Mistral and Sheng over to the entrance to a park. Inside they find a long black line marking the city's old meridian. The two kids walk off in that direction, guessing that the white cupola they see over the treetops belongs to the building they're looking for.

They reach a gate, but it's locked. They have no choice but to walk all the way around. Finally, tired and panting, they reach another iron gate. Mistral tries to open it, but it's locked, too. Sunlight glimmers on its golden spikes, and the French flag beside it flutters in the breeze.

Sheng climbs up a nearby street lamp. "There it is!" he cries.

The observatory is a three-story building with classical architecture and gray, anonymous picture windows. Right outside the entrance is the statue of a man pointing at a small globe in front of him.

Sheng climbs back down and rings the bell at the little porter's cabin nearby. No one answers.

Mistral sighs. "We're out of luck. It's closed."

"But we've got to get in!" Sheng says, clenching his teeth.

Mistral shakes her head. "We'll just have to come back to-morrow morning."

Then they hear whistling. Gravel crunching.

"Hey!" Sheng shouts, grabbing hold of the bars. He sees a man strolling right outside the observatory. "Excuse me! Hey! Could you let us in?"

The man walks up to them, curious. "The observatory's closed, kids," he says.

"We know," says Mistral. "But . . . my boyfriend and I . . ."

Sheng's jaw drops.

"We just want to come in for a minute to take some pictures," she adds calmly.

The man looks over his shoulders, making sure no one's around. "If my colleagues found out about this . . ."

Mistral hunches over, pleading. "At least let us go over to the statue, please?"

"Okay, but make it quick," the man whispers.

The two friends run across the gravel courtyard while the man stands by the gate, ready to shut it behind them when they leave.

"Well?" Mistral asks Sheng. "Do you see your friend Isis any-where?"

His cheeks still red, Sheng studies the base of the statue and discovers that the signs of the zodiac are engraved on it.

"She's right here, see?" he whispers, pointing at the depiction of a woman flanked by two stars.

"Are you sure that's her?"

Sheng isn't sure, but now that he's Mistral's boyfriend, even if only for a few minutes, he doesn't want to look like a wimp. "Let's give it a try."

He positions the clock, points the moon hand at the woman sculpted on the base of the statue, the sun hand at the sun and the star hand toward the east. But before he positions the last hand, he closes his eyes.

Clack. The clock activates for the third time.

Isis is now sitting on a throne in the middle of a lake. Behind her, tree branches. At her feet, tiny men brandishing their weapons in celebration.

"Well, it looks like we've moved on to water."

"Any ideas?"

Mistral shakes her head. The man standing by the gate is starting to look impatient.

"Well, we'd better come up with one, and fast."

Mademoiselle Cybel glides down the stairs of her restaurant, her beaded gown glittering. She has the peevish look of someone who has to deal with a nuisance. And the nuisance is one of her men.

He's hunched over in a white chair, his arm resting on the table, a glass of water in his hand. He's in his underwear.

The moment he sees the woman arrive, he jumps to his feet. A glimmer of pure fear flashes in his eyes, but it isn't clear if it's because of what he's been through or what's in store for him.

One of the restaurant's waiters hands him a robe.

"Well, then? What happened?" Mademoiselle Cybel asks, walking up to him. "What happened?"

"It was a man, mademoiselle!" the man sobs. "Just one man!"

"Just one man? And what was the man like?"

"He had . . . he was wearing . . . a hat . . . and carrying a violin case."

"Goodness gracious! A violin? What a romantic soul!"

Mademoiselle Cybel motions to the young man to follow her upstairs. Then, changing her mind, she has him go up first and stops by the tables in the dining room to greet her patrons. Finally, the woman and her many layers of flab make their way up the stairs and into her office, where the young man in the robe is staring down with terror at the piranhas in the aquarium beneath his feet.

"Would you mind telling me everything from the beginning?" Cybel asks him, sitting down in front of him. "Would you mind? Because I don't think I understand."

The tiny red and green lights on the walls are flickering.

"First he got Fernand at the Arc de Triomphe," the young man begins. "Knocked him out with a single blow."

"Interesting. Interesting . . ."

"Then he got Philippe and André."

"And what happened to them?"

"I don't know. They just disappeared. We'd gone down to take the Métro. The man was at the end of the corridor. He was playing the violin. Like . . . like those people who play music for change. Nobody else was around. When we heard him playing, Philippe and André both froze."

"Froze?"

"They were paralyzed. I . . . I don't know how to explain it, mademoiselle, but . . . you know what snakes look like when they're charmed?"

"Certainly," Mademoiselle Cybel replies. "I know exactly what they look like. Then what happened?"

"The man started walking toward us. He told us to leave the kids alone. He said they were his. He told us to go home."

"And you did, I see. You did."

"I ran away, Mademoiselle Cybel. I was afraid. I turned around and ran up the stairs."

"So you don't know what happened to Philippe and André?"

The man shakes his head desperately. "No. No, I don't."

"What did you do then?"

"I ran out of the Métro and looked for a place, any place, to hide. The Montparnasse Cemetery was right there, so I went in and started running as fast as I could."

"And were you already . . . dressed like that?"

"No, mademoiselle. That happened later."

"When?"

"I calmed down once I was inside the cemetery. Nobody was there. It was nice and warm and sunny, and there was no trace of the man. I stopped by a statue with some sort of big angel on it, and . . . and while I was standing there, catching my breath . . . he appeared out of nowhere! I couldn't do anything to stop him. My brain . . . my brain was completely paralyzed."

"Presuming that it ever worked," Mademoiselle Cybel points out. "That it ever worked."

"The man looked me straight in the eye. I was terrified. I couldn't move. He held his violin bow up to my neck and . . . and he did this!" the young man exclaims, showing her a small, clean slash at the base of his neck. "I thought he was going to kill me, but he didn't. He told me to come see you, mademoiselle."

"See me?"

"Yes, to tell you not to send anyone else. To tell you not to trust Zoe, because she's been betraying people for over a hundred years. He said he knows her better than you. His exact words, mademoiselle: 'I know Zoe better than she does.'"

The remark hurts Mademoiselle Cybel's pride as a seasoned professional in the world of espionage. "What a compliment," she says, scowling. "What a compliment. Did he say anything else?"

"He said he needed my clothes."

"Your waiter's uniform?"

"Yes."

Mademoiselle Cybel slides her hand across the desk slowly. "Is that all?"

"Yes, mademoiselle, that's all. But please be careful. That man . . . that man is so strange. I . . . I've never been so terrified in my life. He was . . . pure evil. Pure evil."

The woman raises her flabby hand. "Oh, my boy, I know what you're talking about." She rises to her feet, gesturing for him to stay seated. "Please, don't get up. Don't get up."

"I'm sorry, mademoiselle!" the young man apologizes. "I shouldn't have left them behind, Philippe, André, the others . . . but believe me, we'd better not go out looking for them. We'd better do what he says."

"We'll see. We'll see . . . ," the woman murmurs as she walks to the door, deep in thought.

"Are you going to fire me, mademoiselle?"

"What?" Cybel replies, snapping out of it. "Oh, no. I'm not going to fire you. Certainly not. I think you'll still be very useful to our restaurant. Now just wait here. I have something to check on. I'll be back soon."

Mademoiselle Cybel closes the door behind her. Then she

presses a button on the remote control she always carries with her.

Back in her office, the tiling over the aquarium beneath the young man's chair slides open.

Wondering what to do next, she goes downstairs and walks around the dining room. She's quite irritated. She'll have to tell all her men to go out and track down the kids, and at once.

Smiling, she heads over to a table of important patrons. "Have you decided, Your Honor? What's that? A second course? I need to check, but I think we still have some of that special meat . . . the succulent kind that falls right off the bone."

It's so nice here at sunset, Fernando Melodia thinks, sitting comfortably at a table outside the Café de Flore, waiting for his drink to arrive.

After visiting the Louvre, he treated himself to a stroll along the Seine and around the tangle of streets in the Saint-Germain-des-Prés area, which kind of reminds him of Rome and his beloved Trastevere quarter, although the French version is cleaner and sweeter smelling.

And what about the café he's chosen? A historic Parisian establishment worthy of a flâneur who wants to savor the atmosphere of the French capital. A newspaper resting on his knee, Fernando smiles as he muses about his afternoon wandering around, the people passing by, the time he's spent relaxing at the café and—why not?—his future as a successful novelist.

Under his breath, he murmurs, "Sooner or later, all the bad memories, disappointments and pains of the past finally disappear, faded by time or carried off by the wind."

Not bad, thinks Fernando, jotting the sentence down in one of his notepads. He'll use it in his book. Maybe he'll give the line to the detective he's been struggling so hard to develop, a sad man with a long beard whose wife has passed away and who, despite everything, finds the will to live again thanks to a lively group of kids pretending to be caught up in international intrigue. *In a way, it's an autobiographical character*, he reflects, fanning himself with his newspaper and pretending to read an article. *But then, people tend to write what they know, don't they?*

Fernando looks up, pleased to see his waiter approaching with his drink. But the young man suddenly puts the tray down on another table.

"Garçon!" Fernando calls out to him. "Over here. That's for me!"

The waiter doesn't even look his way. A second and a third waiter come running out of the café. Across the street, even more waiters are leaving their respective cafés, to the amazement of all the customers.

The owner of the Café de Flore stands in the doorway, crosses his arms and shakes his head, baffled. "This is absurd!" the man grumbles. "And people complain that we don't hire enough young people these days!"

27
THE BOOKSHOP

Mistral has no idea where to start looking for the fourth Isis shown on the clock, but she doesn't intend to give up now. There's water in the picture, but that makes her think of only one place: the Seine, with its boats and islands.

She asks Sheng if they can walk instead of taking the Métro and makes her way down the street with her characteristic long strides.

"Do we have to walk all the way across Paris?" Sheng pants, starting to get a little fed up with running all around the city.

"Come on. The fresh air will help us think."

On rue de l'Odéon, Mistral stops in her tracks. "Get down!" she orders her friend. She hunches over and starts creeping behind the cars.

"What's going on?" he asks.

"Quick, in there!" Mistral tells Sheng, jumping up and pushing him into a small bookshop. She stays near the door, peering out the window.

"What'd you see?"

"Two waiters wearing black ties walking down the street."

"You think they were looking for us?"

"Well, I don't want to find out."

Sheng tries to peek outside, but Mistral, who's taller than he is, is blocking his view. "Where are they?" he asks.

"Ahem . . . May I help you, kids?" comes a voice in French from behind them.

Sheng and Mistral are in a small but charming shop full of books. A friendly-looking old woman with short gray hair and a checkered shirt with the name MONTECRISTO printed on it is smiling at them from the other side of a small counter. Behind her is an entire collection of adventure books by Jules Verne.

"Oh, sorry," says Mistral, moving toward the woman. "We . . . we're—"

"I see them!" Sheng cries, finally able to look out the window.

Mistral smiles sheepishly. "We're on a treasure hunt!"

The old woman claps her hands together daintily. "Why, that's wonderful! I adore adventures like that. What kind of treasure hunt is it, exactly?"

"Well . . . ," Mistral says, stalling. "Actually . . . it's a little complicated. We need to visit different neighborhoods in Paris and . . . and find clues. But we can't let the team wearing black ties catch us."

"What is it you have to find? Can people help you?"

"Well, yes . . . ," Mistral replies, "but it's very, very difficult."

"Why not let me try?"

"All right . . . I think we might need to find a fountain."

"What kind of fountain?"

"One with a woman sitting on a throne. With a pond or lake all around her."

The old woman starts to think. "Is that the only clue you have?"

Mistral shows her the picture on the clock.

The moment she sees it, the woman exclaims, "Oh, heavens. *That* fountain!"

"You know it?"

"Of course!" the old woman says, chuckling, as she starts to look through the many books in her shop. "But I don't think you'll have an easy time finding it."

"Why? Is it far away?"

"No, not really . . ." Finally, the woman goes over to a shelf, rises up on her tiptoes and pulls out a big book with old pictures of Paris. "Do you know where place de la Bastille is?"

"Of course," says Mistral. She turns to Sheng and tells him the news.

"The Bastille!" Sheng cries. "I've heard of that! It's the prison that was stormed at the beginning of the French Revolution."

"And from which only seven people were freed," the woman adds, switching to English for Sheng's benefit. She continues thumbing through the book. Finally, she finds the picture of a fountain that's almost identical to the one on the clock.

"That's it!" cries Mistral.

"The Fountain of Regeneration," the woman nods. "Also known as the Bastille Isis. The problem is . . . well, it's gone. Just like the Bastille."

"So now what do we do?" moans Sheng.

"Does the book say exactly where the fountain used to be, by any chance?"

"Yes, it does," the old woman replies. "It says there's a pillar where the fountain once stood."

"That might work, too, I guess," Sheng says, thinking.

"Thank you so much! We couldn't have done it without you!" Mistral says. Then she looks out the shop window, worried. "Our problem now is that if we leave, the bad guys will see us."

"Then stay here!" the woman chimes. "I close at seven-thirty. You can keep me company until then."

That's definitely not an option, thinks Mistral. *Not with Elettra and Harvey drifting around in that hot-air balloon, Ermete who knows where, and . . .*

"I have an idea," she tells Sheng.

"What?"

"They're looking for the four of us, right?"

"Yeah, I guess so."

"At most, they might be looking for Ermete, too, and maybe Elettra's father."

"So what?"

"So maybe someone else could use the clock for us . . . someone who isn't being watched."

"I can't think of anyone I'd trust with the clock."

"I can, but I need to use your phone."

"Who do you want to call?"

"My mom."

28
THE CRASH

◯

Right after the hot-air balloon drifts past Notre Dame, it makes another sharp turn and an unfavorable wind pushes it back toward the cathedral.

"Harvey!" Elettra shouts when she sees the tall spires drawing dangerously close. "Look out!"

"I see them! I see them!" he says, filling the balloon with as much hot air as he can. He has the impression the bullet hole is getting bigger. "But we're still sinking!"

Curious people point up at the balloon, gathering on both banks of the river and all around the church. French police cars race across the bridges blaring their sirens and honking their horns.

"*Mamma mia!*" Elettra groans, looking down.

"Come on! Shift all your weight over to this side!" Harvey orders her, racing to the left and clinging to the suspension lines, trying to make the balloon veer off in that direction. But it doesn't work. The wind pushes them closer and closer to Notre Dame. The spires on the cathedral look like quills on a stone porcupine.

"We're going to hit them!"

"No, we aren't!"

"Harvey!"

"I'm telling you, we're not going to hit them!"

Harvey climbs up onto the edge of the basket, grabs hold of the suspension lines and leans back until he's almost falling out, desperately trying to coax the balloon over just half a meter, enough to let them pass by. Then he focuses all his attention on the first stony outcrop in their path.

Screams rise up from below, and a policeman shouts something to them in French through a bullhorn. But neither of them pays any attention to that. They're too focused on trying to avoid crashing into the cathedral, which is getting closer and closer. They keep the burners going full blast, but nothing they do seems to help.

"Turn, baby, turn! Turn!" Harvey pleads, leaning back as far as he can.

Elettra squeezes her eyes shut and starts counting. One second. Two seconds. Three . . . Then she opens her eyes and sees the spires passing just twenty centimeters away from the basket. Ten centimeters . . .

But it's enough for them to clear the building.

They hear applause, which makes Elettra's heart swell. "We did it!" she cheers, hugging Harvey.

But Harvey's as pale as a ghost. "Don't speak too soon . . . ," he says. He jumps back down into the basket and stares helplessly at the cathedral's front tower. "We're going to hit this one."

"No! We've got to get higher up!" cries Elettra. "More heat!"

Harvey cranks the burners again. "Go up! Go up!"

Three seconds. Four. Five.

The balloon bobs up only slightly. Harvey shakes his head and angrily switches off the burners. "Let's try again!" he hollers, grabbing hold of the ropes. "Get up here with me!"

Both he and Elettra climb up onto the edge of the basket, shifting all their weight to the outside.

Six. Seven.

They drift into the tower's shadow.

"Harvey!"

"Just when we're about to hit the building, jump down into the basket!"

Notre Dame's tower is a stone barrier standing before them. Only a tiny glimpse of the sky is visible to the right. They can see its stained-glass windows, its stone gargoyles peering down from the upper gallery. Down below, the yard in front of the church is crawling with people snapping pictures, hoping to capture the big moment.

"Brace yourself!" Harvey shouts.

The basket crashes into the gray stone of the cathedral and bounces to the side. The impact only partially cushioned by the basket's light material, both kids are knocked head over heels against its inside walls. Harvey looks up. The top of the balloon starts to drag against the tower's upper arches, and its fabric snags on the building's sharp, pointy ornamentation, letting out a loud ripping noise. The basket bangs against the stone a second time, and the whole balloon comes to a halt with a groan.

* * *

"Excuse me! Excuse me!" Ermete shouts, limping and ignoring people's protests as he pushes his way through the crowd gathered in the nave inside the cathedral. He looks around for the stairs to the north tower and starts climbing the countless steps.

Just when he's made it halfway up, the balloon's giant shadow passes the stained-glass windows, making everyone who notices it scream.

"No, guys, no! Don't crash!" the engineer wails. "Let me through! Gangway!"

The basket's first impact against the thick wall of the cathedral is imperceptible. But then Ermete hears the whole balloon groaning and scraping against the stone. He doubles his pace.

"Elettra? You okay?" Harvey asks her.

"Yeah, you?"

"I'm a little banged up, but it's nothing serious."

"Where are we?"

"Um, dangling off the side of Notre Dame."

"Aaaah!"

The basket lurches and plunges down a meter and a half. When it does, a chorus of screams rises up from the spectators below. Searchlights scan the sky, and the roar of a helicopter comes from far off in the distance.

"We gotta get out of here," Harvey says, clutching the edge of the basket. He looks down. The ground is fifty meters below them. For a moment, he feels dizzy.

Elettra carefully inches over to him.

They both look up.

The balloon is slowly deflating. It's snagged just a few yards away from the upper gallery that runs all the way around the tower. The ropes are tangled up in the row of pillars and decorations below the stained-glass windows. The tower beside the basket is a sheer wall of gray stone that plummets down to the ground. The basket lurches as the suspension lines and fabric slip down even farther.

"There's not much we can do," Harvey whispers, afraid that even talking too loudly may upset their delicate balance. "There's no way down and there's no way up."

"The lines won't hold out very much longer. . . ."

"We need to try to climb down."

"Or cling to the side of the building."

"Guys!" calls a voice from overhead.

Harvey and Elettra recognize it instantly. "Ermete! Ermete! Where are you?"

"I'm right here, above you!"

Harvey leans out just enough to see Ermete looking down at him from between two gargoyles on the gallery. "Elettra! Hand me a rope, quick!"

The girl gives him one.

Harvey dangles his arm out of the basket and shouts, "Ermete! Catch this!"

"Okay, ready!"

Harvey throws it.

"Harder!"

The boy pulls the rope back in and tries again. This time, his throw is well aimed, but the rope passes just centimeters out of Ermete's grasp and falls back down.

With each failed attempt, a groan erupts from the people watching below.

Meanwhile, the helicopter is getting closer and closer.

"We'll never make it!" Elettra wails, afraid the basket will plummet down again any second now.

"Kiss me."

"Harvey, we risk falling and you—"

"Exactly. Kiss me."

Elettra kisses him lightly on the lips.

Then Harvey gets ready to try again. He dangles his arm outside the basket, swings the rope around as hard as he can and finally throws it up high enough for Ermete to catch it.

Timid applause rises up from the crowd.

Ermete ties the rope around the gallery's pillars and calls out, "Okay, done! Come on! Get out of there!"

Harvey passes their end of the rope to Elettra. "You first."

"Harvey—"

"Let's not waste time."

The girl grabs hold of the rope, climbs up onto the edge of the basket and hops out. It's enough to make the basket lurch and the whole balloon groan. Harvey grabs the end of the rope. "Start climbing!"

Her feet braced against the tower wall, Elettra looks down at Harvey, who's still inside the basket.

"Go on! Climb!" he shouts to her.

"You too!"

"I will, but you get up there first!"

"Grab the rope and get out of there!"

"I've got the rope. Just get up there, darn it!"

Harvey's reluctant to put too much weight on the rope. He

isn't sure the stone columns, which are almost a thousand years old, can support both of them at the same time.

Elettra digs her shoes into the stone and takes baby steps, pulling herself up with all her might. It feels like a lifetime, but in less than thirty seconds she's already climbed all the way up to the first gargoyles.

"Way to go, Elettra!" Ermete cheers, helping her over the edge. He puts his arm around her shoulders and moves her over to the safety of the gallery's walkway.

Then the engineer leans over and waves for Harvey to come up. But just then, to his right, the balloon lets out a terrifying groan, shrivels up like dried fruit and crashes down into the yard below.

"Harvey!"

"I'm okay! I'm okay!" the boy yells, dangling from the rope.

In a few seconds, he's climbed up to the gallery and finally leapt to safety.

A helicopter flies by just a few dozen meters away from the cathedral.

"Let's get out of here!" Harvey shouts to his friends.

"I'm afraid that's not going to be easy," Ermete replies. "Practically the whole city's downstairs!"

They hear policemen's excited shouts and footsteps approaching from the stairway. It comes as no surprise. After the gunshot in Les Halles, their theft of the hot-air balloon and the spectacular crash into the cathedral, the authorities have grounds to question them for days.

"There's no way down," Harvey says, groaning.

"Let me take care of this," Ermete suggests. He darts past the two kids, stops at the top of the stairs and spreads his arms out in front of him. He's greeted by a chorus of shouts and the ominous clacks of guns being cocked.

Ermete holds up his hands and yells, in English, "Stop! Everything's okay! Everything's okay! I don't understand you! English! Speak English!"

Behind him, Harvey and Elettra peer around, hugging.

"Better the police than Cybel," Harvey murmurs.

"It was me!" Ermete yells from the top of the stairs. "Yes, it was me! I stole the balloon!"

Nice try, thinks Harvey, *but it's useless*. Hundreds of cameras probably photographed and filmed the two of them as they were dangling from the north tower.

"It looks like we're stuck," he says. "Let's just hope Sheng and Mistral don't get stopped."

"There's nothing electrical here," Elettra says, looking around. "Nothing I can use to create a diversion."

Harvey squeezes her hand. "We shouldn't be afraid."

"Pssst! Hey!" comes a voice from a few steps away. It belongs to a giant man with a bristly beard and an elegant blue suit. He's motioning them over, waving a knotty wooden cane with two snakes entwined around it. "Come, quickly!"

"What does that guy want?" asks Harvey.

"Looks like he wants us to follow him."

The man is standing in front of a tiny, almost invisible spiral staircase leading down between the cathedral's front towers. When Harvey and Elettra reach him, he points at the staircase.

"It's almost never used," he says with a deep voice, "but it's your only way out of here."

"Thanks," says Harvey.

"Yes, thank you . . . but why are you helping us?" Elettra asks.

"Who says I'm helping you?" the man rebuts, pushing them toward the stairs. "Now get moving or I'll end up in trouble, too."

Without saying another word, the two kids do as he says, bending over as they make their way down the secret passageway. Harvey leads the way, with Elettra behind him and the man with the cane behind her. But with each turn, Elettra hears the man lagging behind. By the time they reach the bottom of the stairs, she can't even hear his cane thumping on the steps anymore.

"Where'd he go?" the girl exclaims when she catches up with Harvey.

He doesn't answer. He's standing in front of a tiny, closed door. When he presses on it, it opens with a click.

They find themselves in a dark, shadowy area of the ground floor of Notre Dame. The shafts of colorful light coming in through the stained-glass windows cast tiny kaleidoscopes on the floor. People are looking up toward the stairway Ermete came down. Policemen are everywhere.

"Let's get out of here," Harvey whispers, staying hidden in the shadows.

"What about Ermete?"

"We can't think about him right now."

The two kids take a few cautious steps around an old confessional. Once they've reached the main door, Elettra tugs on Harvey's arm, stopping him. "Look!" she whispers.

Standing right outside the entrance is Zoe.

Keeping their backs pressed against the wall, Harvey and Elettra sneak over to a small side door.

"Zoe?" a harsh voice suddenly asks from behind the woman. The man tips his baseball cap a fraction of an inch. "Remember me?"

Zoe glances over her shoulder without answering and then stares stubbornly at the entrance to Notre Dame.

The man moves closer and stands right behind her. "We met in Iceland, remember? At the hot spring."

Zoe presses her lips together.

"We also met in Shanghai a few months later. To negotiate the price of your betrayal."

"I didn't make a deal with you."

"I didn't make one with you, either."

"They told me you were dead."

"A lot of people said that."

"What do you want?"

"The kids."

"Forget it."

A gleaming violin bow slips into view at the woman's side.

"There's a lot of commotion here," Jacob Mahler hisses. "No one will notice a woman fainting."

"If you wanted to kill me, why didn't you do it before?"

"I don't want to kill you. What I want is for you to call Heremit and tell him it isn't nice to betray friends."

Zoe holds her breath as the bow slowly brushes against her side.

"You'd know all about that, wouldn't—?" the woman asks, whirling around. But all she sees are unfamiliar faces.

Jacob Mahler has already vanished.

Cecile Blanchard received Mistral's call when she was still at work, and now she's come to rue de l'Odéon to meet her daughter in a tiny bookshop specializing in adventure novels.

Mistral is still hiding out there with Sheng. When she sees her mother walk in, she runs over and hugs her. Then, telling her there's no time to explain, she hands her an old clock and asks her to do something for them.

"In place de la Bastille? But why?" her mother asks.

"That's where the fountain used to be," the bookshop owner answers. "Right in the center of the square, where the column is. You know the one I mean?"

Cecile nods, still not understanding. "Why don't you two come with me? The car's right outside and—"

"We can't," Mistral replies. She looks out the window, worried. "They would spot us."

"Sorry, but who are *they*?"

"It's part of their treasure hunt," the elderly shop owner says. "They can't let the others catch them."

Cecile stares at her daughter. With a pleading look in her eyes, the girl begs her not to ask any more questions. "Okay. Let's imagine that I go over to place de la Bastille with this clock and I adjust the hands and everything. Then what? What's supposed to happen?"

"The clock will activate," Sheng explains.

"Oh. What then? Do we all meet up back at home?"

"We'd better not. It might be . . . dangerous."

· "Mistral?"

Another pleading look.

"I just don't understand any of this."

"If things go as planned . . . ," Sheng begins.

Cecile holds up the clock. "You mean if this thing . . . 'activates'?"

"Exactly. If it does, we just need to know what happens."

"Oh, because it might . . . activate . . . in different ways?"

"Yes. Then we'll need you to do us one more favor."

"Kids, I'm not on vacation!"

"But you can do it tomorrow morning before work! You just need to stop by place de l'Opéra for a second and . . ." Sheng lowers his voice to a hush.

When he finishes giving her the bizarre instructions, Cecile bursts out laughing. "You're kidding, right?"

Sheng looks at Mistral.

"It's very important, Mom," she says.

"This treasure hunt certainly sounds complicated, doesn't it?" the woman from the bookshop chimes in.

"How are you involved in all this?" Madame Blanchard asks her.

The shop owner shrugs. "Oh, I just gave them a few leads, and . . ." She casually heads toward the back of the shop, gesturing for Madame Blanchard to follow her. "I've also agreed to give them a ride to place de l'Opéra after I close the shop, but in hiding, so that no one will see them."

Cecile doesn't ask any more questions. She points her finger at her daughter and walks out of the adventure novel bookshop, bewildered.

She drives down the long Parisian boulevards, crosses the Seine, which is lit up by a fiery red sunset, and heads north all the way to place de la Bastille. She parks her car crookedly and gets out.

Dusk is starting to descend over Paris with a mantle of stars.

In the middle of the square is a tall, tall column, at the top of which stands the *Genius of Liberty*, the golden statue of a boy with a star on his head.

"Well . . . ," Cecile murmurs, feeling a little silly.

Before the sun sets completely, she needs to point one hand toward the column built where the Bastille fountain used to be, the sun hand toward the sun, the star hand toward the east . . . and wait to see what happens.

She does it.

The old clock lets out a furious ticking noise.

"It really did activate . . . ," Cecile whispers.

A new picture has appeared on the face of the clock.

She thinks about the second part of her instructions. Tomorrow morning. Place de l'Opéra. "But why?"

Reporters are swarming outside the police headquarters, hoping to capture shots of the hot-air balloon hijacker. The only official statement made by the thirty-year-old man from Rome was "Don't worry, Mom. I'll explain everything."

But the two kids everyone saw climbing up the cathedral tower? What happened to them? And their two friends, who were last seen in the observatory gardens?

217

Six hundred young men and women wearing black ties don't have a clue.

Not to mention that around twenty of them have been taken out of commission by a mysterious gray-haired man who appears and disappears like a phantom.

Elettra and Harvey are cautiously making their way on foot, while Sheng and Mistral are hidden beneath a flowered dog blanket belonging to the old woman from the bookshop, who's driving them to avenue de l'Opéra. They're all going to Mistral's music school, which the tower top told them was a safe place.

When they get out of the car, Sheng and Mistral find Harvey and Elettra hiding just inside the main door. They exchange hugs and go up to the top floor of the building. Barely able to breathe, Mistral takes out the key Madame Cocot gave her, and they all slip inside.

Elettra brought kebab sandwiches for everyone. They eat them sitting on the floor by the piano as the stars begin to twinkle over Paris.

"Summer starts tomorrow," Harvey says, looking outside at the starry night looming over the terrace and then back inside at the pitch-dark music school.

But they still have a lot to do before tomorrow.

"Well, should I go first?" Elettra asks Mistral. She's holding a box of hair dye. The girls disappear into the bathroom, where they switch on a tiny light.

Harvey checks his backpack to make sure everything's still there: the map of the Chaldeans, the five tops, the Ring of Fire, the Star of Stone, the book on the secret language of animals and even Sheng's camera, which survived the trip in the hot-air balloon.

He and Sheng lay out the blue mattresses they'll be sleeping on.

"I'm crashing," Sheng announces. He keeps his promise, instantly falling into a dreamless sleep.

An hour later, the girls come out of the bathroom with their new short, blond hairstyles.

Mistral's wide awake. She runs her fingers through what's left of her hair and texts her mom.

Cecile, who's also having a hard time falling asleep, replies immediately: IT WORKED. SEE YOU TOMORROW. YOU OK? WILL YOU EXPLAIN?

Mistral reads the message and presses the reply button on her cell phone. THANKS. SEE YOU TOMORROW. I'M FINE. YES. LOVE YOU.

"How'd it go?" Sheng grumbles, yawning.

"It worked."

"Mmm . . . Great . . . ," he manages to whisper.

Hoping it'll help make her sleepy, Mistral pores over the pages of the fascinating book about argot and the secret language of animals. She reads the song of the bees and, in the silence of the music school, practices it over and over beneath her breath, nostalgically thinking of the hive outside her bedroom window.

The last thing she sees before she finally closes her eyes is Sheng's sleeping, trusting face.

Elettra slips across the room and joins Harvey, who's leaning against the windowsill. She, too, has cut and dyed her hair, which is now a horrible blondish mop. Harvey tries to avoid looking at her.

"Is it that bad?"

"No, it isn't."

"It'll grow back, you know."

"Uh-huh."

Harvey sighs. Concentrating, he stares at the street below and the lights around place de l'Opéra.

"Hear anything?" Elettra asks him.

"Yeah."

"What?"

"A hissing noise. Like somebody's . . . *blowing*."

"Does it sound scary?"

"No," Harvey says, smiling. "It sounds like the wind about to sweep everything away."

On the other side of the river, someone actually *is* blowing, his lips pursed, his cheeks full. It's a corpulent man with a bristly beard. He's standing near the gargoyles of Notre Dame, leaning on his wooden cane and blowing. When he's done, he chuckles.

In the distance, he sees patches of black clouds growing thicker to the west, like scraps of burnt bread. He hears the music rising up from the bars and cafés on both banks of the Seine.

"Sing, everyone . . . sing!" he says, laughing. He turns and walks away, carefully staying out of sight of the patrol helicopter that flies around the church from time to time. "Paris is music. Paris is singing. Paris is the City of Wind."

Now that the police are gone and the tourists have left, the church of Our Lady of Paris looks like a cloak topped with a crown of thorns. The sun long since set, its stained-glass windows are dark eyes, its gargoyles twisted lumps. The man walks up to one of the many statues and strokes its pointy cap. It's a Phrygian cap, the kind worn by the Chaldean Magi.

The statue peers down at the very center of the church. The few tourists who know of it call it The Alchemist.

The man with the cane smiles and moves on.

He was once known by that name, too.

THIRD STASIMON

"Irene? Can you—"

"Vladimir? Where are you?"

"On a Chinese train headed—Mongolia. I think—get there—five days—"

"The line's breaking up. Vladimir, there are problems in Paris."

"What kind—problems?"

"The worst kind. He knows the secret. It was Zoe!"

"How do you know?"

"Elettra called to check in. She tried to act natural, but she sounded terribly upset. In the background, I overheard the other kids whispering about a mysterious man in Shanghai, and Zoe, and something about her having a gun! Suddenly, it was all very clear: Zoe's trying to track down the object in Paris . . . and she's using the kids to do it!"

"I didn't think—go—such lengths."

"But she did. Alfred was right not to trust her!"

"This means that—"

"Yes. You and I are in serious danger, too."

"—the secret—"

"What did you say?"

"If she revealed the secret, then there's no point in our protecting it any longer."

"No! We need to keep protecting it. That's the Pact! We can't *all* betray the Pact! We haven't lived all these years just to do that!"

"But—must know. We—hand it down. If they kill us, there won't—anyone who can—"

"What on earth was that noise? I didn't hear you, Vladimir. . . ."

Silence.

"Vladimir?"

Silence.

"Vladimir?"

The line goes dead.

29
THE MEETING

AT EIGHT O'CLOCK IN THE MORNING ON JUNE 21, SOMEONE BUZZES
up to the penthouse at 22 rue de l'Abreuvoir. Cecile Blanchard is
having breakfast. Napoléon's gold clock is on the kitchen table
beside her plate.

"Mistral?" she cries into the intercom panel.

But it isn't her daughter. It's a repairman from France Télécom
who says he needs to come up for a moment to check their land
line.

"But you just checked it last month! Besides, I need to
leave. . . . I'm already late."

The man insists, saying it'll only take five minutes. Madame
Blanchard buzzes him up but immediately regrets it. What if he isn't
really a telephone repairman?

Standing behind the door, she nervously peers out at the
young man through the spy hole. She asks to see his identification
and then, feeling foolish for all the precautions, lets him in.

It's exactly as the man promised. Five minutes later, he says
goodbye and leaves. Once he's outside, he calls Mademoiselle
Cybel. "I did it," he says, "but there's a problem."

"A problem? What is it?" the woman bursts out, exasperated. "What kind of problem could there be with planting a bug in the woman's phone?"

The problem is resting in the palm of the hand of the young man who just passed himself off as a repairman from France Télécom. "There was already one there."

"Another bug? Goodness gracious! Who put it there?" Mademoiselle Cybel asks with astonishment.

Across the street, Jacob Mahler is checking the apartment one last time. He mustn't leave any sign that he was there. No fingerprints. No trace at all. At most, someone might vaguely remember hearing him playing the violin during those long nights.

Everything is exactly as Madame Mouffetard left it. Everything's in perfect order. Even the creeping ivy on the terrace.

The sweet aroma of freshly baked croissants and baguettes rises up from the café below and drifts in through the windows.

"Thanks for the hospitality," Jacob Mahler whispers before closing the door behind him.

On the little table by the door is some sheet music. He didn't leave it there by accident. It's his signature.

It's the music to Mahler's Symphony no. 2.

Also known as *The Resurrection.*

As she slips into the Métro station, Cecile Blanchard wonders whether her daughter has gone crazy or something serious really is going on. Whatever the case may be, she decided to follow the girl's instructions and called the office to tell them she was taking the day off.

She gets off at the Opéra stop and walks over to the center of the square, which is crowded and bathed in sunshine.

What now? she wonders. Does she really need to do what Sheng asked her to?

Just then, a parade of musicians playing accordions, trumpets and trombones passes in front of her. Today the city is celebrating its big music festival.

Cecile looks at them distractedly. Then she gapes. A note is taped to one of the musicians' backs.

It reads:

> *Please, Mom, dance!*
> *Then go to the Brasserie*
> *le Vaudeville at noon.*

Cecile catches up with the man and stops him. She's never seen him before in her life. She rips the note off his back and looks around. *This is crazy,* she thinks. *This is absolutely crazy.*

She pulls the gold clock out of her purse, holds it high over her head and begins to whirl around in the center of the square.

"She's gone nuts," one of the men wearing a black tie who's been following her says into a microphone.

"Maybe not," Zoe replies from the other end. "Go get that note!"

There's only one thing more exciting than being delivered a package at your hotel room, looking for a few coins as a tip, opening the package and finding a cell phone inside.

The only thing more exciting than that is when the cell phone rings the moment you pick it up.

"Elettra?" Fernando Melodia says, answering it. "Where are you? What—"

"Please, Dad, don't ask any questions. I need to give you some instructions."

"Instructions? What do you mean, instructions?"

"Don't talk so loud. They might hear you."

"They who?"

"You're being watched. And followed."

"What are you talking about?"

"They know who you are, and they want to get to me. Watch out for waiters. They might be spies."

"Speaking of waiters, yesterday—"

"I know. They were looking for us."

"Elettra, I think your little joke has gone far enough."

"It's no joke. I need you to go for lunch at the Brasserie le Vaudeville at noon. You've got two hours to try to shake everyone who's following you."

"But why—"

"Mistral's mom will be there. Have lunch with her."

"Elettra—"

"End of the instructions. Now turn off the phone and never turn it on again."

"Did you get it?" Elettra asks Sheng, who's crouching down on the music school's terrace, camera in hand.

"I think so."

Just to be sure, he snaps another dozen shots. Then he goes inside and looks at the display. On the tiny LCD he sees Mistral's mom holding Napoléon's Clock over her head.

"I don't think this is going to work," Elettra mumbles.

"Get away from me, before you melt my camera!" Sheng snaps, searching through the display commands. First he zooms in on Mistral's mother's arms, then her hands, then the clock and finally the clock face, which is incredibly clear through his lens.

"It activated," is the first thing he says. "And here's the last clue."

Another picture of Isis has appeared in the fifth section of the clock face. She's dressed in black and is turned the other way. Her hands are raised imperiously, like an orchestra conductor's, toward something that looks like a cluster of trees.

"What are those, pillars?" Mistral asks.

"No," Harvey answers. "They aren't pillars. . . ."

They're organ pipes.

Noon.

"I—I'm sorry . . . ," Fernando Melodia stammers, walking up to a table at the Brasserie le Vaudeville. "Am I mistaken, or are you—"

"Fernando?" the woman sitting at the table greets him, pushing back her chair.

"No, please, don't get up!"

Le Vaudeville is a small, smoky, tastefully furnished restaurant full of people who look like they've come over from the nearby banks. Stiff-backed waiters are serving plates piled high with shellfish.

Looking a bit awkward, Fernando smiles and takes a seat. "This . . . this is definitely an unusual situation, I'd say. But it's fun, too, if you ask me."

Also because Cecile Blanchard is a truly delightful woman, he thinks.

Cecile nods toward a waiter. "Shall we order?"

As the waiter walks by their table, Fernando raises his voice loud enough to be overheard, saying "And go immediately to number five boulevard Voltaire."

When the waiter walks away, he smiles.

"My daughter told me to watch out for waiters," Fernando explains in a hushed voice.

"Then why did they have us meet in a brasserie, of all places?"

"According to my guidebook, this one's been run by the same family for almost thirty years. All the waiters are members of the family."

"Great. Well, then, what do we do now?"

"The first thing," Fernando suggests, "is to order their famous smoked salmon."

Which they do.

"I'm going to the ladies' room," Madame Blanchard says a moment later.

The instant Cecile stands up, Fernando rises to his feet for a few seconds. Then he rather nervously waits for her to come back.

"Your turn," the woman says when she finally sits down at the table again.

"Oh, well . . . actually, I don't—"

"I'm telling you, *it's your turn,*" Cecile repeats slowly.

Fernando stands up rigidly, looks around for the men's room, slips past a few telephone booths, pushes open the elegant wood and glass door to the bathroom and steps inside.

A few minutes later, he's back at the table, his face crimson. "You'll never believe it—" he starts out.

"There was one in mine, too!" Madame Blanchard says. "How did they do it?"

"I don't know. What did your message say?"

They peer around, but the restaurant is so noisy that no one can overhear them.

"I have to go to the church of Saint-Séverin to look at its organ," the woman explains, "and ask if there are any statues of the goddess Isis there."

Fernando nods. "For me, it's the church of Saint-Gervais. The city's oldest pipe organ. But do you know why we need to do it?" His nose detects the first of their two salmon dishes, which is served a second later. "Oh, thank you."

"I thought you knew!"

"Me? How could I? I haven't seen my daughter for days! Not since she sneaked off the train and—"

"She sneaked off the train?" Cecile smiles with satisfaction as her salmon dish is placed before her.

"But . . . it's like we're in some kind of spy story!"

"You may be right," Madame Blanchard agrees, amused.

"And you're still smiling?"

"Oh, don't get me wrong. I'm simply happy not to be at work. I forgot how nice it is to stroll down the streets in the morning without needing to be anywhere . . . and how nice it is to enjoy a delicious meal like this."

"Ah, yes, to live like a flâneur," Fernando whispers with a

literary tone. He sees a young blond girl walk out of the brasserie. Then he raises his fork and says, "The thing is, one of our kids must've left those messages in the restrooms, don't you think?"

"I suppose so."

"I think it was your daughter."

"Why's that?"

"Call it intuition, Madame Blanchard. . . . Careful! A waiter's coming our way!" he adds.

They laugh.

"You seem to be in a good mood, too," Cecile points out.

Fernando nods. "You want to know what I think?"

"What?"

"I think our kids are playing a joke on us." He dips his knife into the butter and spreads it over a slice of toasted bread. "You know, like those pranks with the hidden cameras? I think there might be a few somewhere in here, filming us."

Cecile frowns slightly. "I hadn't thought of that. Well . . . yes, it could be. So what do you suggest we do?"

"Let's just sit here and play along with it," Fernando suggests.

Also because he thinks having lunch with Cecile is a delightful game.

Mistral smiles, walking toward avenue de l'Opéra as quickly as she can in her silver sandals. She's just left the brasserie where her mom and Elettra's dad are eating lunch together. If they didn't recognize her, she can rest assured that her new hairstyle is a perfectly spy-proof disguise.

She stops on the corner and waits for the light to change. Across the street, a man is playing a slow melody on a barrel organ. When the light turns green, the organ-grinder crosses the street, but Mistral doesn't.

Something just dawned on her. A detail that doesn't make sense. A missing piece. The bridge top hasn't told them anything useful. Not in New York, where it indicated some connection between Siberia and Paris, and not now, in Paris, where it indicated Passage du Perron. But why? Where did they go wrong?

Maybe the bridge top doesn't work like the others, or maybe when they visited the passageway they didn't notice what they were supposed to see. Or hear. Or feel. Or smell . . .

The light turns red, and Mistral isn't sure what to do. She checks her watch. It takes fifteen minutes to get from avenue de l'Opéra to the Palais-Royal on foot. It's a quarter past twelve now. Maybe there's still time for her to go take a look and come back. If she runs, she can make it. Or she can keep striding along through the crowd with her long, lean legs and forget all about it.

Mistral pulls her hat down a little farther over her blond hair and, keeping her head down low, rushes toward rue de Beaujolais.

Linda Melodia is in her room, lost in thought. She's looking through a stack of photographs. Photographs that unexpectedly turned up yesterday in the basement.

Assunta, the Sinhalese maid, was trying to move a rickety old bureau. One of its legs was broken and the bureau lurched over, making one of its drawers fall to the floor.

Linda went down immediately to check and was relieved to find that no serious damage was done. A bunch of old documents were simply scattered on the floor. As she was helping Assunta stand the bureau back upright, she happened to look into the gap left by the drawer, where she saw a crumbling, worm-eaten false bottom. Linda slipped her hand inside and discovered that the false bottom contained a zinc box.

She took it out and opened it.

It was full of photographs. Very, very old photographs.

Black-and-white photos from twenty, thirty, fifty years ago.

Photos of Linda as a little girl.

And photos of Irene.

She took them upstairs to her room and went back down to the basement to work with Assunta, forgetting about them for the rest of the day.

These are the photos Linda Melodia is studying right now. And something doesn't make sense. The pictures have rounded edges and are very, very old. The first one is of a young woman who looks like Irene. She's bundled up in a thermal suit and is surrounded by ice. The others are snapshots of people Linda's never seen before.

How could it be? she wonders when she thinks she recognizes her sister in two of the other pictures. Maybe it isn't her sister after all. Maybe it's their mother, whom Linda never knew. If it's her, then who's the gaunt-looking man standing beside her in the old picture taken at the edge of a forest? Her father?

In another picture, Linda sees four kids. In the middle are two girls, one blond and the other with long, black hair. On the ends, two boys. Written on the back of the photo is 1907.

After thinking it over for a long while, Linda gets up, puts on her house slippers and goes into her sister's room. "Sorry, Irene?"

she asks, resting the stack of photographs on her knee. "These turned up yesterday in the basement. Do you know who these people are?"

Irene stares at the photos. "Goodness. How did you find them?"

"They were hidden in a zinc box behind the drawer of an old bureau."

"Were there any others?"

Linda hands her sister the old, yellowed envelope and sits down beside her. "I thought they were pictures of Mom and Dad when they were young. Or maybe our grandparents. But why were they hidden? Do you think they were just forgotten down there?"

"No," Irene says, smiling. "I'm sure they weren't."

"Well? Do you know who these people are?"

Irene lets out a long sigh. "Yes, I do. . . ."

"Who are they?"

"This boy here, the heavier-set one . . . his name was Alfred. This other boy, the really thin one . . . his name is Vladimir."

"His name *was*, you mean. These people would be a hundred years old by now."

"The girl with black hair, on the other side, is Zoe."

"And the blond girl?"

"That's me."

30
THE MUSIC BOX

"I WANT TO SEE THEM AGAIN," ZOE ORDERS, SITTING AT THE computer.

Standing behind her, Mademoiselle Cybel jingles her bracelets with exasperation. She grumbles peevishly, "My dear, would you mind stopping now? Would you mind? This must be the tenth time we've seen all the photographs from start to finish!"

"Then this'll be the eleventh," Zoe snaps.

The train of Mademoiselle Cybel's silk gown glides across the floor until it reaches the little door leading into the green room. "Why don't you just admit that the kids got away right under your nose, hmm? Right under your nose!"

"They didn't elude me. They eluded you and your useless spiderweb of snitches."

"Eluded . . . eluded . . . that's a big word!" Mademoiselle Cybel sneers, opening the door and disappearing into the other room.

"I don't want any of your little monsters in this room, thank you."

"So sorry, my fussy little archaeologist. My fussy little archae-ologist."

"From the beginning," Zoe insists, clicking the mouse.

"What is it you're hoping to find, anyway?" Cybel calls out from the green room.

"I don't know yet, but those two didn't meet by chance." The photographs taken at the Brasserie le Vaudeville flash up on the screen in front of her. Neither Cecile nor Fernando has any papers, notes or drawings with them. Nothing at all. "What are they doing, dammit?"

"Take my advice: Grab them, bring them here and lock them up with Marcel. They'll tell you everything you want to know in a matter of hours. Isn't that right, Marcel? Did you like that delicious-looking American boy? Did you like him?"

"Would you cut it out?" shouts Zoe.

"Cut it out, my dear?" Mademoiselle Cybel asks, reappearing in the doorway, a snake coiled around her flabby arms. "Cut what out?"

"We can't just kidnap them and torture them!" Zoe exclaims.

"Why not? Because they're just children, perhaps?"

"No, because they might be the only ones capable of finding the object hidden in Paris."

"Why's that? Do they have magical powers?"

"There's no such thing as magical powers."

"Then they're simply better than you are?" Mademoiselle Cybel asks sourly. "And they'll manage to do what you couldn't?"

"What would you know?"

"I know many things, don't you think?" Then she adds, looking the snake in the eyes, "What does she think, Marcel, hmm?

That we don't know anything? That we don't know that she once tried to find the ship that was hidden in Paris during the revolution? Well, we do know that!" Mademoiselle Cybel turns to look at the woman sitting at the computer. "We know that perfectly well."

Zoe clenches her fists, trying to ignore her. One by one, pictures of Cecile Blanchard whirling around in place de l'Opéra flash up on the screen.

"Take my advice, Zoe. Go get everything they have—those ridiculous tops, the objects you told me about, everything—and give them to Heremit. He'll take care of the rest."

"The ship needs to be found right away," Zoe snaps.

"But why? If it's been hidden for two hundred years, it can wait a few more months!"

"It needs to be found right away," Zoe repeats, "because summer's starting."

Mademoiselle Cybel raises her braceleted wrists in the air. "Then what are you worried about? Summer may be starting now, but it's going to last three whole months! That's ample time for you to find your little toy. Isn't that right, Marcel?"

Zoe would kill her if she could, partly because her own plan failed so miserably. Calling Professor Miller and pretending to be an old acquaintance of his, faking Harvey's rescue in order to earn his trust, giving the kids Alfred Van Der Berger's things, being nice to that stupid engineer from Rome . . . it's all been a total waste of time! And Zoe hates doing something for nothing.

She stares at the photographs taken in the square outside the opera house. Why is the woman dancing around with the clock? There must be an explanation. A logical explanation.

"Wait," she says, pointing at a picture that flashes up on the screen. "There . . ."

The orchestra that fills the square is heading down avenue de l'Opéra, toward the Seine.

She enlarges a detail. She enlarges a glimmer of light. She enlarges it even further.

It's a reflection coming from one of the buildings on the corner.

She enlarges it even more.

It looks like a binocular lens. No. It's a camera lens. It's the camera lens of someone crouching on a terrace. A boy.

"Found them!" Zoe cries.

Passage du Perron is very small but very easy to find. Mistral goes down the steps of the building where the great French novelist Colette once lived and turns down a very short corridor with a low ceiling and a few shop windows. At the far end of it, she sees the glimmering light of the Palais-Royal gardens.

Nothing unusual here, she thinks.

Once she reaches the corner, she stops. The last little shop captures her attention. It's the Maison Anna Joliet. On display in its red-framed picture window are lots of little music boxes. When Mistral sees them, she smiles. Among the many different boxes with bright, bold colors and precious antique cases, one in particular catches her eye. It's neither pretty nor valuable, but it looks just like the music box on the cover of the book Agatha sent her, the one with animals riding rainbows out of it.

Rainbows.

That is, bridges.

The girl doesn't think twice. She walks into the shop and asks how much it costs. When she hears the price, she gulps. It's the exact same amount as the meager savings in her bank account.

"May I listen to it?" she asks, slowly raising the lid.

After listening to the music box's melody, she hands the owner of the shop her debit card.

"Is it a gift? Shall I wrap it?"

Mistral shakes her head. "No, it's for me."

Her heart thumping, she walks out of the Maison Anna Joliet and runs over to the nearby park. On a bench is a beautiful bouquet of wilted flowers. Flowers still full of nectar, which the bees would happily turn into honey.

Mistral sits down beside it and stares at the music box, her fingers trembling. There's no doubt about it. It's the same one. The same, identical music box as the one on the cover of the book.

Holding her breath, the girl opens it again. Inside the box is a lady wearing a long, embroidered gown. The moment the lid is pushed all the way back, the woman begins to dance in a circle on a pedestal in the shape of the Earth. The brass cylinder inside the box lets out a sweet, simple melody, just a few notes repeated in a slow, ancient refrain.

This must be the song of nature, Mistral thinks, fascinated, as she stares at the tiny woman dancing around, poised on top of the world. *Harmony, music, balance. That's the whole secret.*

Feeling both foolish and exhilarated, Mistral tries to delve into that secret. She uses the words she's read in the book on argot. She uses the secret language of the animals. She closes her eyes.

And she sings.

She sings along with the notes the music box is playing. She feels a wind pick up all around her, a wind that was hidden in the bushes, lingering in the shade of the bridges. A wind tired of blowing without anyone listening to it, weary of the dullness of the modern world.

Mistral is perfectly aware that it's only a dream, a sensation . . . but it's a nice sensation, so she savors it to the fullest.

Then a scream coming from behind Mistral makes her open her eyes and stop singing.

She leaps to her feet, frightened.

She's surrounded by bees. Hundreds of bees, which are buzzing around her and the bouquet of wilted flowers.

31

THE FALL

MADAME BLANCHARD STROLLS THROUGH THE TALL, DARK CORNERS of the church of Saint-Séverin like a hesitant tourist, like someone walking without any hope of reaching the end of her journey.

What is she supposed to find there in the church, exactly? She can't say. Maybe just being there is enough. Maybe it's just a little trick Mistral is playing to get her mother to enjoy a little free time. With this in mind, she slowly explores the dimly lit aisles, thinking about all the things in Paris she's long forgotten.

Time is suspended around her like the tiny specks of dust floating in the shafts of light, and Cecile Blanchard rediscovers it as if it's something new. She savors it as she walks through the church's choir, which smells of incense and things sacred. It's a scent that can't be worn like perfume because it's impalpable, made only of thoughts and intentions rising upward.

The choir area is elegant, with unadorned columns as dense as a forest and as slender as cypresses. It's captivatingly beautiful, soothing, full of shadows.

However, while she's admiring the little church, Cecile becomes convinced that her daughter isn't playing a joke on her.

Maybe someone really is following her. Two young men walked in after she did, and now they're sitting on a pew bathed in the white light that's streaming in through the windows. They almost seem to be waiting for her.

"The organ," Mistral told her. She needs to look at the organ. And find out if there's a statue of the goddess Isis in the church.

She approaches a monk dressed in a white robe, who's walking barefoot across the uneven floor, and asks him in a hushed voice.

"No, ma'am," he replies kindly. "There's no statue of Isis here at Saint-Séverin."

Cecile Blanchard hears a pew creaking. She turns around just in time to catch sight of the two young men who were following her as they rush outside.

On the other side of town, Fernando Melodia frowns, not sure what to do next. He's making his third trip around the outside of the church the kids told him to visit, but he hasn't seen anything unusual, let alone Isis. However, he's now certain, without a doubt, that two people really are following him. It was hard for him to believe it at first, but he's finally convinced there must be some truth in what the kids told him.

Or it might be like in that movie The Game, *he thinks. It could all be a big, elaborate charade. But who set it up?*

In any case, he'd better play his part and act like a real spy . . . or a spy novelist. After all, that's why he came to this city in the first place.

"Paris! Oh, Paris!" he exclaims, startling some nearby pigeons, who fly away.

Knowing he's being followed gives Fernando just the right

dose of adrenaline and curiosity. He starts doing strange things, like walking in and out of shops and changing streets constantly . . . all for the sheer pleasure of driving whoever's following him crazy.

They stay on his trail, but that's fine with him. He wants to wear them down. For the time being, it doesn't matter why they're doing it. For him, it's enough to know that they're doing it.

Then, on his fourth trip around the church, as he's looking at his reflection in a shop window, he notices that the two men are talking on their phones. They look worried.

Something must've happened.

They race off toward the Métro.

Fernando runs after them.

Cat and mouse have traded places.

No, no, no, no! thinks Mistral when she finally returns to avenue de l'Opéra. *Something's happened.*

There are too many people.

A small crowd has gathered outside the building's main door. They're talking excitedly. A gust of wind rises up, making flyers and scraps of paper whirl around at their feet. The women cover their heads with their hands, holding their coiffures in place. Everyone is looking up at the music school's terrace.

No! Mistral thinks again.

The French doors to the terrace are open.

She sees young men and women wearing black ties and white shirts on every corner, guarding the area. If she had any doubts before, they're gone.

They've been discovered.

Knowing her dyed hair won't protect her for very much longer, Mistral slips into the group of curious onlookers to hide. The music box clutched in her hands, she turns to the people beside her. "What's going on?" she asks.

They point at the terrace. "There were gunshots!"

"Gunshots?" Mistral feels dizzy. "Where?"

"Up there."

"On the top floor."

"There's a music school up there."

"They teach dancing, too."

"Listen!" someone shouts.

"What?"

"I don't hear anything!"

"Shhh!"

Random keys banged on the piano. A gunshot. Harvey shouting as he rushes at someone.

Mistral covers her mouth with her hand. "Oh, no!"

"They're fighting!"

"Yes, in English!"

"Look!" screams a woman, pointing.

Someone's appeared on the terrace.

Mistral raises the visor on her hat. Very clearly, she hears Elettra screaming in Italian, "Leave him alone!"

"There's an Italian," someone remarks.

"And a Chinese boy," another points out.

Oh, no! Mistral thinks again, finally recognizing the person who's come out onto the terrace. It's Sheng.

"What's he doing?"

"He's holding something!"

Sheng is backing up, holding the map of the Chaldeans high over his head.

It can't be! thinks Mistral. *Someone got into the music school. But that's impossible. It was supposed to be a safe place!*

She stands there watching. She feels paralyzed.

Sheng's back is pressed up against the railing. A young man with a black tie comes out through the French doors and heads straight toward him.

"No, never!" Sheng exclaims.

"That man's threatening him!" the crowd of curious onlookers cries.

"He's after that box!"

"They're fighting!"

"What's the Chinese boy doing? Is he crazy?"

"He's going to jump!"

Sheng has leapt over the railing and is on the outer side of the terrace, holding on with one hand and the toes of his gym shoes.

"I think he wants to jump onto that other terrace. . . ."

"He'll never make it!"

It's too far away, Sheng! thinks Mistral, her fingers instinctively opening the music box.

"Look out!" someone beside her screams.

The window beside the terrace shatters with a deafening crash. A face flashes in the empty window frame before disappearing a second later. The crowd shouts and backs up into the street as shards of glass rain down onto the sidewalk.

"Hang in there, Sheng!" Harvey hollers from inside.

There's another crash.

"Let's go! Let's go!" someone shouts.

245

Mistral gulps, recognizing the voice.

It's Zoe.

A black car makes its way around the square and pulls up near the main door. Nobody seems to notice it. Everyone's attention is glued to what's happening up on the terrace. The Chinese boy is waving around the wooden box, hitting the man with it and trying to keep him from getting it at the same time. All the while, he steals desperate glances at the neighboring terrace.

The street transforms into a chorus of voices. A number of drivers have stopped their cars to watch. Horns are blaring.

"Sheng! Don't jump!" Mistral pleads. She can't tell whether she says this under her breath or just in her mind. Her ears are ringing. There's a wild confusion of shouts, car horns . . . and then, traces of music drifting in on the wind. The notes of a violin.

"He got him!" a woman screams.

The man has grabbed Sheng's arm and is trying to yank him back onto the terrace with all his might.

Mistral suddenly feels surrounded by silence. Her heart is a metronome beating faster and faster. The music box is lying open in her hands. The tiny woman is dancing around, perched atop the world. The cylinder and pins inside are playing the song of nature. The notes of a violin are sweeping in on the wind.

Mistral turns around. Standing on the corner, a man with a violin tucked under his chin is playing the same melody as her music box.

The girl's jaw drops.

The violinist looks over at her.

They recognize each other.

Jacob Mahler is moving his lips. He's speaking to Mistral, but she can't make out a single word he's saying.

A woman screams.

Mistral whirls around and looks up at the terrace on the top floor. Sheng is free again. He managed to hit the man with the wooden map and break free from his grip.

"Sheng!" Mistral finally manages to scream. "No!"

The Chinese boy looks down at the street. Only then does he seem to realize where he is.

She can tell Sheng's finally noticed her.

Their eyes meet.

She sees him smile. Her friend's white teeth sparkle. Sheng's always smiling.

He's always optimistic.

Sheng's about to jump.

Mistral pushes her way out of the crowd, takes a few steps forward and starts running.

As Mistral runs, she sings.

She sings with all the air she has in her lungs.

Sheng crouches down, bending his knees, ready to jump.

Mistral reaches the main door, right below the terrace.

The boy takes a deep breath and thinks, *I'm Sheng.*

The terrace he wants to jump over to is less than two meters away. He doesn't look down again. Mistral's down there. Nothing bad can happen.

A bell tolls from Notre Dame.

Sheng clutches the map of the Chaldeans.

And he jumps.

It all happens in a flash. The wind rushes against his face. Someone's singing.

Sheng reaches out his hand toward the other terrace. His fingers brush against it. He feels the railing under his fingertips.

There.

He did it.

Then he feels the void beneath his feet.

His fingers slip.

And he plummets down toward the street.

"You have a visitor," the prison guard says in broken Italian.

Ermete looks up from his newspaper. The hot-air balloon crashing into Notre Dame is on the front page. The mass exodus of all the waiters from the city's cafés is on page 15. And no one except him and the kids knows that the two events are connected.

"Someone came to see me?" He stands up, curious.

Despite his night in prison, Ermete's in a good mood. A very polite French attorney explained to him that he'll be released later today, or tomorrow at the latest, and that not only has the balloon company dropped all the charges but they've even offered to pay for the damages. They got more publicity in a single day than they had over the past several years, and all it took was losing one of their balloons to the cathedral's spires.

As he's walking down the hallway to the visiting area, Ermete imagines it may be a representative of the balloon company who's come to see him, maybe to offer him a contract for a testimonial. If that's true, how much should he ask them for? After all, he's famous. He became the Fountain Man back in New York, and now he's the Mad Balloon Bandit of Paris. Maybe he can convince them to give him his very own hot-air balloon to keep in his yard. Just imagine, showing up to appointments from the sky!

Or maybe it's a reporter, he thinks as he walks into the visitors' hall, which is divided by a glass partition, like the ones he's seen on thousands of TV shows.

His visitor is a disheveled man with dark bags under his eyes, who's wearing a bizarre-looking wool coat and is clutching a hat in his dirty hands.

Ermete sits down on his side of the glass partition. He picks up the phone, looks the strange man in the eye and says hello.

"Hey! Nice to meet you. Ermete De Panfilis."

The other man doesn't even blink. Through the glass, Ermete gestures for him to pick up the phone, and only after a few tries does the man finally imitate him.

"Ermete De Panfilis," the engineer says, introducing himself again.

The man on the other side of the glass checks the article in the newspaper he's brought with him. *"Da, da."* He nods, seeing that it's the same person. He rests his wool hat on the counter in front of him, picks up an old Paris guidebook and flips to the French glossary at the back of it. The man has already written down a few sentences, which he starts to read slowly.

"Stop! Stop!" Ermete says, interrupting him. "Wait! I don't understand! I can't speak French very well. Italian!"

The man looks at him. "Italian?"

"Yes, Italian. Rome. Spaghetti. Francesco Totti . . ."

The man nods. *"Da, da.* Italian."

Then he starts to read his sentences in French again.

Ermete asks the guard for help, but the man explains that it's against the rules for him to listen in on prisoners' conversations.

Ermete insists. "I'm Italian, he's Russian and he's speaking to me in French," he explains in English. "Without your help, this'll never work!"

They decide that Ermete will repeat aloud what he hears over the phone and the guard will try to translate it.

The first sentence the guard translates is, "He saw you yesterday in the white balloon. . . ."

"Yes, yes. *Da.*" Ermete nods, gesturing. "That was me. *Da.*"

The man on the other side of the glass seems pleased with his answer. He reads the second sentence.

"And he wants to know if you're one of the children . . . of the . . . what do you call it . . . that animal with big teeth that . . . that sleeps in the winter?" the guard asks Ermete.

"A beaver?" the engineer guesses. "The one that makes dams?"

"No, bigger! Much, much bigger!"

"A bear?"

"Yes, yes! Bear. He wants to know if you or the children are the Children of the Bear."

Ermete stares at the man through the glass. Maybe that wasn't exactly what he meant to ask. He probably saw Harvey and Elettra climbing out of the hot-air balloon and is wondering if they're his children. His children, who were in the balloon with the bear on it. He smiles. Close enough.

"Yes, yes. *Da.* Me. Me."

A broad smile spreads across the man's face. He claps his hands joyfully. Then he reads a third sentence.

"He says that in that case, he has a gift for the Children of the Bear. A gift that comes from far, far away," the guard translates.

"What is it? What is it, and where does it come from?"

"It's from Siberia," the guard tells him a few seconds later.

Ermete leaps to his feet. "Oh, man!" he exclaims. "I'll take it! *Da! Da!* But who are you? Do you understand? Who are you?"

The man doesn't reply. He holds his threadbare hat out to Ermete.

The guard has it passed through a security device. Then he gives it to Ermete.

Inside the hat is a wooden top.

Engraved on it is a bleeding heart.

32
THE REAWAKENING

WHEN MISTRAL WAKES UP, SHE SEES JACOB MAHLER'S FACE, HIS PALE blue eyes, his eerie smile. People are standing around him. Mistral's lying on the sidewalk. Her back hurts.

The final toll of a bell comes from Notre Dame.

This isn't happening, she thinks.

She closes her eyes.

When she wakes up the second time, she's in her room, lying on her bed. She recognizes the ceiling, the sheets, the furniture, the window, the beehive.

"Help!" she screams.

The door to her room bursts open. Her mother rushes in, followed by Harvey and then Elettra.

Elettra's hair is bleached and very short.

Mistral touches her head. Her hair is bleached and badly cut, too.

They all gather around the foot of her bed. Light is coming in through the window. It's hot.

It's daytime.

Mistral looks at her mom, Elettra and Harvey.

"Where's Sheng?" she asks.

They don't answer.

"It was unbelievable," Harvey finally says. One of his hands is wrapped in a white bandage.

Mistral shakes her head.

No, no, no, no, she thinks. *It can't be. It was a safe place. The top with the tower on it said it was a safe place.*

Instead, they found them. They got inside. Zoe was there. Jacob Mahler was there. Sheng tried to jump. To save the map, their oracle. Their only chance to discover the secret.

Suddenly, the bedroom window bursts open with a crash and the curtains dance wildly in the wind. A powerful wind.

"It was supposed to be a safe place," Mistral sobs as Cecile hurries over to shut the window.

"And it was," comes a voice from the doorway.

Mistral can't see who said it. At the foot of her bed, Elettra and Harvey are blocking her view. Then they slowly step aside, and the girl recognizes a row of white teeth smiling at her from beneath two unusually blue eyes.

Mistral is so overjoyed she can barely speak.

"Sheng?" she whispers. She looks over at her mom, seeking reassurance. "I'm not dreaming, am I?"

Cecile smiles. "No, Mistral. You aren't dreaming. It's Sheng."

The girl plops back on her pillow. She suddenly feels exhausted again. "But . . . the terrace?"

Elettra's father, Fernando, appears behind Sheng and rests a hand on his shoulder.

"It was unbelievable," Harvey says again.

"Get some more rest," her mother suggests. "You're home now. We're all home. There's nothing to be afraid of."

There's nothing to be afraid of.

Except the whirlpool.

Mistral closes her eyes. She can still hear them talking.

For a moment, at least.

"Did you know there's a wind called Mistral?" Sheng asks.

It's the last thing she hears before she falls asleep.

When Mistral wakes up for the third time, it's dusk. The delicious aroma of roasted potatoes lures her out of bed and over to the kitchen, where she finds all the others sitting around the table.

"What time is it?" she asks, rubbing her eyes.

"Nine."

"I slept nine hours?"

"You slept a day and nine hours," her mother corrects her, smiling.

Mistral sits down. She looks at the others. She waits.

Finally, she bursts out, *"Well?"*

"When we heard someone knock, we assumed it was you," Elettra says, "so we opened the door without even checking."

"But it wasn't you," Harvey continues. "It was four of Cybel's waiters. And Zoe too." The boy shrugs. "End of story. There wasn't much we could do. We were outnumbered and they were a lot bigger than us."

Elettra rests her hand on his shoulder. "Harvey's being modest. Before giving up, he knocked two of them out and smashed another one into the window."

Harvey raises his bandaged hand. "Yeah, and here's what I got for it."

Mistral looks at Sheng. "What about you?"

The kids exchange a worried look and turn to the two adults, as if asking for their permission to explain. Mistral's mother is the first to nod.

"We're not exactly sure . . . ," Elettra murmurs.

"We were inside fighting . . . ," Harvey says.

"And your mom and I were out searching the churches . . . ," Fernando adds. He rests his hand on Cecile's wrist and then pulls it away, embarrassed.

"But people are still talking about it."

"It's in all the papers."

"What is?"

Elettra smooths back her short hair. "Listen, I'll tell you what we think happened," she says, "but you need to try to stay calm."

Naturally, all this beating around the bush simply makes Mistral nervous.

"When we were back in Rome and I told you I could make mirrors go dull, you thought I was kidding, remember?" Elettra continues. "Harvey didn't want to accept the fact that he had some kind of special connection with plants and the earth. He didn't even like being called Star of Stone, like the professor. Remember?"

Mistral nods. "And . . . ?"

"Well, here's the thing: From what people are saying, just before Sheng fell from the top floor, you were singing."

That's true, thinks Mistral. *I remember that.*

"They also say that the moment Sheng fell from the terrace, you screamed . . . and all of a sudden, avenue de l'Opéra got dark."

"Dark?"

"A massive swarm of bees flew in from every corner of Paris. Some say it was like a tornado, a hurricane. In any case, they swarmed in and flew away again."

"Crazy, huh?"

Mistral shakes her head. "No," she says softly. "That's what I wanted to happen."

"You see?" Elettra cries, turning to Harvey. "I told you it was her!"

Mistral looks at her mom. "I'd summoned the bees before. I did it half an hour before that, in the gardens of the Palais-Royal. I summoned them . . . by singing."

"By the time the bees flew away, you'd fainted and Sheng was lying on the sidewalk," Elettra goes on. "Safe and sound."

"But how?"

"Show her your back, Sheng."

The Chinese boy lifts up his pajama top. His back is covered with lots of puffy red splotches.

"Oh!" Mistral gasps. "You mean the bees held you up?"

"They slowed me down," Sheng says, quickly lowering his top.

"Does it hurt?"

"A little," he admits, "but it's way better than smashing down onto the sidewalk!"

"Did you realize what was going on?"

Sheng shrugs. "When I knew I was falling, I closed my eyes. All I felt was a big gust of wind and a funny tingling on my back. And when I opened my eyes again—"

"What about the map?" Mistral suddenly asks. "You were holding the map. What happened to it?"

The kids' eyes drop to the floor and a grim silence fills the room.

"Guys?" Mistral asks, her voice little more than a hush. "What happened to . . ."

Since no one else seems willing to answer, Fernando speaks up. "We think . . . Well, we think *they* took everything."

33
THE TRAITOR

AT 8:16 THE NEXT MORNING, MADAME BLANCHARD FLINGS OPEN
the apartment door and rushes down the stairs to the ground floor.
She's sorry to leave Mistral, but she can't afford to miss another
day of work. Besides, Fernando can look after the kids.

As she walks out the main door, she tries to remember where
she parked the car. Incredibly, she remembers. She left it on a
steep lane in the direction of Saint-Denis. She slips her purse over
her shoulder and starts walking that way when a voice calls out
to her.

"Madame Blanchard?"

She's heard the voice before. And recently, too. It belongs to
the man who stopped her a few days earlier, the one carrying a
violin case and wearing a baseball cap.

"Oh, it's you," she says, smiling, "Mr. Now-You-See-Him-
Now-You-Don't!"

The man's eyes are ice-cold, his smile odd.

"I asked you to do me a favor the other day, remember?" he
says, moving toward her.

Instinctively, Cecile Blanchard takes a step back but finds a wall right behind her. "Oh, yes. The sheet music . . . ," she says, suddenly remembering. "I'm afraid I completely forgot to give it to her. I'm sorry."

"Apologize to your daughter, not to me. Is she feeling better?"

Cecile gapes. "How did you know she—"

"Don't use your phone," the man says, cutting her off. "They might be listening in on your calls, although by now they probably aren't very interested in anything you have to say. I think you're all free now."

"You—"

"If you'd done what I asked you to," Jacob Mahler continues, taking off his cap, "your daughter might've realized sooner that she shouldn't trust Zoe. Check the music. On it you'll find the date of her first betrayal."

"Betrayal? Sorry, but what are you talking about?"

"You let me down, Madame Blanchard. Or perhaps I should call you *Mademoiselle* Blanchard?"

Cecile realizes there's nowhere for her to run. "You're scaring me. Stay back or I'll scream."

"Go ahead and scream if you like. It won't do you much good."

Somewhere deep in her heart, Cecile Blanchard finds the courage to look her aggressor in the eye. "Why are you here?"

"To give you a second chance, mademoiselle."

With this, he hands her a square object not much bigger than a book, which is wrapped in white cloth. "Take this to your daughter."

Too frightened to do anything else, Cecile nods nervously. When the man has walked away a few steps, she starts breathing again.

Then Jacob Mahler stops and holds up his violin case. "One last thing," he says, turning around and walking back to her. "Would you be so kind as to tell her something for me?"

Once again, all Cecile Blanchard can do is nod.

"Tell her that the enemies of my enemies are my friends . . . and in case they're interested, their enemy's name is Heremit Devil."

"It's the map!" Elettra says, even before they take it out of the cloth.

Astonished, the kids stare at the map of the Chaldeans, which is theirs once again.

"Jacob Mahler gave it back to us?"

"He must've picked it up after I fell. Look! This corner's all smashed up."

Actually, it's much more than just the corner. The fall from the terrace splintered away almost a third of the map, revealing the many overlapping layers of wood inside.

"He was there," says Mistral. "I saw him. He was in the square."

And he was playing music, she thinks, but she doesn't tell the others this. Because what Mahler was playing was the melody from her music box. As if he knew. As if he were helping her.

"Here," Madame Blanchard says to Elettra, handing the girl a coffeepot and a tin of coffee. "I want it just like you make it in Italy. Nice and strong." Then she sits down. "I've never met anyone so frightening before!"

"He broke two of my ribs," Fernando says, frowning.

The kids steal glances at each other, keeping the fact that he kidnapped Mistral a secret.

"What I don't get," Sheng says, "is why he gave us the map back, now that he finally had his hands on it!"

"Because he isn't working for Zoe and Cybel," says Harvey. "'The enemies of my enemies are my friends.' . . ."

"And our enemy's name is Heremit Devil."

"That can only mean one thing: After what happened in Rome, Mahler rebelled."

"I thought he was dead," Mistral murmurs.

"But instead, he came back to take revenge," Sheng adds. "And he's using us to do it."

"I almost forgot!" Mistral's mother exclaims, rummaging through her purse. "The other day, just outside our building, that man gave me something else for you."

"Something for me? You mean you'd seen him before?"

"Yes . . . oh, where did I put it?"

Cecile disappears into her bedroom. Her daughter follows her. "You ran into Jacob Mahler and you didn't tell me?"

"So that's why the whirlpool top pointed to your house!" Elettra guesses.

Cecile reappears in the doorway, holding the sheet music. "Let's get one thing straight: I'm a busy woman with a lot on my mind, and I have no intention of being criticized."

"But, Mom . . . !"

Her mother tosses the sheet music onto the table. "He said that the date written on it is when Zoe made her first betrayal."

Sheng looks at the cover. "1907?" he says, astonished. "It can't be! That would make her about a hundred years old!"

"Just like Professor Van Der Berger," Elettra points out.

The phone rings.

Mistral goes to answer it, but Cecile bars her way. "Don't! He said our phone was tapped. I'll take care of this!" She grabs the receiver. "Hello?" She pauses. "Who is this?" she demands, turning around to face the others. "Cover your ears, everybody."

The kids do as she says. So does Fernando.

Cecile Blanchard vents all her anxiety in the longest series of insults she's ever made in her entire life.

A few minutes later, Harvey's cell phone rings.

"Hey . . ."

"Ermete!"

"I'm glad you answered," the engineer says, his voice shaking. "You can't imagine what just happened! A minute ago, I called Mistral's house and . . ."

Twenty minutes later, Ermete is there with them.

"Would you like some coffee?" Cecile offers. "I'm warning you, it's really strong,"

"*Viva l'Italian* style!" Ermete cheers, accepting a cup. The moment he sees Elettra, he cringes. "Oh, man! What did you do to your hair?" Then he notices Mistral. "What is this? Some crazy new trend?"

"We need to fill you in on a few things, Ermete."

"No, wait!" the engineer exclaims. "Me first!"

With this, he shows them the top with the heart on it.

* * *

262

The explanations have all been made. The top is lying in the middle of the table, beside the battered remains of the map of the Chaldeans.

"I think we should try it anyway," Mistral suggests.

Harvey nods.

So does Elettra.

Sheng agrees. "We'll need another map of Paris."

They find one and spread it out over the ancient oracle of the Chaldeans.

"So, who casts this one?"

"What do you think this heart stands for, Ermete?" asks Mistral.

"The heart symbolizes life. It's the beginning of everything."

"And how does life begin?" Mistral insists.

"Well . . ." Ermete scratches his head hesitantly. "It begins when . . . when we're born."

Mistral looks at her friends. "Then there's only one person here who can really use this top."

And she holds it out to her mother.

The heart gyrates sluggishly, like a toy that needs winding. It slowly moves all the way down the Seine, veers away from it just before the Eiffel Tower and starts drifting along the narrow roads of Saint-Germain-des-Prés.

It's the area where Zoe and Harvey spoke for the first time. The quiet place where they went after leaving Cybel's. The top comes to a halt on the old abbey.

"The oldest church in Paris," Cecile Blanchard says softly, looking at the others.

34

THE VEIL

IN MADEMOISELLE CYBEL'S OFFICE, GREEN AND RED LIGHTS ARE
blinking. Her desk has been cleared off to make room for a series
of bizarre objects: an old, bronze mirror; an egg-shaped stone; a
book about the secret language of animals; a poster of the Egyptian zodiac at the Louvre; five wooden tops; a gold clock from the
1700s; a white veil; a digital camera; and a reproduction of the
Bibliothèque Nationale's Parisian coat of arms.

"Goodness gracious!" Mademoiselle Cybel exclaims, scratching her nose, deep in thought. "What an incredible collection of
rubbish."

As she walks over to her desk, the piranhas in the aquarium
follow her, snapping at the glass flooring. "It looks like we have
everything. We have everything."

"No, two things are missing: the Parisian ship and the wooden
map."

"Don't worry about the ship. I had someone buy a small, attractive one from an antiques dealer who's a friend of mine."

"I'll pretend I didn't hear you say that."

"It's a ship, my dear, and it's from Paris. What more could you want?"

"What about the map of the Chaldeans?"

"Oh!" Mademoiselle Cybel grumbles. "My men told me it shattered on the sidewalk when that revolting swarm of bees appeared. That revolting swarm of bees. It was very old, wasn't it? It must have ended up in a thousand pieces. Some curious passerby must have taken them. We can run an ad in the papers, if you like. 'Missing: Hunks of wood that fell from the sky onto avenue de l'Opéra on June twenty-first. Generous reward offered. Fake hunks of wood unwelcome.'"

"That isn't funny," Zoe snaps, picking up Napoléon's Clock and studying it carefully, noticing that its face has changed.

Meanwhile, Mademoiselle Cybel picks up the Ring of Fire. "This mirror looks perfectly ancient. Perfectly ancient."

"The mirror itself, maybe," Zoe replies distractedly, "but the frame isn't even a hundred years old. Alfred had it made by a sculptor friend of his at the beginning of the last century. Ever heard of Paul Manship, the man who designed the Prometheus statue at Rockefeller Center?"

Mademoiselle Cybel stares into space for a moment and shakes her head. "No, sorry. When I think of Rockefeller Center, all that comes to mind is Dior. And Armani. What about this big rock, my dear? Is this recent, too?"

"It's only a few million years old."

"Magnificent. Truly magnificent," Cybel remarks, brushing her fingers against its rough inner surface. "And why is it so important, hmm?"

"It's one of the meteorites that mankind may have descended from, but I think it'd be too difficult to explain it all to you," Zoe grumbles, still trying to interpret the final picture on the clock.

"You mean we didn't descend from the apes?"

Irritated, Zoe looks up at her. "No, Cybel. It's possible that we didn't. In fact, they might have descended from us."

"A fascinating theory . . . ," the woman coos, leaning her misshapen body over the desk. "What a wonderful improvement on mankind! A wonderful improvement!" She brushes her ring-studded fingers over the wooden tops. "And these? They're clearly ancient, too. Am I right?"

"The internal parts are Chaldean, dating back three or four thousand years." Zoe jots down a few notes in a journal beside the clock. "Their wooden cases are more recent. When I first examined them, I estimated that they couldn't be more than a thousand years old."

"You mean you've studied them before, dear?" Mademoiselle Cybel asks, feigning surprise. "You studied them and then you *lost* them?"

"Yes, Cybel, I studied them before. But I didn't lose them. I left them with my . . . my friends, so that everything could be set up again for the Pact."

" 'Friends' sounds like an exaggeration to me. At most, we could say you left them with that Alfred fellow, the professor . . . and the antiques dealer . . . and the woman. What is it the woman does?"

"She sits around in a wheelchair," Zoe grumbles. "And now, if you don't mind, would you leave me alone for five minutes?

I'm trying to figure out what the picture on the clock face means!"

"What about this white veil?" Mademoiselle Cybel asks.

"I have no idea what that is, where it came from or what's behind—" Zoe snatches up the veil.

Behind it is an old wooden galleon, coiled around which is a snake. Before Zoe even has time to pull her hand away, the reptile lunges out and bites her.

"Heavens! So that's where I left him!" Mademoiselle Cybel exclaims, her bracelets jingling. "How thoughtless of me!"

"What have you done?" Zoe asks, staring at her hand, terrified.

"Me? Why, I didn't do anything, my dear! You did it all by yourself. . . ."

"What bit me? What kind of snake?" Zoe gasps, staggering backward. She plops down heavily on the chair. The closely set fang marks on her hand are glistening.

"Who, him? Oh, he's a perfect darling, believe me! But may I ask you a question, my dear? There's something I don't understand. If you really are an archaeologist who's more than a hundred years old . . . does that mean you're immortal?"

"I'm . . . not . . . immortal."

"You see? That's exactly what I thought. Exactly what I thought. You're simply a woman who does things slowly. My little darling is perfect, then. His venom will cause neuromuscular paralysis in, let's say, sixty seconds. At that point, you should begin to suffocate. And then, after another minute or minute and a half at the most . . ."

Zoe's face suddenly turns white. Her eyes grow enormous. "Heremit . . . will . . . kill you," Zoe rasps feebly.

Mademoiselle Cybel moves closer and leans over her. "What's that, my dear? Would you say that a little louder? I don't think I heard you."

"He'll . . . kill . . . you . . . ," Zoe hisses.

"Oh, but why should he, my dear? I'm about to give him everything he's been looking for, including this beautiful ship from Paris. Do you like it?"

"That . . . isn't . . . it. . . ."

"But he'll never know that, my dear!"

With all the strength she has left, Zoe gasps, "He . . ."

"What? Oh, what a terrible thing old age is! What a terrible thing! I simply can't hear you! In any case, what do you think of my new little darling? Snakes like him are very hard to come by, you know? And he's so beautiful! Why, he's probably the rarest, most beautiful snake you'll ever see in your whole life," Mademoiselle Cybel says. "In your whole life . . ."

From the outside, thinks Mistral, the abbey of Saint-Germain-des-Prés doesn't look at all like Paris's oldest church.

It was entirely rebuilt after the French Revolution, during which it set the stage for one of the furious mobs' many massacres. Three hundred and eighteen priests lost their lives, and the whole church was burnt down after that.

"Where's that music coming from?" Sheng asks as they cross under a low, sculpted architrave and walk through the main double doors.

"Inside. Somebody's playing."

"It's an organ," Mistral whispers.

It's like venturing into a golden chest worn by time.

Above the tapered columns are Gothic arches and dark frescoes. Shrouded in half-light, a starry ceiling glimmers high above. Everything seems to resonate with the organ's harmonic scales. From behind a forest of fiery red columns, the light streaming in through the choir windows looks like it has the consistency of alabaster. The doors close behind the kids with a thud just as a bell tolls.

The church is deserted. Candelabras flicker in the distance. The golden figures on the columns are the only audience for the unknown musician whose fingers are gliding across the ivory keys. The organ is a silvery body below the starry skies of the night-blue frescoes above. Quivering with notes, the six main clusters of pipes seem to support the whole church. They resound with majestic chords, notes that slice through the air like sabers, scales that ascend to dizzying heights.

Mistral suddenly feels light-headed. Moved by the suggestive music, she stares at the columns, mesmerized. On them are the faces of women, surrounded by birds and animals. "Look at this . . . ," she whispers, but the others have split up and are off exploring different areas of the church.

When he's halfway down the nave, Harvey's head starts to throb.

"Everything okay?" Elettra asks him.

"There are voices here," the boy whispers, his eyes closed.

"Voices?"

"Yeah. Lots of people . . . ," Harvey whispers. "People who were killed . . ."

"What are they saying?"

"They were . . . listening to the music. . . . Then they heard us come in. . . . They're quiet now. They stopped talking. There's only one voice left . . . only one."

"What's it saying?"

Harvey shakes his head, trying to understand the deep, ancient voice coming from the earth. "He's saying . . . that he's a king. The ancient king of the French . . ."

Harvey listens. He listens some more. Then he smiles.

"What is it?"

"He wants us to know we're welcome here." He squeezes Elettra's hand. "In fact, they've been expecting us."

"I've never been here before," Cecile admits.

Cecile and Fernando are standing by the front door, reading a pamphlet that describes the church's history. Ermete is using one of the pamphlets to fan himself.

"It's beautiful," says Fernando. "The colors are . . . There's something . . ."

"Yes. It gives me the same feeling," Cecile nods.

Their eyes meet for a moment. Then they both look away, embarrassed.

"Well," says Ermete, standing beside them. "This church was founded in the year 542 by King Childebert, one of the earliest Merovingian kings. The tombs of the kings are somewhere in its underground levels. They say the church was built over a much older temple, where they used to worship a statue of a black woman. It was on display until 1514, when it was removed. It hasn't been seen since." Ermete smiles. "What a coincidence."

"What is?" Fernando and Cecile ask in unison.

Ermete points at the kids walking around the church. "Isis."

Mistral has walked all the way around the church and is back at the entrance. Near it, she sees the door to the stairs leading up to the organ. It's open.

She slowly tiptoes up the narrow stairway.

Moments later, she's just a few steps away from the musician.

From the organ balcony, Mistral enjoys a breathtaking view of the church. She sees the others down below. Sheng is looking up at a column with a crowned head on its top. Elettra and Harvey are in the middle of the nave.

"Excuse me . . . ," Mistral says to the organist.

He instantly stops playing. He's young, with short blond hair and blue eyes, and wears glasses with rectangular aluminum frames.

"Yes?" he asks, smiling at Mistral and pushing back his stool. He's shorter than she is but has strong, broad shoulders.

"I'm sorry . . . I . . . I hate to interrupt you, but . . ."

"Don't worry. That's all right. I was just practicing for the concert."

"A concert? Really?"

"Yes, it's tonight at eight-thirty. Part of the music festival. There should be a program around here somewhere." As the organist shuffles through some pamphlets lying on the floor, he asks, "Did you come up here for anything in particular?"

Mistral blushes. She did come up here for a reason. As she was walking through the church, she had an idea, a hunch. But now she finds it terribly embarrassing.

"Actually . . . ," she begins to say, but then she stops. Her face turns even redder. She runs her fingers through her horrible blond hair and shakes her head. "No, never mind. It's nothing."

"No, go on. Tell me."

Mistral looks out at the church below her and rests a finger on the tip of her nose. "Could I ask you to play something?"

"If I know the song, I'd be happy to."

"Actually, I think it's very . . . simple."

She steps over to him and shows him the little music box.

"I'd like you to play this," she says, opening the lid.

35

THE SHIP

THE ORGAN'S LOW, MAJESTIC CHORDS JOIN THE LIGHT JINGLING OF the music box, at first simply accompanying it and then drowning it out entirely. Finally, atop its own magnificent foundation, the organ begins to repeat the music box's melody, note by note. They're harmonious notes that whirl out like the wind, washing over the vaulted ceilings, the buttresses, the stained-glass windows. It's a deep, powerful melody, simple yet complex. Its refrain makes them all feel they've heard it somewhere before at least once in their lives.

It's a refrain quite like a circle, something that's born, grows and then dies only to be born another time. It's like the wind. The tides. The plants. Animals. People.

Like the stars.

It's like everything that needs to move if it is to circle back to the origin of its own movement. Like ideas that rise up only to return to the realm of ideas. It's earth sinking down into the fiery depths of the planet. It's the song of the world, the song of life.

A simple song.

And yet a secret one.

Sheng, Harvey, Elettra, Ermete, Fernando and Cecile listen to the refrain, letting the emotions flow all around them, letting them take form and shape. They find it indescribably perfect for this church. And when the ancient tones of the organ are joined by Mistral's voice, they could almost weep.

Yet the effect of Mistral's singing goes far beyond mere emotion. Because inside the church's ancient organ, the keys composing the refrain and the air rushing through the vertical pipes trigger a mechanism that's almost five hundred years old.

And with this, a secret compartment swings open among the silver shafts.

"Oh, no!" cries the organist, who stops playing the moment he sees the compartment open, thinking something just broke. Instead, some of the pipes are actually false fronts. "What happened?"

"I don't know," Mistral admits, kneeling down beside the organ. She rests her hands on the little door of the compartment made of silver pipes and discovers a tiny plaque: MONSEIGNEUR BRICCONET, 1514.

Mistral tries to peek inside, but she can't see anything. She slides her hand into the nook.

It's empty.

"What did you find?" the organist asks, leaning over her shoulder.

"Nothing . . . not yet."

Then Mistral's fingertips brush against something soft. It isn't very big. "I found it," the girl says.

"Found what?"

Mistral wraps her fingers around the object and pulls it out. It's a bundle of folded white cloth. She stands up and rests it on the railing of the organ balcony.

"Would you help me, please?" she asks the blond boy.

Together, they unfold the cloth once, holding it by its corners. Then they unfold it again. And again.

"What are you guys doing?" Elettra, Harvey and Sheng ask, watching them from the floor below.

Mistral and the organist let the cloth drape down from the balcony.

"Whoa!" Harvey exclaims the moment he figures out what it is.

It's a ship's sail.

Elettra starts laughing.

Above her, Mistral laughs, too. As she's laughing, her eyes meet the musician's. He shrugs, not knowing what else to do.

Not the ship but its sail.

Not water but wind.

This is what they were supposed to discover in Paris.

Because Paris isn't the city of water, like Zoe thought. It's the city of wind.

The Veil of Isis. Her ship's sail.

Something dawns on Mistral. She reaches back into the dark nook and feels around, sliding her long arm in even farther. Just when she's beginning to think she's wrong, her hand brushes against something rough. She grasps it firmly and pulls it out.

It's a statue in black wood.

The statue of a woman whose face is worn from time. She wears a long gown covered with engravings. She's holding an ancient musical instrument in one hand and a wooden board that looks like the map of the Chaldeans in the other. On her head is a crown of golden wheat.

It's the woman Sheng dreams about constantly.

Mistral caresses the wooden statue, wondering how old it is. Then she looks at the organist. "What now?" she asks.

"Heremit," the man hisses, answering the phone. His voice is sharp. Like slivers of stone under the fingernails.

Heremit Devil is standing stock-still before the picture window in his study. He stares out at the endless expanse of his native city but sees nothing that interests him in the slightest. He may be around forty years old. He has no wrinkles, like someone who's never shown any emotion on his face. He sees nothing of interest. Nothing worth leaving the building for. No one remembers ever seeing him leave it, for that matter.

Heremit Devil listens to the person on the other end of the line and finally says, "No need to tell me twice. I understand."

More words. More useless words from old Cybel.

"Fine," Heremit Devil concludes. "Bring me everything immediately."

He doesn't say goodbye.

He doesn't even know how it's done.

He simply hangs up.

Five tops, he thinks, walking across the room.

He opens a drawer and stares at a picture of the Big Dipper. The constellation has seven bright stars.

Seven stars.

Five tops.

276

Are two still missing?

No.

Not two.

Only one's missing.

Only one top is missing, plus the map, which shattered against the sidewalk on avenue de l'Opéra.

Heremit switches on the telescope screen. High above, thousands of miles away, in an orbiting region devoid of oxygen, a massive mechanical eye slides open. Its twenty-five-meter lens probes the depths of the universe. In the location where the tail of a comet lit up months ago, he now sees utter darkness. But it's only a matter of time.

"Century tells us where we came from and where we're going. And for how much longer . . ."

If he knew how to laugh, he probably would. The kids have lost everything. Two of the Four Magi, Alfred and Zoe, are dead. Vladimir is about to meet with the same fate. The last one is paralyzed and confined to a wheelchair.

Four truly terrible enemies, thinks Heremit.

By tomorrow, he'll have in his possession the first three objects needed to discover the secret: the mirror, the stone, the ship. He doesn't know what he needs to do with them. Nevertheless, he's worked very hard to prepare for the task.

"What difference does it make which road you follow as you seek the truth? Such a great secret is not to be reached by a single path. If you find it, you must guard it with care and keep others from discovering it as well. This is the secret of Century. . . ."

And whoever knows the secret, thinks Heremit Devil, *knows things that others couldn't even imagine.*

Carefully guarded since time immemorial, the secret of Century will be revealed only during a particular astral conjunction. Every hundred years, they said. And only with the objects that lead to the secret.

What could it be? Immortality? Omniscience? Infinite wealth?

Heremit doesn't know yet. But he does know that, whatever it is, it's his now.

He gets up from the telescope monitor and presses a button on the intercom. "I want ice."

Then he changes his mind and presses the button again.

"Never mind. I'm going down to eat."

The moment the news is heard, panic breaks out among the employees on the sixty-two floors below. The twelve restaurants, Olympic swimming pool, nine movie theaters, fitness centers and malls all leap into action. A whisper goes round. "He's coming down! He's coming down!" Dozens of people race across the halls, cleaning everything, which is already perfectly clean, moving chairs, straightening paintings, spraying air freshener, checking the temperatures of the rooms.

Heremit Devil pushes the elevator button. The doors slide open. Just as he's about to step in, a shiver unexpectedly runs up his spine.

He turns around, walks through his study and steps into a long, narrow hallway.

There aren't any doors or lights on the high walls. Instead, they're covered with drawings and inscriptions in red, scrawled with a childish hand. The man walks all the way down the hall, opens the tiny door at the end of it, crouches down and goes into a small bedroom. He crosses it with three paces and ducks through another tiny doorway that leads to the entrance to the top floor of the building.

The door at the top of the stairs is hermetically sealed. He needs to wait a few seconds before he can walk in.

"I'm so close," he whispers.

The room is virtually empty. Beneath his feet is a world map that covers almost the entire floor. Dozens of lines in different colors cross through various parts of the globe. Heremit walks over the continents, causing a series of ticks and tiny blinking lights. A small glass table rests right on top of Shanghai. And on the table, in a protective case, is a top.

"I'm missing the map, but I have this map," Heremit whispers. "And I have this top. . . ."

He strokes the glass with something that vaguely resembles affection. Maybe he's thinking about when his father gave it to him.

The first top he ever owned.

His top.

A wooden top.

A very old one. Ancient.

A top with a skull on it.

The two Melodia sisters are sitting in Irene's bedroom, facing each other. The older one says, "I think the time has come to tell you something, Linda. Although, after all these years, I don't know where to begin."

"Then begin at the beginning."

"Here it is: The two of us aren't really . . . sisters," Irene confesses.

Linda stares straight in front of her and presses her lips

together, her eyes filling with tears. "I knew it," she says, wiping them away. "I knew it. I was always afraid of that. But . . . I never wanted to ask you, because . . ." Her voice trails off.

"Do you remember what I was like when you were a little girl?" Irene asks.

"You were a lot older than me."

"Yes, but back then I still looked much younger than my real age. Before the accident, I looked much, much younger. I looked like a girl myself. Like your sister, that is . . . But I wasn't."

"What about our parents . . . I mean . . . your parents? M-mine? If I'm not your sister . . . who . . . who am I?"

Irene leans over and clasps Linda's hands in her own. "The problem isn't who you are, Linda, but who I am."

"And who are you?"

"Quite possibly, the last of the Four Magi."

"The Four Magi? What . . . What does that mean?"

"It means it's a long story, Linda. I wish I didn't even have to tell you about it, but things are coming to a head and I think you need to know everything. For our own good: mine, yours and Elettra's."

"So she has something to do with all this? And with what happened in New York, too?"

"Yes, it's all connected." Irene glances at the door and whispers, "I was born on February twenty-ninth, 1896." She holds up a photograph. "This is me when I was eleven years old." Then she hands Linda the photo of a young woman dressed in a thermal suit. "In this one, taken years later, I was in the Russian steppes."

"What were you doing in the Russian steppes?"

"I was going to get your mother."

Linda Melodia springs to her feet. "You're joking! You're just talking nonsense!"

"No, Linda. It isn't nonsense. But before I tell you the rest," Irene says, pointing at the bedroom door, which is ajar, "we'd better make sure there's no one else in the house."

Linda Melodia storms out, comes back in and slams the door behind her, both furious and frightened. "We're alone," she says.

"Where do you want me to begin?"

"At the beginning?"

"That would be the Four Magi who came before us, then," Irene replies. She begins to tell the tale.

36

THE GOODBYES

○

GOLDEN SUNLIGHT WASHES OVER THE BRANCHES OF THE PLANE trees and the columns flanking the water-lily pond in parc Monceau. A gentle breeze murmurs in the air. Harvey and Elettra are walking along, their arms around each other. Harvey's going back to New York tomorrow, so it's time for them to say goodbye again.

They've hidden the sail in Mistral's house, agreeing that it will be up to her to keep the third object safe. The wooden statue of Isis, on the other hand, is in the abbey of Saint-Germain-des-Prés, entrusted to the care of its head priest. They thought it would be pointless, even sacrilegious, to take it away from the church after all the years it watched over the faithful, although in hiding.

They spent the whole night thinking and talking, but Elettra, Harvey, Mistral and Sheng still haven't figured out what the sail, that is, the Veil of Isis, is supposed to do. Just like they haven't figured out what the Ring of Fire and the Star of Stone are for.

When Elettra looked at her reflection in the first object on New Year's Eve, Rome lit up in a burst of blinding light. In Harvey's hands, the second revealed its contents: four ancient seeds and, Zoe claims, traces of human DNA that fell to Earth from the stars. Could it be true? More research is needed. More proof that they aren't merely pieces in a big puzzle. More evidence that they have a far deeper significance.

Then what might be behind the ship's sail?

Apparently nothing. Even when analyzed under a microscope, nothing turns up. It's a simple, sturdy, tightly woven cloth. Simple cloth yellowed with time.

The sail, the heart top and what's left of the ancient map of the Chaldeans. After their many months of searching, that's all the kids have left. The sail, the top, the map . . . and a general feeling of discouragement.

Despite everything, there are two things Elettra and Harvey want to do. The first is to take the seed Harvey brought with him from New York, hidden in the coin pocket of his jeans, and carefully plant it in the earth so that it will grow into a very special tree, one that will watch over Paris.

"When you invite me back to Rome," Harvey says, "I'll plant a tree there, too."

"You're welcome to come back to Rome whenever you like," Elettra replies.

The second thing they want to do is share a long, long kiss.

The sun is slowly turning crimson on the horizon, its warm, glowing light tingeing the clouds over Paris and streaming through the city's windows like golden branches.

Sheng is sitting in the lotus position in room 12 *bis* of the Louvre museum. He's staring up at the Zodiac of Dendera. The poster explained that each of the figures represents a known star or planet.

All of them, that is, except one: It's a man with a staff who follows a strange course through the other constellations, concluding his journey beside the Earth. The planet Earth is depicted as a circle within which are four adults and four children, who almost look as if they're sleeping.

Four Magi and four disciples.

Sheng sits there in the lotus position, staring at the zodiac until his eyes start to water. He wants them to turn yellow. He wants to talk to the museum guard again. He wants to see things others can't see. He wants to understand. He needs to, because he'll soon be going home to Shanghai, the city where their great enemy is. The man called Heremit Devil.

Sheng sighs. He feels all alone. Elettra, Harvey and Mistral have completed their searches. In the process, they've awakened within themselves abilities they didn't even realize they had. Maybe that's what they were supposed to do the whole time. Maybe it was even more important than tracking down the objects hidden in the three cities. But what's his purpose? And when is he going to discover it?

What is it they're really risking their lives for?

There aren't any answers to these questions. Not yet, at least.

As he sits there on the floor of the Louvre, Sheng hears footsteps draw near. Imagining it's one of the rare visitors who stray into that area of the museum from time to time, he doesn't bother to turn around. But then the footsteps come to a halt right behind him.

"We need to come up with a plan," a voice says.

Sheng snaps out of his own thoughts. He looks over his shoulder. He tries to stand up.

"You and I don't have much time," Jacob Mahler adds, taking off his baseball cap, "before he discovers I'm still alive."

Sheng opens his mouth but finds he can't talk. Or scream. Or even run away. He doesn't ask any questions. He just listens.

Standing there in front of him, Jacob Mahler tells him everything he knows about Heremit Devil and about what's going on in Shanghai.

Later, much later, Sheng tries calling his friends' cell phones. "I know what it is! I know what it is!" he shouts excitedly. "It's called Century!"

But Harvey and Elettra's phones are lying in the grass in parc Monceau. They're switched off.

The cell phone in Mistral's pocket is silent. Without letting out an ill-timed ring, its screen lights up and goes dark again, unnoticed.

The girl is staring straight ahead, letting herself be whisked away in the sea of emotions conjured up by the organ in Saint-Germain.

And by the hands of the organist playing it.

37

THE OBSERVER

"Nice to meet you!" Professor Miller shouts, holding his hat down on his head. Everything around him risks being swept away by the helicopter's whirling rotor blades. He climbs in and buckles up.

"It's a pleasure, Professor Miller!" a giant, heavyset islander says, shaking his hand. "I'm Paul Magareva, from the Polynesian Oceanographic Institute. Welcome aboard!"

With his other hand, the burly man motions to the pilot, who switches on the radio, saying, "Alpha Foxtrot Charlie one-four-two ready for takeoff."

"Sorry I'm late," Professor Miller adds, looking out the side door, which has been left open.

The helicopter lifts off from the ground tail-first, breaks free from the grassy landing pad and heads toward the ocean. Harvey's father takes off his hat and lets the sweet wind from the Pacific tousle his hair.

"This your first time to the Pacific?"

"No, but it's been years."

The giant man beside him looks at his watch. "We'll be on the ship in a couple of hours. Did you have a good trip?"

"It was uneventful," Professor Miller replies. The helicopter zooms over the ocean and its endless succession of blue waves. "From up here, it almost looks healthy," he jokes.

"That's like saying I almost look thin, Professor Miller!"

The two men laugh like teammates who've just lost the championship through no fault of their own.

"The tidal data collected over the past year is totally abnormal," Paul Magareva continues. "The numbers are off the charts. As for the temperatures . . . well, I imagine you've already seen those."

"I thought a series of submarine eruptions might be behind it," Professor Miller says, frowning.

His traveling companion shakes his head. "The instruments haven't detected any telluric disturbances, and there haven't been any unusual reports of deepwater-fish mortality."

"Baffling."

Paul Magareva sighs. "I came up with a possible explanation, but it's totally ridiculous. . . ."

"Let's hear it."

"The ocean's undergoing an anomalous gravitational pull. It's like there are two moons, not one."

"But what could account for that?"

"Like I said, it's totally ridiculous . . . unless there's a big meteorite heading straight toward us, one whose gravitational field is starting to interfere with ours."

"It'd have to be awfully large. So large we'd be able to see it."

"That's what I figure, too. But . . ." Paul hands Professor Miller a newspaper article.

"What's this?"

"See for yourself."

"'Grab your pen and start rewriting the textbooks,' jokes Brown, head of the Pasadena Planetary Astronomy Unit, 'because we've discovered UB-313,'" Harvey's father reads aloud. "Meaning . . . ?"

"Meaning an extra planet in our solar system. A perfectly anomalous planet. One that's dragging clusters of satellites and debris along with it, kind of like a ring around Saturn. When it passes near a star and solar rays hit the debris, its ring catches fire, making it look like a comet. Under any other circumstances, it's completely invisible. It's just a giant black ball revolving around the sun in a highly elliptical orbit, passing by the Earth every, let's say, three thousand six hundred years. The ancient Egyptians, Sumerians and Chaldeans all talked about it. They called it Nibiru. The planet of the skull. The hobbling planet. According to NASA, UB-313 was a few million kilometers away from Earth in 2003."

"And today?"

"It might be a whole lot closer than that."

CREDITS

© Othon Alexandrakis/iStockphoto.com (p. 13, photo 40).

© AM29/iStockphoto.com (p. 7, photo 18).

© Norbert Bieberstein/iStockphoto.com (p. 5, photo 6).

© Iocopo Bruno (p. 3, photo 1; p. 4, photo 4; p. 4, photo 5; p. 5, photo 9; p. 5, photo 11; p. 6, photo 12; p. 6, photo 14; p. 7, photo 16; p. 7, photo 17; p. 7, photo 20; p. 9, photo 23; p. 9, photo 24; p. 10, photo 26; p. 11, photo 30; p. 11, photo 32; p. 12, photo 34 top; p. 12, photo 35; p. 13, photo 39; p. 15 tickets).

© James Curtis/iStockphoto.com (p. 4, photo 3).

© Matthew Dixon/iStockphoto.com (p. 15 left).

© Steve Geer/iStockphoto.com (p. 10, photo 29 right).

© Ekaterina Hashbarger/iStockphoto.com (p. 6, photos 13 and 15).

© Karen Hermann/iStockphoto.com (p. 8, photo 22).

© Andrew Howe/iStockphoto.com (p. 4, photo 2).

© Ian Ilotte/iStockphoto.com (p. 13, photo 41).

© Andre Klaassen/iStockphoto.com (p. 5, photo 7).

ABOUT THE AUTHOR

PIERDOMENICO BACCALARIO was born in Acqui Terme, a beautiful little town in the Piedmont region of northern Italy. He grew up in the middle of the woods with his three dogs and his black bicycle.

He started writing in high school. When lessons got particularly boring, he'd pretend he was taking notes, but he was actually coming up with stories. He also met a group of friends who were crazy about role-playing games, and with them he invented and explored dozens of fantastic worlds.

He studied law at university but kept writing and began publishing novels. After he graduated, he also worked with museums and cultural projects, trying to make dusty old objects tell interesting stories. He began to travel and change horizons: Celle Ligure, Pisa, Rome, Verona . . .

He loves seeing new places and discovering new lifestyles, although, in the end, he always returns to the comfort of familiar ones.